angel child

angel child

MARK STEADMAN

 Peachtree Publishers, Ltd.

Published by
PEACHTREE PUBLISHERS, LTD.
494 Armour Circle, N.E.
Atlanta, GA 30324

Copyright © 1987 Mark Steadman

Manufactured in the United States of America

10 9 8 7 6 5 4 3 2 1

Library of Congress Catalog Card Number 87-80967

ISBN 0-934601-28-3

For Jo...all by herself

ACKNOWLEDGMENTS

Chapter One appeared in slightly different form in the Summer 1986 issue of *The Southern Review*.

Significant time for writing this book was provided by a Creative Writing Fellowship Grant from the National Endowment for the Arts.

I owe a lot of people for their support in this undertaking, but especially Bob Hill, Ron Moran, Tom Inge, Bill Koon, and Ron Rash who kept telling me not only that I could do it, but that I should—which is another thing altogether.

Also Chuck Perry, my editor at Peachtree Publishers, who showed me how to make it a better book, and Jane Hill, who helped make it right.

And Lois Wallace, of course.

angel child

"People are wonderful as they are."
— George Grosz —

"Glory be to God for dappled things."
— Gerard Manley Hopkins —

April 12, 1963

THE MAN WAS GNOMELIKE AND TWISTED, and the expression on his face indicated pain of long duration. The appearance of the woman was less grotesque, but more startling. Her hair was a tangled mass, like copper wire with electricity humming in it, and her crossed eyes were a bright, metallic yellow. The two of them were sitting with their arms around their knees at the top of a run of six wooden steps without risers that led up to the back porch of a green clapboard house. The house was old and the paint was peeling off, showing patches of the grey, weathered boards beneath. On the porch there were a wringer washing machine, a stack of wooden cases of empty Dr Pepper bottles, and head high piles of old newspapers. There were also various other items that had an abandoned and used up look about them. On the bottom step was a spindly and blossomless petunia plant in a gallon can. Huge crepe myrtle bushes grew at both corners of the house.

The man and woman were watching a boy of about three playing with a Donald Duck beach pail and shovel in the loose dirt of the back yard. The yard was shaded by three large oak trees. One of the trees had short boards nailed to it, making a step ladder that rose to a tree house which was roofed with a piece of corrugated metal sheeting. A rope swing looped down from the first high limb and was wrapped around the porch railing. Spanish moss hung from the limbs of the trees, and patches of it had lodged in the eaves of the house.

"I told you you'd get used to him," said the woman. She spoke without looking at the man. In contrast to her looks, her voice was gentle and melodious.

At the sound of the woman's voice, the child looked up at the two sitting on the porch and smiled. His eyes were a clear, soft blue, and the features of his face were fine and regular. He was a beautiful child.

"Don't put your fingers in your mouth, Gabriel," said the man. He spoke in admonition, but gently. "No telling what all germs in that dirt."

The woman leaned her shoulder against the man in a gesture of affection. "He's your eyeball," she said. "That's what he is. I knew how it would be."

For a minute the man didn't speak. "I don't hardly think what he looks like no more," he said, speaking slowly and thoughtfully. "I don't really see him, you know. After awhile it gets to be that way." He sucked at his lip. "Just all I can think about is the sweetness." He turned his head and looked at the woman for a minute, then he looked back at the child. "That there's the sweetest child God ever put on this earth. It wouldn't matter *what* he looked like."

The woman smiled and put her arm through his, hugging it to her. "And *beautiful.*" She put her head on the man's misshapen shoulder. "He's our angel child," she said, speaking softly, as if she were whispering a secret. "That's what he is. Our angel child."

Our Angel Child indeed.

"Yes," said the man. "Ours..."

Part 1

July 4, 1922 - June 20, 1959

One

LANGSTON JAMES McHENRY WAS BORN in a two-room sharecropper's cabin outside Whippet, Georgia, on the night of July 4, 1922. His father to be, Angus Lachlin McHenry, spent the six hours of his wife's labor seated on the top step of the cabin's porch, with his feet together and his hands on his knees. At intervals he would rise, descend the steps and walk in a tight circle around the swept earth of the cabin's front yard, breathing through his mouth and counting as he went. When he reached five hundred, he would return to his seat on the step and listen to the beating of insects against the panes of the closed windows, and to his wife's moans in the back room of the cabin.

The midwife on the occasion was Jocasta Wingate—a tall, angular woman, with an undershot jaw and a carapace of heavy, blue-black hair, parted in the middle and wound in a bun at the nape of her neck. If the circumstances of her life had been different— the calling she followed and, in particular, the rural county of

Georgia where she performed it—she might have been an elegant woman. Elegance had been the promise of her youth. Only small shadows of that promise had survived into her middle age—a brittle serenity and a deliberateness of manner that bordered on the grim. She was a very erect woman, not often surprised, nor even easily moved, by the general unfairness of life as she had known it in her time and place. But, while she was forced to acknowledge the depressing facts of existence, she never allowed herself to become resigned to them.

When she came to the door of the cabin after the delivery, Lachlin McHenry stood and removed his hat.

"Would you step this way, Mister McHenry?" she said. In her dealings with men, Jocasta was more than ever inclined to be precise and businesslike.

Mr. McHenry entered the front room without speaking. Inside, he put his hat back on his head.

"It's a male child, Mister McHenry," she said. In her high-heeled shoes, Jocasta was taller than Lachlin by half a head.

"Yes, Ma'm," he said. "Much obliged."

"He was born with a caul."

Mr. McHenry thought about this for a minute. "I ain't got but the regular two dollars," he said at last.

"I don't charge extra for cauls."

"I could maybe get up another dollar," he said. "Fifty cents for sure. We wasn't expecting no extra expense."

"Cauls are part of the business, Mister McHenry. I don't charge extra for cauls."

"I see," he said.

"Cauls are generally a good sign. You don't have to worry about a caul."

"Cauls is nothing to worry about, eh?"

"John Milton was born with a caul."

Mr. McHenry pursed his mouth and looked at her for a minute, thinking. "Is that a fact?" he said at last.

For a moment the two of them stood there without speaking. Finally Mr. McHenry held out his hand with the two dollars folded into a packet the size of a three-cent stamp. "Much obliged," he said.

Jocasta accepted the money without looking at it. For a minute she hesitated, then she looked at Mr. McHenry in an uncommonly serious way. "I hate to say it, Mister McHenry, but it's an ugly child." She paused to contemplate her truthfulness, then added, "Your wife's doing fine."

"I reckon it was the caul?" he said.

"What?"

"What's ugly about it? Is it the caul?"

"No. It's not the caul. I took that off already. It's just an ugly child, you know, *all over.*"

"Well," said Mr. McHenry. "Would it look better if you put it back on?"

"What?"

"I was thinking . . . you know . . . maybe it would look better *with* the caul. What do you think?"

She thought for a minute, then nodded her head. "I think you're right," she said. "But I told you already. I couldn't put it back on. Now let's just don't worry about that caul."

Mr. McHenry darted his eyes around the room then brought them to rest on the part in her hair. "*Real* ugly?" he said.

"Yes," she said. "In my experience, I'd say that's a real ugly child in there. I wouldn't have brought it up otherwise."

"I don't reckon there's nothing you could do?"

"Ain't nobody but the Lord God can cure ugly, Mister McHenry." She looked at him for a minute. "It's not so bad for a male child." She gave him a serious look. "I didn't *have* to tell you, only I thought you ought to know."

"What's she say, Lachlin?" Mrs. McHenry called out from the

bedroom. "Something wrong with our treasure?"

"No offense meant, honey," said Jocasta, speaking over her shoulder. "The Lord don't give us no more'n we can bear." Then she added, "...*Usually*."

After Jocasta left, Mr. McHenry went into the bedroom to take a closer look at his new son. He put his head down and examined the infant's face. "Looks all right to me," he said at last. "I ain't *real* strong on babies no way."

Mrs. McHenry propped up on an elbow and looked at Langston James. "I think he's adorable," she said.

Which was the first and last time anyone ever used *that* word in reference to Langston James McHenry. The next morning when she took him out onto the porch and examined him in broad daylight, even she wanted to take it back.

* * *

Langston James weighed five and a half pounds at birth, with facial features that brought him in about one step ahead of the Rhesus monkey in the evolution parade. Still, the afflictions of his birth were, so to speak, only the beginning. Fate had other little tricks to play on Langston James.

Out of general consideration and a hesitation to disturb him, his parents neglected to turn him in his crib so that his skull sutures closed lopsided, with his head cocked over to the left, like he had been whacked with a board. In certain lights and moods it gave him a pensive look...though those lights and moods were few and far between.

Just before his fifth birthday, his left eye went out of focus and began walling off to the left. Mrs. McHenry took notice and called it to the attention of her husband.

"Look at that eye, Lachlin. What you reckon?"

Mr. McHenry stooped down and put his face up close.

"Well...," he said, "I'll swan."

When she and Mr. McHenry were sitting around in the evenings listening to the radio and admiring the pattern in the linoleum, she undertook to correct the defect by holding Langston James on her lap and tapping him gently on the left side of his head. The tapping gave him a terrible squint and a permanent look of apprehension. It also perforated his eardrum so that he lost his hearing on that side. However, it had no effect on the eye, which continued its lateral movement into his cranial recesses.

When he was six, the front porch of the cabin collapsed on the right side of his head while he was twirling doodlebugs underneath it. After they dug him out, his head was more lopsided than ever, and over the next few months, a mysterious contraction developed on the left side of his body. Mr. and Mrs. McHenry watched thoughtfully as his left arm and leg hunched toward one another. When it finally stopped, Mrs. McHenry heaved a sigh of relief. "Well, Lachlin. What you reckon?"

"I don't know," said Mr. McHenry, "looks like a tow sack to me."

That was as far as the diagnosis ever went. A doctor might have found the illness less of a mystery, but they never called one in. Their view of the world put everything pretty much in God's hands, and they were too poor to get in on the march of science. Besides, Langston James didn't seem to be in any pain.

"I love him just the way he is," said Mrs. McHenry.

"Maybe he'll draw up on the other side and it'll even out," said Mr. McHenry, turning optimistic in his thoughts. "If it don't, he's going to walk like a crab."

Walking like a crab would have been a godsend for Langston James. A crab was poetry in motion and grace defined, compared to the flailing, knee-hobbled shuffle that propelled Langston James through the world. Getting from here to there was ninety percent effort and ten percent progress for Langston James.

"Anyway," said Mrs. McHenry, "he's a sweet child."

Once again she took him to her lap, this time rubbing him with turpentine, which was, unfortunately, the universal specific in rural areas. Where she rubbed turned raw, then healed purple. As he grew older, the purple patch spread up his neck, engulfing his deaf left ear and causing his hair to fall out in an arrowhead pattern on the side of his head. At ten, the hair came back in, but it came in white and curly. The rest of his hair was black and straight.

Through all of his afflictions, Langston James maintained a langorous sweetness of disposition which was uncanny. Love, especially the love of his mother, was his balm and recompense. As with most children, he thought of himself as just like everybody else. In fact, he thought of himself as swell. However, once he started school the world closed in on him and adjusted his concept of himself to more realistic proportions.

The one-room schoolhouse that Langston James attended was not up-to-date in its treatment of the disadvantaged, nor was the teacher very finely attuned to the needs of the afflicted. Miss Fulmer was not cruel nor by nature distracted; it was only that she had enough sadness of her own to occupy her attention. She was a small, distraught looking woman, who kept a diary in which she pressed flowers that she picked herself. Every evening, in the privacy of the room she rented, she made entries in it while she chain-smoked Avalon cigarettes and sipped bourbon whiskey out of a cut-glass tumbler. As the night wore on, she would turn out the lights and lie in her bed with the skirt of her nightgown pulled up to her waist, listening to out-of-town stations on the radio. Sometimes, when her longing became unbearable, she cried. As she grew older she cried less often.

Miss Fulmer's impulses were good, but the misery of her own life kept her from paying much attention to the problems of others, especially her students. Since they were young, they had futures before them. That thought alone made her hate them a little.

The world she lived in was a serious one, and she did her job in it with as much grace and fairness as she could. She was a plain woman, unloved and alone, who had been raised to an ethic of truthfulness as hard and painful as surgical steel. At the age of thirty-eight all reasonable hope of marriage had died, even in her most secret midnight dreams, and she was left to confront the barrenness of her spinsterhood in a society which ranked fecundity—of the earth, of beasts of the field, and of women—as the first of duties among many, and the last of joys among few.

* * *

"Cripples sit up to the front, Langston James," she said. It was his first day of school. "I need you right there where I can keep an eye on you."

"Ma'm?" he said.

"Take that seat there so I can keep up with you," she said, pointing to a desk on the front row.

"Yes, Ma'm."

"You don't throw fits too, do you?"

"Ma'm?"

"Will Ed Freemont there throws fits," she said, pointing to a large, unhappy looking boy with a slack mouth. "You sit next to Will Ed so I can keep an eye on you."

Langston James looked at Will Ed apprehensively. "You throw fits?" he said.

Will Ed gave him a sullen look. "You kiss my ass," he said.

Miss Fulmer brandished her ruler. "I told you about that, Will Ed." A vein stood out on her forehead as she spoke. "I'm not putting up with any of your dirty mouth this year." She whizzed the ruler around in the air to emphasize her remarks.

After she calmed down, she gave the class a little lecture, taking the opportunity to present Langston James as an object lesson.

"Sometimes...," she said, standing behind Langston James at the front of the class with her hands on his shoulders, "sometimes the Good Lord puts an affliction on us so we can tell he means business. I want you children to look at Langston James here and think about what all He can do if He takes a mind to it." Langston James was embarrassed, not by what she said, but because he was having to stand up before the class and let everybody look at him. He smiled in a twisted way and stared at the floor.

"Stand up straight, Langston James," she said. "Being deformed wasn't never your fault. No need for *you* to be ashamed."

Miss Fulmer was the first of a large number of people Langston James would meet whose kind impulses were most often thwarted by a preoccupation turned inward and stilled by a lack of volition. Though not always.

"Do you hurt, child?" she asked. There was a momentary gentleness in her voice.

"No, Ma'm," he said. "Not hardly." His embarrassment at having to stand in front of the class was softened somewhat by the comfort he felt in the touch of her hands on his shoulders.

"Well," she said, "that's something."

His little schoolmates were frank and forthright in their cruelty, and relentless in their expression of it—until they lost interest in him and ignored him altogether. All, that is, except Will Ed Freemont, who was fascinated by the range of afflictions besetting Langston James. They were greater than his own, and he took a dim comfort in the fact. Every day, just before the bell rang for class to begin, Will Ed would lean over and whisper in Langston James's ear, "The doctor give me *medicine* for my fits." Then he would sit back and smile to himself in a satisfied way. Every day he did that. For four years. It was his daily moment of satisfaction and happiness. He would have done it for *more* than four years, but after the fourth grade, when he turned sixteen, he dropped out of school and took a job loading sacks of fertilizer at the roller mill. Hundred pound sacks. Will Ed sat on the left side of Langston James—his deaf side—and he never knew that his little joke beat lifeless and unheard in the dead air between them.

Langston James was not particularly unhappy at school; still the accumulation of faces, either hostile or indifferent, that was presented to him by the world outside cast in him a preference for home and solitary activity. Langston James was ugly, but he was not stupid.

* * *

In 1933 his family moved into town. Mr. McHenry had inherited the family home on Price Decant Street when his older brother, Vandell McHenry, was struck by lightning while in the act of blaspheming the preacher and total congregation of the New Wine Missionary Baptist Church. The house was a green frame structure with a veranda on three sides and a hall down the middle that occupied nearly a third of the floor plan. It was going down off its brick piers in an easterly direction, a result of the fact that the prevailing winds were from the west. But it had been Mr. McHenry's childhood home, and it was free, except for thirty-five dollars a year tax money.

Mr. McHenry got a job with the state highway department, helping paint stripes down the centerlines of the roads which were being built as part of the public works program that Roosevelt had initiated to bring prosperity back to the country.

Mrs. McHenry tried to help out by selling *Liberty* magazines, but Whippet was not much of a town for reading. Nor was Mrs. McHenry much of a one for selling, even with Langston James along to help her fill out the forms. Most of the magazines ended up as wadding in the cracks that were opening up between the floors and walls of the house.

"Don't you worry none, honey," said Mr. McHenry. "A pretty woman needn't do aught, but be herself."

Mr. McHenry passed on in the spring of 1934 as the result of a curious accident. He was standing too close during a concrete pour and fell into the form, ending up as part of the bridge abutment when State Road 41 went over the Oakmulgie River into McAfee County. Eubank Kelsey, the gang foreman, took a stick and wrote Mr. McHenry's name and the date of the occurrence into the wet concrete. He sent a man to town to get the birthdate and an epitaph from Mrs. McHenry, but the temperature was ninety-seven degrees Fahrenheit, and by the time the man got back the concrete had taken its set. Mrs. McHenry was disconsolate, but when the District Engineer authorized a payment of one hundred dollars if she didn't make them chisel him out, she had to make one of those terrible choices that poverty forces on people. The thought of her responsibility to Langston James choked her heart, and she felt she had to take the money.

The check got them through the summer, but for the next two years she and her son led a hand-to-mouth existence. The people of Whippet were charitable folk, but charity naturally waxes and wanes. Sometimes it thinned out until it almost wasn't there. Then, in the summer of 1936, when he was fourteen, something happened to Langston James which opened a vista for him.

What happened was that he got run over by Mrs. Adelaide Fanshaw in her new Packard automobile. Mrs. Fanshaw was the wife of the president of Whippet's biggest bank, and a tenderhearted woman on nearly all occasions. The accident did mostly damage to the left side of Langston James, which wasn't of much use to him anyway, and the concern of Mrs. Fanshaw, augmented by the cash settlement which her husband arranged, indicated to him that the road of life might lead up as well as down.

He talked to his mother about it.

"Say I jump two cars a week." He got a pencil and a piece of paper. "Mizres Fanshaw give me ten dollars...and that's twenty dollars a week." He wrote the figures on the piece of paper and contemplated them.

"It's sweet of you to think about it, Langston James, but you needn't go to jumping. We'll make do."

"Couldn't we live off no twenty dollars a week?"

"Son, I hate to tell you, but we're living off twenty dollars a *month* this minute."

"Mama," he said, standing up and looking her in the eye, "twenty dollars a month ain't good enough for you."

"The Lord provides, son. The Lord provides."

"Mama," he said, "you're a jewel in this world. You got better coming to you is what I mean."

She stared at her hands folded in her lap for a minute. "Once a week would do it, son," she said at last. "No need to run it in the ground. It ain't worth your getting hurt over."

"I got a knack for it, Mama." He patted her knee. "You needn't to worry about me none."

For half a year it worked. After that the whole town was onto him and the police adopted a condescending attitude towards his complaints. Seeing his means of livelihood disappearing, he was led by greed and desperation into making a big mistake. The mistake he made was that he jumped Elrod Sweat for the second time. Langston James was already into Elrod for twenty-five dollars, and jumping him twice was an imposition. Elrod Sweat was not a man to be imposed upon. Elrod was the John Deere dealer and a man of very little patience with people—except when it came to selling them farm machinery. When Langston James took his second dive under Elrod's automobile, Elrod put the car into reverse, backed up and ran over him on purpose.

"Once is enough, Jumper," he said, as his tires thumped over Langston James. "I'm going to get my goddamn money's worth this time."

The profits he had accumulated up to that point went for the medical bills, but it turned out to be money well spent. The stay in the hospital was a time of reflection for Langston James. When he came out after the treatment, he had a new and deeper outlook on life. It was the result of a simple truth that had come to him as he hung there in traction while his bones were knitting themselves back together. The truth was that you can't impose on people indefinitely and get away with it. And you certainly can't impose on people and get away with it if they *know* you are doing it. Over the long pull you have to give some kind of value in order to avoid the world's contempt.

"You can't get something for nothing, Mama," he said. "No way you can do it in this world. Respect . . . that's what it's all about."

"Ummmmm," she said.

"I can see it all now. Jumping ain't respectable." He limped back and forth in front of her in the living room with his good hand in his pocket. "Respect, Mama. Respect is the name of the game."

"Yes," said his mother, wringing her hands. "We sure going to miss that twenty dollars a week."

He took a job delivering newspapers and began to think about the problem. As he limped the streets of Whippet, fighting off dogs and lobbing tightly rolled copies of the Braxton County *Excaliber Blade* into the shrubbery, he worked at it single-mindedly. Eventually he factored the quality of respect into three elements— industriousness, dependability, and humbleness. Those also happened to be the three elements which defined the Protestant ethic of the inhabitants of Whippet, and, in fact, of the entire population of South Georgia at the time. Especially when applied to people who were poor or ugly.

Armed with his new truth, he set about projecting an image of life's not getting him down, in spite of his afflictions. He resolved that he would be always ready to do his share of the work for the civic good. By his deeds would he be known and loved and respected.

Once embarked on that noble path, he quickly discovered that the word is often taken for the deed. And, in his case, the word was generally preferred. Having him *serve* as a volunteer fireman was a terrible liability for everyone concerned. He flailed and stumbled, tangled himself in the hose and generally got in the way. But having him *offer* to serve, repeatedly, softened the hearts of the community towards him in ways that he found could be carried to the bank. Over a period of time he won the respect he was after, in recognition of the fact that he was always ready and willing, if not often able.

Nowhere did this principle work more to his advantage than in his attempts to join the armed forces during World War II. When Pearl Harbor was bombed, he was nineteen years old, but, considering the catalog of afflictions he could muster, getting caught in the draft was the last thing he had to worry about. That being the case, he tried, time after time, to volunteer for all four services. He became the most conspicuous patriot in a region that fairly boiled with them.

He started at the top—with the Marines.

"You want me to call an ambulance, buddy?" said the recruiting sergeant. "It ain't but two blocks to the hospital."

"I want to kill me some Japs," said Langston James, drawing his left side up as far as it would go.

The sergeant looked him over. "We could maybe wave you around on a pole and scare some to death," he said at last. He took the cigar out of his mouth. "You ain't being serious, are you, buddy?"

"I can shoot good."

The sergeant went back to reading his copy of *Titter* magazine. "This here is a serious war, son. Go start a paper drive."

The Army, Navy, and Coast Guard recruiters had less style, but their reactions were substantially the same.

Mrs. McHenry never did understand the war very well. She couldn't read unless the need was dire, and was an inattentive radio listener—except for a mild interest in *Lum 'N' Abner.* Langston James made the mistake of taking her to see *The Wizard of Oz* when it finally came to Whippet in 1945, and there she saw a newsreel report on the battle of Iwo Jima. She came out of the picture show with her brow furrowed in concern over the American soldiers being killed by the Japanese.

"Is *that* what the war is, son?" she asked.

"That's about it, Mama. You needn't to worry yourself none. We're winning."

"Whereabouts is Japan?" she asked.

Langston James thought a minute. "Over thatta way, Mama," he said, pointing.

"They're funny looking little fellers."

"Yes, Mama. You needn't to worry yourself about it none. Everybody says it's almost over."

"But they're killing *our* boys," she said.

"Mama," he said, "we're killing theirs too."

"I should *hope* so," she said. "Sweet Jesus, what a world."

Mrs. McHenry took onto herself all at once the accumulated grief of four full years of the war, puzzling over the conundrum through the winter and spring of 1946 and sinking steadily all the while. She finally died of unrelieved woe on the first anniversary of the bombing of Hiroshima in the summer of 1946, leaving Langston James an orphan at the age of twenty-three.

On the evening before the funeral, Langston James drove out to the Oakmulgie bridge and broke a piece off the concrete abutment that contained his father. The next day he dropped the piece into the grave beside his mother's coffin before the grave diggers filled it in.

It took more than a week of roaming the empty house for him

to get himself under control and go down to the Whippet Monument and Funerary Adornment Company to arrange for a grave marker. He took with him a little sketch he had made to show Wicklow Grant what he had in mind.

"Are you sure?" Wicklow said, shaking his head over the drawing. "That thing looks like a bridge abutment."

"Do it like I say, Wicklow. I'm paying for it."

"Yes. But I'm the one got to make it. How about a Maltese cross with a dove?"

"It's *my* money, Wicklow."

"The dove will be flying."

"What would I want with a Maltese cross, Wicklow? I ain't even *that* much of a Baptist."

"Maltese crosses is very popular right now. You'd be up to date with a Maltese cross."

Langston James shook his head. "No," he said.

"Listen," said Wicklow. "I got me a professional reputation I need to think about." He held the drawing at arm's length, studying it. "I'll do it if you'll let me put a dove on it."

"How much you going to hit me for the dove?"

Wicklow thought a minute. "Twenty-five dollars," he said at last.

"How big of a dove?"

Wicklow held up his hands to measure the size. "Eight inches."

Langston James studied the space between Wicklow's hands.

"That's minimum proportions, Eljay. You couldn't even see what it was if I made it littler than that."

Finally Langston James nodded. "Okay," he said. "I'll go for the dove."

"You won't regret it," said Wicklow.

"Uh huh," said Langston James.

Two

AN ORPHAN OF TWENTY-THREE IS no less an orphan and no less alone. Langston James was accustomed to isolation, but he found that the total blankness of solitude was more than he could bear. He missed his mother and her sounds in the house. Though he had hardly talked to her at all when she was alive, she had talked to him constantly, and the silence and emptiness that met him at the doorstep were a wall of remembrance through which he had to step as he came and went in the house. He found himself holding conversations with his reflection in the bathroom mirror, and talking into his coffee cup at the kitchen table. Her cooking had been mediocre on her best days, but his own was worse, and he pined for her soggy, overcooked collards and greasy cornbread with too much sugar in it.

With September the fall rains began and in the cooling weather the house started to creak and moan as it adjusted itself to the new season. In the sound of rain on the tin roof and the movement of timber against timber, Langston James heard a cadenza of woe.

Then, just at the time when he felt he could stand it no longer, salvation presented itself in the form of G. Doal Kicklighter, a representative of the circulation department of the Atlanta newspapers. He was looking for someone to handle the distribution and act as agent for the *Journal* and *Constitution* in Braxton County. Willard George, the editor of the *Excaliber Blade*, recommended Langston James.

G. Doal wore a leather flight jacket with his name on a patch over the breast pocket, and a grey fedora hat. He also smoked Old Gold cigarettes, which Langston James took for a good sign, since that was the brand he smoked himself.

"You'll run a circuit out of Whippet to Breedville, Fly, and Wilkes. The main thing is you'll make the rural deliveries, but we want you to carry the bundles for the delivery boys in those towns too. You got a car?" He looked at Langston James's left side. "I reckon you can drive, can't you?"

Langston James nodded. "I got me a Hudson," he said. Then he added. "Course I can drive."

G. Doal looked at him thoughtfully, then went on. "We'll pay the regular rate for the papers you deliver and a nickel a mile for the car."

"How many miles?"

"You can drive it any way you want to, but we figured the shortest route is seventy-eight miles. That's what you'll be paid for."

"A nickel a mile?"

"That's right. We'll give you a penny a paper for the bundles you drop in Breedville, Fly, and Wilkes. Right now that's three hundred and sixteen papers. Breedville's getting a fertilizer plant, so it ought to go up some."

Langston James nodded, trying to work out the figures in his head.

"The hard part is you got to keep your delivery boys happy. If one of them quits, it'll be up to you to find a replacement."

"How many papers I throw?"

"The *Constitution* route's got three hundred and ninety-seven. Two hundred and eighty-four for the *Journal*." He paused. "Farmers get going early."

"I know."

"You get twenty cents on the collection, but you don't have to do the collecting. The customers mail that in." He looked at Langston James again. "You sure you can drive?"

"You want a demonstration?" He took out his wallet. "This here's my driver's license."

G. Doal took the license and looked at it closely. "That's okay," he said, handing it back. "I don't expect you'll want to throw both papers, but it'll be up to you to find somebody who will."

"I can handle both of them."

"I don't think so. But I'll let you decide."

Langston James nodded. "Sounds okay."

"Well, do what you want. Just don't expect me to be coming down here to straighten things out for you every week or so."

"I can handle it."

"Mister George thinks you can."

"He knows my work."

"If I was you I'd get rid of the Hudson and buy me something more dependable."

"I'm going to see to it right away."

After G. Doal left, Langston James went around to the office of the *Excaliber Blade* and thanked Willard George for his confidence. "I ain't going to let you down, Mister George. You can count on me. And it won't interfere with throwing your paper. With me the *Excaliber Blade* comes first."

The next day he drove the Hudson down to Waycross and traded it for a 1940 Chrysler Windsor with an A sticker on the windshield. After he took the back seat out, it made a fine automobile to run the route in.

Taking on the Atlanta papers tripled his income and moved him into the upper reaches of entrepreneurship. He saw himself in a new and pleasing light as a man of substance, a person to be reckoned with, one who teetered on the very brink of tycoondom. All of these developments made him happy, of course, but the best thing about his new responsibilities was that he had to shake a leg to keep up with them and was too busy to hear the silence in the house.

His day began at two o'clock in the morning when the truck from Atlanta dropped his bundles of the *Constitution* under the marquee of the Star theater. Actually it began a quarter of an hour earlier than that, since he liked to be standing on the spot when the truck arrived. It took him thirty minutes to roll the papers he had to deliver, then four and a half hours to drive the route. He could have driven it in an hour and a half easily—even obeying the speed limit signs at the speed traps along the way, and dodging the livestock that wandered around on the roads in those days. But in 1946, nobody in South Georgia had yet learned how much customers would put up with. Even the shortages of the war hadn't imparted that bit of wisdom. The Depression was still too close to them. It never occurred to Langston James that he had an option—that his service was exclusive and the people he served had to like it or lump it. In some of the larger cities the germ of that idea was already taking hold—proprietors and clerks were beginning to savor the joys of being disdainful. But in Braxton County it was still the customer who was always right. Three extra hours was the price he paid for not being up-to-date—three hours of crawling from mailbox to mailbox, grinding the gears of the Chrysler and meticulously stuffing papers into the tubes provided free by the Atlanta office—into the tubes or into other more sturdy and refined receptacles, many of them homemade.

Anyone who had survived the thirties in South Georgia was likely to be left with a deep sense of the seriousness of life — its tentative and precarious nature. The little metal tubes provided to the customers to attach to their mailbox posts were serviceable enough, but to an eye habitually tuned in to the disasters of the world they had an insubstantial look. A good many of Langston James's customers couldn't bring themselves to trust them, and so fabricated receptacles more in keeping with their sense of the lurking contingencies of woe.

One customer had welded up his receptacle out of four-inch galvanized pipe — a sturdy and workmanlike job which no doubt let him sleep soundly, secure in the knowledge that if an asteroid hit it, or a B-29, or any other of the multitude of menacing objects that roamed the skies above him, he wouldn't be deprived of his farm and market report. Another customer, more mechanically inclined, but no less tuned in on the hum of impending disaster, had constructed one that involved an intricate sequence of gears and escapements that were set in motion by pulling a lever, and ended with the opening and closing of an aperture for the paper that had the menace and finality of a guillotine. The simplest of all in conception, but by far the most irritating to deal with, was a one hundred and fifty-five millimeter shell casing which was brazed to the top of an eight-foot steel post. Langston James had to pull the Chrysler up close beside the post, then climb onto the roof of the car and stand on tiptoe to reach it.

Some of the special instructions he received also got pretty elaborate. One customer had a different place to put the paper for every day of the week.

"You move it around and ain't nobody going to steal it," he said.

Langston James couldn't argue with his logic. "Yes, sir," he said. "That certainly is right." So he kept his mouth shut and made up a chart to keep track of the shifting locations. The most cautious customer of all wouldn't trust him with *any* instructions ahead of time. Instead he left notes in the mailbox telling him the place of concealment for the day—notes beginning with things like, "walk east seventy-five paces to the chinaberry tree...."

He got back to Whippet at seven o'clock, just in time to pick up his bundles of the *Excaliber Blade*, which took until eight-thirty to deliver. Back at the house, he cooked a huge breakfast, using all four burners on the stove and the oven as well—bacon, eggs, Cream of Wheat, sweet rolls, corn bread, and chili con carne with extra Tabasco sauce. While he ate he read both papers from cover to cover, then went out and sat on the back steps and smoked five or six cigarettes in a row, finishing up the pack of Old Golds he had opened when he had gotten out of bed that morning. By then the fire in his stomach was up to maximum heat and he needed to move around to get it distributed in a more general way. To do that he busied himself in the house, making up the bed and washing the dishes. It would be getting on towards eleven o'clock after all that, so he'd get into the Chrysler and drive down to the Billups station to gas up and buy his second pack of Old Golds for the day. At eleven-thirty he would be parked in the alley beside the Star theater, smoking the first cigarette out of the fresh pack and listening to Arthur Godfrey on the radio. Before the program was over, sleep would overcome him like a poleaxe between the eyes.

He would wake up with a start when the first bundle of *Journals* hit the sidewalk at one o'clock in the afternoon. Waking up started a coughing fit that lasted for two or three minutes, flailing him around on the front seat of the car, until he could jam himself in against the dash long enough to light up another cigarette, which would stop it.

Delivering the *Journal* was not so demanding as the *Constitution*. Besides the fact that there were not as many papers on the route, daylight inspired trust and made his afternoon customers less apprehensive so that he had fewer special instructions about where to put them. With one or two exceptions, he could stay inside the car the whole time. By five-thirty he was back off the run and sitting in the Day-Is-Done Diner, eating pork barbeque on rice with side orders of brunswick stew, cole slaw, and strawberry jam on slices of white bread. Shortly after six o'clock he pulled into his drive on Price Decant Street talking to himself in a serious manner with his eyes focussed on the hood ornament of the car. Pretty often he forgot to turn off the motor, but would leave it idling in the side yard until it ran out of gas sometime around midnight. He was making more money than he knew what to do with, and gasoline was selling for seventeen cents a gallon. But on top of all that, being wasteful had a certain attraction for him in itself.

The wear and tear on his body was fierce, but he actually enjoyed driving the loop—especially the *Constitution* route. The morning darkness gave him time to himself insulated in the moving car. Not time he used to think about anything, but time carved out and encased. Keeping up with the special instructions filled his head comfortably, and not having to think was restful. He liked listening to out-of-town stations on the radio, and watching the centerline roll up under the hood of the car.

Over the fall and winter he settled into the routine, becoming more and more adjusted to it, until finally the strain went out of it altogether. With the slackness of habit, the feeling of loneliness came back and he began to notice the silence in the house again. Money was piling up on him at a furious rate. There was nothing in particular that he wanted or felt he needed, and he had no time to look around for things or accumulate desires. Finally, in the spring, he decided to take on a helper to get his mind off himself. The helper he took on was Will Ed Freemont.

Will Ed had grown into one of those constitutional vagrants who float around small towns, getting passed along from one employer to another as a community responsibility—a kind of presumption on the sense of duty among God-fearing people. Even minimal competence at the simplest tasks exceeded his capacities. He couldn't be taught to load watermelons or dig potatoes, and multiplying seven by three would keep him occupied for most of an afternoon. But that wasn't the problem. Unmitigated stupidity can sometimes be charming and even endearing, bringing out the best in those who have to confront it. The need to protect is one of the most attractive aspects of common humanity, and a true innocent, one who finds it impossible to cope with the world, can cause even a callous person to rise above his limitations and discover his true potential as a human being. Will Ed Freemont inspired none of those noble sentiments. Will Ed was a genuine pain in the ass.

The trouble was not Will Ed's stupidity, it was his attitude. The value he set on himself could not be reckoned in silver and gold. To his own way of thinking, he was a pearl without price. If by some miracle he had found himself ensconced as president of General Motors, he would have thought the job was beneath him. Rising above it all was his one talent, but in that department he could have opened vistas for Louis the Fourteenth.

Langston James hired Will Ed mostly because he was available, but also because he felt it was his turn to take him on. He remembered sitting beside Will Ed on the front row of Miss Fulmer's class, and he decided that maybe he owed himself something for old time's sake. Frankly, there was a large portion of genuine spite among his nobler motives. Langston James imagined it might be pleasant to be Will Ed's boss. Since there wasn't anything else to spend his money on, he would lay out some of it just for the pleasure of seeing the big oaf step and fetch. The way Langston James looked at it, ordering him around had a cash value. Of course he reckoned without taking Will Ed's nature into consideration, or at least without taking it into consideration *enough*. Though Will Ed felt generally superior to *everybody*, Langston

James was the person in the world that he felt most superior to of all.

The problems Will Ed presented as a hired hand were immediate and persistent. Just teaching him to roll papers was a project of monstrous proportions. Training a gorilla to pack china would have been child's play by comparison. Over and over Langston James demonstrated the series of folds necessary to reduce the paper to stuffable dimensions. Will Ed watched with his eyebrows slightly raised and an insufferable half smile on his face.

"Got it," he'd say, taking a paper in hand and crushing it down to a size that would pass through a soda straw.

"Easy...*EASY*. You ain't got to wring water out of it, Will Ed. People don't want to stuff a noodle with it. They want to *read* the goddamn thing."

"Got it," Will Ed would say, smiling and reaching for another paper.

Eventually he caught on to the sequence of movements, but he caught on in exactly the way a gorilla would have done it — one step at a time, and with no conception of what the steps were leading to or what the outcome was supposed to be. Toward the end of the delivery run, little mistakes would begin to accumulate, turning the final product into a fused and wadded mass that was a miracle of compaction, but needed four hours in boiling water to get it open again. If Langston James had stuffed the papers into a cannon and fired them into the tubes he would have made a neater job of it.

Will Ed could never get it through his head that they weren't sitting on the front row of Miss Fulmer's class. To Will Ed the fourteen intervening years were as but a day.

"That left arm you got there ain't much good to you, is it?"

Langston James had developed a technique of steering with his left elbow and winging the papers out the window with his right hand. "It's better than nothing, Will Ed. I had twenty-three years to get used to it."

"Yes," said Will Ed, smiling. "A man can get use to anything, I reckon. If you ain't whole, you got to come along on what they is left of you."

Langston James didn't say anything.

"Doctors done helped me a lot. They given me pills I can take."

"Ummmmm."

"I got yaller ones and pink ones and a real nice blue one." Will Ed thought for a minute. "I like the blue one best," he said. "Momma, she says I'm cured good as new."

"I'm glad to hear it, Will Ed. Your momma said what them pills cured you *of*?"

"Sure did."

Langston James waited. "Well?" he said at last.

"They cured me of what they given me the pills *for*." Will Ed leaned back on the seat, smiling his satisfied smile while he mangled another paper. "I reckon it's a shame they ain't got no pills can straighten out that cripple arm you got." He nodded. "Nothing they can do about *that*." He thought a minute. "Nor that leg neither," he added. "You could take ever color pill they is and I don't reckon it'd do no good."

Langston James kept his eyes on the highway and drove for awhile in silence. "You want me to drive?" Will Ed asked. "What with being a cripple and all, ain't you afraid you'll wreck the car?"

"You got a driver's license?" Langston James sounded surprised.

"No," said Will Ed. "They wouldn't give me one because of the epileptic fits. I can drive though. Momma says I caught on real good."

"Listen," said Langston James. "This is *my* car."

"I just thought you might feel better about it if I was to take over."

"Will Ed," said Langston James, "you're working for *me*."

"Glad to do it," said Will Ed. "You needn't to thank me none.

Momma says helping out the less fortunate is just the Christian thing to do."

Langston James swerved to keep from hitting a possum. "What you call somebody you're working for, Will Ed? I mean somebody who hires you and pays you good money to, you know, do things he says for you to?"

Will Ed furrowed his brow in thought. A minute passed by. Then another minute. "I can't think of it just now," he said at last.

"Maybe you need you some other color pills."

"*What?*" said Will Ed. "What color pills?"

The note of panic in Will Ed's voice had a terrible effect on Langston James. It made him feel sorry for Will Ed—just as his irritation with him was hitting a peak.

"I taken me ever color pill they is already." Will Ed leaned forward and turned the dial on the radio. When he spoke he was beginning to sound condescending again. "Momma says hillbilly music is common. Let's see can't we find something more refined."

Being whiplashed from pity to exasperation was hard on Langston James. "Wouldn't you call somebody that you work for a *boss?*" he said.

The smile of superiority came back to Will Ed's face. "You know," he said, "that was just on the *tip* of my tongue."

Pills or no pills, once every five or six days Will Ed would have an epileptic seizure. A very dramatic one that stiffened him out with his feet jammed against the floor under the dash and his head pushing against the roof of the cab. For a minute or so he would be stretched out that way, his back arched and his fists clenched, making bleating noises through his teeth like a sheep. When he came out of it, he would huddle against the door, covering his face with his hands and whimpering. Sometimes he cried out loud. For the next half hour he wouldn't move or say anything. These episodes beat up a froth in the brain of Langston James. They always seemed to come just as he was reaching a high point in his irritation with Will Ed. He sometimes wondered if it was his irritation that brought on Will Ed's fits. At any rate Langston James would spend the time while Will Ed was recovering sucking on the roof of his mouth and trying to sort out the mixture of emotions he was feeling.

Inevitably pity would win, because, given enough time to think it over, Langston James was a soft-hearted person. But, just as inevitably, after Will Ed had pulled himself together, he would come up with some contemptible remark, spoken out of the side of his mouth, that would leave Langston James with dried out mucous membranes and an ongoing rearrangement of his vital organs.

The emotional wear and tear were fearsome, and most evenings Langston James would come off the run inhaling thirty times to the minute, with his Day-Is-Done barbecue supper laying in his stomach like a red-hot cannon ball. He would stomp through the house, kicking the furniture and slamming doors, then flop onto the bed for a night of sleep too fitful to be of any use to him. One morning he woke up under the back porch, another time face down in the bathtub, with no idea how he gotten to either place. Over and over he reminded himself that he didn't have to put up with any of this—still, he could never keep up his resolve long enough to fire Will Ed. Something pitiful was always sure to happen and turn him aside.

After two months of this he was down to ninety-two pounds and his good eye had a constant twitch in it. Then, just as he was reaching the absolute breaking point, Will Ed solved the problem for him. He quit.

"Momma says a paper route ain't no job for a grown man," he said, by way of explanation. "Especially if I got to ride around in no automobile with a cripple behind of the wheel. She says it's a miracle you ain't done killed the both of us already." Will Ed paused to let the point sink in. "We going to go on the welfare for awhile and think things out."

Even Will Ed's leaving on him was a mixed blessing. The one real pleasure he might have gotten out of the arrangement would have been firing him. But he had to admit that he was relieved at the turn of events.

"If I'd given him the boot, I'd of been ashamed about it for the rest of my life," he told himself in consolation. It really would have been that way, because the meaning of life was starting to shape up for Langston James. "Ain't nothing whole cloth one way or the other—long as you got to look out for the other fella." He shook his head. "And there ain't no way you *cain't* look out for him."

For a month he drove the routes alone, recovering his calm, catching up on his sleep and getting his weight back up to his normal one hundred and twelve pounds. But then, in the calmness that led to reflection, the well of loneliness began to fill up again, and his thoughts turned once more to the need for companionship.

He was in this frame of mind when he met Cowie Retch Vanessy.

Three

THE REASON HE MET COWIE RETCH VANESSEY was that she had taken over the Breedville *Constitution* route of her younger brother, Barberau Vanessey, when he came down with what was probably the last diagnosed case of diptheria in South Georgia. It was not exactly love at first sight, and, in fact, the first glimpse Langston James got of her in the predawn darkness almost caused him to levitate. She looked like something put together out of spare parts left over from a Boris Karloff movie. He recovered from it quickly, however, and once the initial shock had worn off, the way she looked was a major attraction to him. Before Barberau was up and around and able to deliver papers again, three weeks had gone by. The first week wasn't over before thoughts of matrimony began to flicker in Langston James's mind. By the end of the third week he was burning with more candle power than the Edisto lighthouse.

The view that Langston James took of the world, all he had

learned of it from personal experience, inclined him to ugliness and deformity. With those he felt comfortable and easy. The fair line of beauty was alien to him. It made him sad and ill at ease at best—at worst he felt it as a menace. For all those reasons, Cowie Retch was a fit wife for him. She was poor and ugly and looking for love. She also didn't seem to notice any of Langston James's afflictions. But, of course, she wasn't in any position to be choosy.

Her hair was red like a rusty Brillo pad, and she had a mouth full of teeth that would have given pause to a man-eating shark. Her eyes were a startling golden color, like recently polished brass, crossed in a gaze that was permanently fixed on the bridge of her nose. The way she looked had kept suitors at bay for all of her twenty-three years—the way she looked and her father—a huge, confused man with the disposition of a ground hornet and major illusions about the desirability of his daughter as an object of dalliance. It never occurred to him that anyone would ever want to marry her, so when Langston James first came calling, Mister Vanessey simply couldn't believe that his intentions were serious and honorable.

"You mean you want to *marry* her? Cowie Retch? Where you come from, Mister?"

"Whippet."

"You from *Whippet*? That ain't but seventeen mile away." Mr. Vanessey figured the least radius he would have to get outside of would be about two hundred miles. Up to that limit he assumed that Cowie's reputation would go before her. During the war he had hoped for a downed German bomber crew—with some members preferably blinded in the crash. When that didn't materialize, he thought in terms of a returning veteran with *some* of his faculties impaired.

Once he realized that Langston James was in earnest, he couldn't wait for the marriage to take place, and all but locked him in the house while he went for the preacher.

"Listen, buddy," he said. "You think this over *careful*. You marry her and she's *yours*. I ain't going to take her back. Vanesseys don't hold with divorce."

"Nor do McHenrys," said Langston James.

"Shake on it," said Mr. Vanessey, holding out his hand.

After the ceremony, the newlyweds drove down to Waycross for the honeymoon, which lasted two hours and took place in the Heart of Okefenokee Motel. Two hours was one hour and fifty-eight minutes more than it took to consummate the union, and, anyway, it was all Langston James could spare, since he had to be back in Whippet by two A.M. to pick up his *Constitutions*.

To be ugly is a greater affliction for a woman than a man, but Cowie had learned early to take up her bed and walk. Still, it pleased her when Langston James said to her, "Ma'm, it ain't your looks I'm interested in. . . . It's your *qualities*." Those he found to his liking.

Cowie was an extremely placid and gentle woman, with small touches of grace in her movements, and a natural inclination to affection, which Langston James saw could fill the void left by his dead mother and father. She pleased him, and his pleasure pleased her.

As dowry, she brought with her a 1940 Ford pickup truck with two spare tires, a washing machine with a wringer attachment, and an old Baldwin upright, which she played in a rolling, rag-time style that he found deeply appealing. Her cooking was to his taste, and, after he brought her into his newspaper delivery business, he discovered that she could do sums in her head.

"Seventeen thousand, nine-hundred and seventy-one dollars and twenty cents."

"What?" Langston James had casually mentioned the number of newspaper customers he had and the weekly rate they paid. The figure she gave him was the yearly total on his collections. She had produced it immediately and without seeming to think about it. Just like that.

"That's what it comes to," she said. "Seven hundred and sixty-eight papers, times forty-five cents a week, times fifty-two weeks in a year is seventeen thousand, nine hundred and seventy-one dollars and twenty cents.

He went and got a pencil and a piece of paper and worked it out.

"Goddamn, Cowie. You're right!"

"Certainly," she said.

"How'd you do that?"

"I don't know," she said. "It's natural."

He looked at her steadily. "Three thousand fifty-nine times six hundred ninety-five," he said.

"Two million, one hundred twenty-six thousand, aught, aught, five," she said, without hesitation.

He worked it out on paper, then went over and kissed her on the mouth. "Hot damn!" he said. "Looky what I got me here."

Twenty-four was late for matrimony to come to him. Early maturity and the weight of responsibility—those were the signs of the times, for men *and* women, though for women the strictures were more binding. According to the standards of the day, children should begin to arrive as soon as possible, lest vitality be lost. But not out of wedlock. That was very specific. A woman of sixteen who was unmarried was courting spinsterhood. At twenty-one she had already betrayed her function and could expect nothing better than halfwits and monsters and other flawed offspring bestowed by a vengeful God. Cowie was a perilous twenty-three.

For Langston James, his duty was clear, and his sexual awakening commenced with a roll of drums. He set about the business of procreation with the single-minded consciousness of years lost and gone, afraid that his time had run out already. And if not his, then Cowie's.

At the beginning, Cowie was delighted by his ardor.

"You're something else, honey lamb," she said, clasping him

to her, awash in thoughts of maternity, which she had been convinced would never come her way. "That's a truly virile member you got there. I would say *truly*." Then she added, "Trulytrulytruly," with a rising inflection.

"Truly" indeed. It was the proper word. After the recitation of vows that made him fully a man, Langston James became nine-tenths tumescent member, dragging behind it the lame and broken body—a prong of flesh impelled by a blind biological urge and a social imperative.

"Yes," he would say. "Well...ummmmm...I had it on my mind, you know, for some time now."

"I always did think married life was going to suit me," she said. "If I ever got me a chance at it."

"This here is your personal chance," he said. "Could you move a little to the left?"

"Left?"

"Left."

"Whatever you say, honey lamb. Just so it suits you."

"I mean to tell you, it suits me to a tee."

"Don't it though," she said. "Dontitdontitdontit . . ." She trailed off in a high-pitched wail that made his hair stand on end.

The fact that Cowie, such a placid woman at other times, turned into a screamer during their lovemaking startled him at first. After that it interested him—for awhile. It gave *dimension* to their experiences together. But gradually it wore on him, and finally it put his nerves permanently on edge.

"Listen, honey," he said. "Don't you reckon you could hold it down a little? I mean, we going to have the fire department in here on us if you keep up that way."

"Uh huh," she said.

He tried stuffing the edge of the pillow into her mouth—then the sheet—then the quilt. In the throes of her passion she ate large pieces of all three. He worried about the expense, but he also didn't like the distraction, which interfered with his own enjoyment. And, anyway, nothing worked.

"It's my natural inclination, Eljay," she said. "I don't hardly know I'm doing it."

"Yes, well, everbody this side of town *does* know it. You sound like the Russians has landed and you passing the word."

"Well," she said.

"This here's an old house, Cowie. It can't take them kind of vibrations. You're backing the nails out the sheetrock."

"You got to take the rough with the smooth, honey lamb. How you going to fight nature?"

"Yes, well. I hate to complain. It's mighty good otherwise. Mighty good."

"Truly it is," she said.

"Why don't you see can't you do something to, you know, *curtail* it a little?" He paused and looked at the expression on her face. "Maybe you could moan instead. It wouldn't *carry* so far."

"It's nature unbeknownst," she said. "My mind is deep as a well. I don't do no thinking just then. All I see is colors."

"Try blue," he said.

She pouted and didn't answer.

"Nature ain't always got to have the last word," he said. "All I'm asking is just to give it a try."

"Well," she said. "I'll see what I could do."

As a mechanical aid, he carved a wooden plug for her to clamp her teeth on, thinking it would help keep her mouth shut, or at least focus her attention. The first time he tried it, she ate the plug.

"Where *is* it?"

"I don't remember, Eljay. I wasn't keeping up with it. You don't notice a thing like that in your moment of delight. I saw purple."

He pulled back the bedclothes and looked. "Don't tell me you et that plug," he said. "It couldn't of been nothing like that."

"Look down toward the foot," she said, raising a pillow and looking under it. "We was moving around pretty good."

"Open your mouth," he said. He looked inside. There were a few splinters, and a smell like a summer fireplace. "Sweet Jesus, Cowie. I carved that out of a hickory ax handle. You done et a hickory plug."

She ran her tongue around inside her mouth. "It's got a twang," she said.

For a minute he looked at her, then he hugged her to him. "I never hearn of a set of teeth like that," he said. "You some kind of woman, Cowie. Do sums in your head and eat a hickory plug."

"Play the pianer as well," she said. "By ear."

"Ain't it the truth?" he said, and kissed her on the mouth.

Eventually she learned to keep her mouth shut in her passion, and as a consideration for the neighbors, the moaning was pretty much of an improvement. But as far as Langston James's personal feelings went, it wasn't a lot of help. He felt like he was doing something unpleasant to her, and after a month or so a certain grimness crept into their lovemaking.

When she confirmed in October that she had missed her third period, he stopped his advances. Cowie didn't protest the neglect, because, to tell the truth, she needed the rest herself.

"We going to quit for awhile now?" she asked.

"If it's all the same to you, honey. That moaning gets on my nerves something awful. It's took a lot out of me."

"That's what you said about the screaming."

"Yes," he said. "That certainly is right. It's a whole heap better than the screaming. Of the two, I'd go for the moaning ever time."

"I was keeping it in mind, you know. Leastways as much as I could."

"I know you was." He thought a minute. "I wouldn't want no thoughts of deprivation working at you. If you need it say so."

"I'll tell you what's a fact, honey lamb," she said. "I could use a rest. You're acting like the guarantee on that thing is about to run out."

"You *sure* about your period now?"

She looked at him. "I can count, Eljay. I *said* I was, didn't I? You want me to put it in writing?"

"No need," he said. He thought a minute. "I never could stand a smart-mouth woman, Cowie. It don't go with the female nature. You know what I mean?"

"You got a mouth on you your ownself, Eljay."

"Well," he said. "I want this here child to be born in love."

"I want it to be born in a *hurry*," she said.

"See what I mean?" he said.

She smiled and touched his arm. "Bring me some Red Hots from the store."

He called on Jocasta Wingate to make arrangements for the delivery. Babies and Jocasta were naturally associated in his mind, and he didn't realize that more than ten years had passed by since he had seen her last. He found her an old woman who didn't recognize him at first.

"Langston James *McHenry*?" she said, leaning closer to peer at him. She carried her head erectly, but her eyes were bleared and watery. Her hair was still heavy and full, still parted in the middle and wound at the back, but iron grey now. "Lord God," she said. "You're uglier than I remember."

"Well," he said. "Me and Cowie is about to have issue."

"Cowie?"

"Cowie's my wife. She's in the family way."

"You old enough to be married, Langston James? What in the *world* does your wife look like?"

"Some of her points're right fine," he said. He paused. "Some ain't. It evens out I reckon. Her eyes're crossed, but she can do sums in her head."

"What?"

"She's got right smart of a touch on the pianer as well."

"I don't reckon you were counting on no Gloria Swanson, were you?"

"Listen," he said. "What I come to see you about is the birthing."

"You talking about a baby, Langston James? You going to be a father?"

"Yes, ma'm. Like I said, me and Cowie is about to have issue."

She shook her head and leaned back in her chair. "I don't do midwifing no more, Langston James." Then she added, "I'm happy to say. That's not my line these days. I get fifty-two dollars and seventy-nine cents a month from the old age pension." She rocked a time or two. "These days I'm concentrating on getting old and ugly." She paused. "How you think I'm doing?"

Langston James looked at her, considering her question seriously. "Well," he said at last, "you ain't what I would call ugly, Miss Jocasta. Not *exactly*. You've drawed up a little from what I remember. You used to be a tall woman."

"I used to be a *young* woman," she said. "I never was all that much to look at, but I wasn't never ugly." She rocked a minute. "Langston James," she said at last, "you ever looked at yourself nekked?"

"What?" he said. "Ma'm?"

"A while back I got nekked and looked at myself in my mirror."

Langston James wet his lips and looked off to the side. "I don't know if you should be telling me about this, Miss Jocasta."

"How you reckon I looked?" she said.

"Listen," said Langston James. "How would I know how you looked? I come to see you on account of this here baby."

"I must have looked at myself for an hour or more. I took note of every little thing there was."

"You did?"

"My hair's all right," she said.

"Don't tell me about your hair, Miss Jocasta." Langston James spoke quickly. "Please, ma'm."

"Head hair, Langston James. *Head* hair." She shook her head slowly. "I still got a full head of hair." She paused. "On the whole I'd have to say I was an ugly thing to look at." She squinted her eyes and looked at him. "I don't know just when it happened. My hair was all right. I always set right smart stock by my hair."

"You got a fine head of hair," he said.

"But I never gave much thought to the rest of me." She paused. "Not having a man around, you know." She rocked for a minute. "I never did think of myself as ugly before." For a minute Langston James thought she might cry, then the line of her mouth hardened and she went on. "I guess it happened a long time ago, only I never noticed just how it was." Her lips trembled slightly. "I wasn't all *that* much to look at to start with. Charles Dana Gibson never would have wanted to draw *my* picture. But I wasn't, you know...ugly. Something like that comes up on you a step at the time. I couldn't tell just when it happened. It must have been a good while ago. I hadn't looked at myself close to since I was just a young girl."

Langston James shuffled his feet and looked around the room.

"I had a beau once," she said. "You didn't know that, did you?"

"No, ma'm," he said. "I never did."

"I'm not lying to you, Langston James. His name was Walter Pretorius."

"Walter Pretorius," he said.

"Walt was a fair looking figger of a man. He went off to Cuba with Teddy Roosevelt and never came back. One of his buddies wrote me a letter about it, though we weren't even engaged really at the time. Some friend of his he met in Tampa while they were waiting to go. He told me Walter had caught the fever and died." She thought a minute. "He said that my name was on Walter's lips just before he passed on." She put her hand to her hair, daintily, the way a young girl would do it. "On his lips..." For a minute she didn't speak. "Yellow fever, I guess. All he said was *the fever*. They put him in the ground down there in Cuba. I thought one day I might be able to make the trip just to see where he was buried, but I never could get up the money." She paused. "I guess I could have bought the ticket if I'd truly wanted to. There didn't seem to be any reason to go really. We never were engaged, you know."

"Well," said Langston James, "I'm sorry to hear this, Miss Jocasta." She rocked a minute. "It's old business now, Langston James. Old business. Everybody was young once. Old people get morbid."

"Yes," he said. "Listen. You ain't going to help with the baby?"

"I haven't done a baby in ten years or more. My eyes aren't any good for it now. Besides," she said, "somebody will just start a war and kill it."

"She can't do it by herself."

"She don't have to. Get you a doctor, Langston James. That's the way they do it nowadays. In a hospital and everything. You know, modern."

"How much does that cost?"

"They'll work it out for you." She rocked a minute. "You know what?" she said.

"No, ma'm."

"I sure would like to see that child when it does come. You say your wife's cross-eyed?"

"Yes, ma'm."

"Sweet Jesus, Langston James. The Lord moves in mysterious ways."

"I got to think about this, Miss Jocasta."

"You should have thought about it before now. The time for thinking is past."

"Well," Langston James said, rising to leave.

"And, listen," she said, "you let me know when that baby gets here."

"Yes, ma'm," he said, moving toward the door.

"I want to get a look at that child when it comes."

Four

TEN MONTHS AFTER THE MARRIAGE, in the summer of
1948, Cowie gave birth to a male child in the Braxton County
Memorial Hospital. They named him Halstead Lamar, a name
which Langston James thought had a thoroughly respectable
sound.

When Langston James took him around for Jocasta to see, she
held him up close and examined his face for a long time. "Well,"
she said at last. "Not as bad as I thought." Then she handed him
back to Langston James. "Near as I can see."

Halstead was not deformed, nor even particularly ugly as an
infant, but there was, from the first, a debilitated air about him — a
kind of fragile weariness which became more and more pronounced
as he grew into childhood. He never looked young, not even in
the cradle. And anyone over the age of twenty who met him on
the street was immediately reminded of his own mortality. Only
Cyrus Degraff, the undertaker, took an interest in him, but of

course his interest was professional and morbid.

"I can't get over how natural he looks," said Cyrus. Then he added, "Of course he *is* alive."

Langston James would have been more comfortable with the physical deformity of a twisted arm or leg, but he gradually adapted himself to the abstract terms of Halstead's affliction. In the long run he found his son's air of gloom a good substitute, and was rather pleased with him on the whole.

They made a happy family, if a somewhat grotesque one, and by pulling together they expanded their newspaper delivery business and raised their level of prosperity steadily over the years.

In the spring of 1956, Langston James had the good fortune to be the aggrieved party in a car wreck when he was hit by a Cadillac automobile with Pennsylvania license plates—always an occasion for rejoicing in the rural counties of Georgia. The car was driven by a middle-aged man in expensive clothes accompanied by his two hundred-pound wife, whose clothes were even more expensive and who gasped when she talked.

Langston James saw his chance and took it. Before the police arrived, the tourist was convinced that the wreck of a man standing before him had been—up to the moment of impact—well, if not Robert Taylor, at least hale and hearty. Even without a critical eye, he could see he didn't stand a ghost of a chance. So he paid the patrolman in cash for the fine, gave him the name of his insurance company, and whacked his wife on the back to get her breathing back to normal. He then asked directions to Florida and left.

The insurance company chose to contend the case, and sent a lawyer down from Atlanta to argue it. The lawyer, a young man with dark hair and pale, oily skin, made the serious mistake of appearing in the Braxton County Courthouse wearing a camel hair sport coat and tasselled loafers. He could have made a bigger mistake only if he had appeared in a taffeta evening gown with a flower in his hair. He took a good look at the disapproving face of the judge, who was wearing a Sears Roebuck shirt with a clip-on tie, and at the knot of men called for jury duty, all of whom were dressed in overalls, then motioned Langston James out into the corridor where he settled for twenty thousand dollars.

With the money, Langston James bought a Motorola television set for the family and a pair of black and red tooled leather cowboy boots for himself. Also a white Stetson hat with a snakeskin band. His childhood admiration for Gene Autry got fulfilled, so to speak, at both ends. And if what went in between looked like something out of a funhouse mirror, Langston James didn't worry about it. He was used to marching to his own drummer.

Most of the money went for a lease on an empty building in a side street near the courthouse square, which he vaguely planned to turn into a store of some kind, an enterprise which never quite defined itself.

Cowie and Halstead liked the television set and the loose feeling they got from going down to the store and picking up things without having to pay for them.

The building had been unoccupied for some time, but had once been a drugstore — a rather grand one at that. With a black-and-white octagon tile floor, three ceiling fans, and an elaborate soda fountain with a marble counter which had been left, probably because it was too large to pass through any of the openings after the building had been modernized. There were shelves on the walls in mahogany, and elaborate paneling back to the point where the prescription counter had been. Behind that loomed a vast empty space with bare brick walls and a concrete floor. Langston James put a rocking chair just at the point where the tile ended and the concrete began. After he delivered his papers in the morning, he would sit and rock in the nearly empty building, relaxing and enjoying a generalized sense of proprietorship. Finally the place turned out to be more a haven than a business.

Just inside the entrance, he put a glass-front display case and a rack for magazines. Possibly out of deference to the history of the place—he never took them himself—he laid in a supply of patent medicines, and, for Cowie and Halstead, an assortment of novelty items and candy. At that point he lost the momentum of his inspiration and never carried it further. Occasionally a customer would wander in and buy a bottle of Hadacol or a package of cigarettes, paying the money into Langston James's hand, while he made change out of his pocket.

As it turned out, the chief benefit the place bestowed on him was that it brought him together with Bodine Polite.

Bodine was a black man, somewhat older than Langston James—in his mid-forties, he said—with a grave and serious manner. His skin was a stark blue-black, but his features were finely drawn—Nubian. Except for his color, even a citizen of Whippet would have admitted that he was a handsome man. He carried himself with an air of fastidiousness and restraint, and his movements were elegant and refined. His customary expression was one of pained thoughtfulness, which was a little misleading. Bodine was shrewd, but not particularly smart—and certainly uneducated. He thought that Mexico was one of the forty-eight states, but that Texas was a foreign country. He had never been able to go to school, but had taught himself to read—though he did it laboriously and only if the need was great. Since the Star theater in Whippet did not have a balcony, he had never seen a motion picture or a newsreel. He did not own a radio.

When Langston James tried to recall later just how the attachment had been formed, he could never be sure exactly how it had come about. He did remember, clearly, the first time that Bodine had appeared in the store. It had been a weekday in August of 1956, though he couldn't remember precisely which day. He did remember that it had been a hot one, even by the high standards of Braxton County. Bodine was dressed in clean, pressed overalls over a white shirt buttoned at the collar without a tie. On his head was a snap-brim driving cap of grey tweed—like the ones James Cagney used to wear in the gangster movies of the thirties. He did not acknowledge Langston James, but stood in front of the glass case, looking at it as if something were happening inside. Langston James was sitting in his rocking chair toward the back of the store. The yellow light from the street pounded outside the window, outlining Bodine as a black silhouette. Because of his movements and his fine facial features, Langston James thought at first that he was a white man. The sweep of the ceiling fans made a soft whispering sound in the shadowed gloom. In his recollection, Langston James remembered the sound in the stillness. Bodine stood very erect with his hands folded inside the bib of his overalls. Several minutes went by.

"You going to buy something?" Langston James said at last.

Bodine didn't look at him. For a minute he didn't answer. "Ain't got no money," he said.

As soon as he spoke Langston James knew he was black, and his voice relaxed. "I give credit," he said. He didn't get up from his chair. Having to display his spastic walk to customers was hateful to him, though he did stand and move for the white ones. "You got a job?"

Bodine continued to look into the case for a minute, then he turned to face Langston James. "I reckon not," he said.

For awhile neither of them said anything. Bodine stood with his hands folded inside his bib, looking around at the empty shelves of the store. Old papers had begun to accumulate in piles against the back wall.

"What you need? Ain't nothing you see going to cost you much."

Bodine looked up at the fan rotating slowly above his head. "It be nice and cool in here," he said at last. "You got you a nice cool place." He took off his hat and fanned himself with it. "Reckon I could sit down for a spell?" he said at last. "It awful hot and glary out there." He gestured toward the window with the hat, then put it back on his head.

Langston James frowned and thought about it. The request took him off guard. "Take that chair there," he said at last, pointing to a lyre-backed drugstore chair. He sounded exasperated when he spoke.

Bodine lifted the chair delicately, carrying it with both hands, as if he were going to practice a dance step with it. "Much obliged," he said. He put it down facing Langston James in his rocker, then took a red bandanna handkerchief from his hip pocket and dusted the seat with dainty flourishes.

"Put it over there," said Langston James, pointing to the back of the store.

Bodine picked up the chair and walked it to the back. When he put it down, he dusted it with his handkerchief again. He sat down slowly and deliberately, then crossed his legs and placed both hands on his knee—a stiff and self-conscious pose. The two men sat for awhile in silence, making a tableau, as if they were waiting for something to happen. Each sat looking at the wall opposite.

Finally Bodine took out a can of Tube Rose snuff. He held out the can to Langston James. "Have some?" he said, not looking at him.

"I don't dip."

Bodine nodded, then took a large pinch and put it inside his cheek. Langston James got up and hobbled to the soda fountain. He came back with a Dixie cup which he handed to Bodine. "Don't spit on the floor," he said. Again there was the sound of exasperation in his voice.

"I don't spit on *no* floor." Bodine was emphatic when he spoke, and he looked Langston James in the eye as he took the cup. "Much obliged."

They sat for awhile, facing, but not looking at each other—

each contemplating his wall. Neither spoke for a long time.

"You got a name?" Langston James said at last.

"Absolutely."

"Well...?" he said. "Don't get funny with me."

"Polite." Bodine put the accent on the "*Po*."

"Po-light what?"

"Bodine Polite." He looked up at the ceiling fan. "It ain't Polite what. It *what* Polite. Polite my *last* name." He paused. "It go...P—O—L—I—T—E."

"Oh," said Langston James, raising his eyebrows. "Smart fella. Know how to cipher and everything."

"I can do my own name."

"Think that's a big advantage, do you?"

"I can sign myself when I got to."

Langston James nodded. "C—A—T," he said.

"What?"

"I said, 'C—A—T.' That strike a note on you? Don't think about it too long."

Bodine gave him a long look, but didn't reply.

"How you spell 'Bodine'? Or maybe you ain't got that far yet."

"I *said* I could sign myself."

"Okay."

"B—O—D—I—N—E. You satisfied? I get me some kind of a prize now?"

"'D—I—N—E'? That don't spell Bo-*deen*. You sure about it now?"

"It *my* name, ain't it?"

Langston James looked at him for a minute. "How old are you, Bodine?"

"Fawty-three last June. What that got to do with it?"

"I was wondering how you got to be fawty-three years old in Whippet with a mouth on you like you got."

"I keep it to myself when I got to."

"You got a pretty risky *manner* about you as well."

Bodine didn't say anything.

"How come you figure it's okay to let it run just now?"

Bodine sat swinging his foot and looking at the wall. "Well," he said at last. "You ain't ezackly *main* stream, Mister M'Hennery."

Langston James sat back in his chair and rocked a time or two. "You know my name?" he said.

"I reckon you got to be Mister M'Hennery."

"Close enough." Langston James pursed his lips. "You worked all this out ahead of time? Or you just making it up as you go along?"

"I just lookin' for me a cool place."

"Well . . . I'm going to give you a little more time while I figure you out. You know. Before I throw your black ass out that door yonder." He pointed to the door in the back wall of the store. Langston James took out his pack of Old Golds. "You want a cigarette?" He held it out to Bodine.

"Better not," he said. He touched his index finger to the bulge in his cheek. "I likes snuff gen'rally. Leastways I don't take my weed but one way at the time."

"Old Golds got 'Apple Honey,'" he said. "Cured with 'Apple Honey.'"

"That so?"

"Says so right there on the pack." He pointed with his finger and held up the package for Bodine to see.

Bodine glanced at the package. "Prob'bly," he said flatly.

"I like the yaller package too." Langston James looked at the package, then tapped out a cigarette and lit it. "Bodine," he said, "you make me curious." He blew smoke towards the fan. "How long you lived in Whippet?"

Bodine spat into the Dixie cup, a long, drooling blob of saliva. He held the cup in this right hand, placing his left on his chest with the fingers splayed as he leaned over. "Fawty-three years," he said. "I done told you."

"I got no use for a smartass, Bodine. You on mighty thin ice anyways."

Bodine took out his bandanna and wiped his mouth. "You the one tried to be in the waw," he said.

"What?"

"You tried and tried."

"That's a long time ago. How you know about that?"

"I pays attention."

Langston James thought a minute. "Was *you* in the arm service?"

"It wasn't nothing to do with me. I was farming at the time."

"You done your part?"

"I reckon."

"Colored folks didn't have to go, did they? Not in Braxton County they didn't."

"*Some* went."

"I mean *have* to go?"

"Cripples neither."

"What?"

"You didn't go your ownself."

"I tried."

"Like I said."

Langston James rocked for awhile, blowing smoke at the fan.

"You got you something off that Nawthen feller too," Bodine spoke at last. He rolled his eyes, looking around at the walls of the store.

Langston James looked at him intently. "Uh huh," he said. "It's going to come to me. Any minute now."

Bodine looked at him, then he put the Dixie cup down on the floor slowly and carefully. He stood up. "I reckon I be getting along now," he said.

Langston James looked up at him for a long minute, a serious expression on his face. Suddenly he gave a loud hiccoughing laugh. Bodine frowned. "You jumping me, ain't you, Bodine?"

For a minute Bodine didn't answer. "Not ezackly," he said. He was almost smiling, but not quite. "I knows about that too."

"You running a goddamn close line, buster. You think you know what you doing?"

"It caught my eye is all. The way you getting on. You don't mind folks taking notice, do you?"

Langston James held out his hand. "Gimme that cup," he said. Bodine picked it up and brought it over to him. He dropped his cigarette butt into it, then gave it back. "It don't hurt the tile none," he said. "Stomping it out on the tile. It's the principle of the thing. I don't like it." He picked a piece of tobacco off his tongue.

Bodine stood over him nodding.

Langston James rocked for awhile, drumming his fingers on the arm of the chair and looking up at Bodine. "Bring your chair over here," he said, pointing to a spot opposite.

Bodine brought the chair and stood watching him. "Sit down, Bodine," he said at last. "Maybe we got us some business here."

Bodine sat down.

"Would you say you was a smart nigger, Bodine?"

Bodine looked up at the fan, pursing his lips and thinking about the question. "Hunh uh," he said at last. "I wouldn't say that."

Langston James nodded. "I didn't think you would. And you ain't no *uppity* nigger neither, wouldn't you say?"

"Not me."

Langston James nodded, working his mouth. "You want a job?" he said at last.

Bodine shook his head. "All I want me is a cool place."

"Cool *and* quiet?"

"That'd be nice," he said. "Cool *and* quiet be real nice indeed."

Langston James nodded. "See that cooler up there?" He pointed to the front of the store.

"Yassah."

Langston James looked at Bodine. "Gimme a 'Yassah *Bossman*,'" he said.

"BOSSMAN," said Bodine elaborately.

"That's the ticket." He pointed again. "Go get us two Co-colas out that cooler. We going to sit here and drink Co-colas and smoke cigarettes while I find out about you."

"I'll have me a Dr Pepper."

"Get us one."

They sat and drank their Dr Peppers and smoked two Old Golds apiece, passing the cup back and forth between them for an ashtray.

"What I can't figure out is how you managed to get by all these years and keep your head out a rope. How come the Klan never took no notice of you?"

"I done time."

"You got off easy. What you done time *for?*"

"Stole me a hawg."

"How soon they catch you?"

"I got me a meal off him."

"What they give you?"

"Five. I done three."

"I hope that hawg was a good one."

"He's pretty sweet."

"Five years sweet? Sounds dumb to me, Bodine."

"I only done three. I was hongry."

"That's high meat any way you figure it."

"They ain't going to leave a nigger alone in Braxton County till he done time. I be free and clear now."

"They don't have to pay you welfare if you done time."

Bodine nodded.

"How long ago that happen?"

"I been out eighteen years."

"Eighteen years?"

"Eighteen years come October."

"I thought it was recent."

"It stays in your mind. They put the chains on us back then."

For awhile they sat without speaking, each looking past the other at his wall.

Finally Langston James spoke. "How come you ain't been by sooner?"

"Come by *what*? You taken social visits from colored folks on Price De-Cant Street?"

"Earl Warren says it's all equal now."

Bodine looked at him. "That be bullshit." His voice had an edge on it. He looked away. "Anyway, I been busy."

"Doing what?"

"I got me some punch boards. Run a few numbers."

"It would just naturally be a hustle, wouldn't it?"

"I run 'em honest. No need to cheat. The advantage goes to the board."

"Naturally."

"Damn right 'naturally.' I ain't no smart nigger, but I ain't no dumbass neither."

Langston James looked at him for awhile. "Let me tell you about the newspaper business," he said at last.

* * *

Langston James never could decide just what it was about Bodine that appealed to him. He didn't ask himself questions about it all that much, but when he did he never could get the answer. It might have been the way Bodine looked, which was, surely, not according to any constitutional or inherited way of thinking that was available to Langston James. Black people were there, but beyond the range of values like that — sometimes a care but never a consideration. A handsome black man was simply a contradiction of terms—a hot that was cold, an up that was down. It might have been the way Bodine talked—or didn't talk—in the hours they spent together, and the restfulness of never having to explain himself or say things twice or think about the words he was choosing. It might even have been the clean-pressed overalls or the cap he wore. The idea of friendship with a Negro never entered the lopsided head of Langston James, and certainly the word itself never did. He *loved* Cowie. And Halstead was his natural son. But obligations and duty clung there, if ever so faintly. Except for his dead mother—and that only during his childhood—Bodine was the one human being he had come across in his life who didn't put a weight across his shoulders or wear him out.

Serious introspection was never a strong point with Langston James. Five straight minutes of it glued his tongue to the roof of his mouth and put a twitch in his optic nerve. His deepest inclination was to let things go.

"Well," he'd say, sucking the juices back into his oral cavity, "I *like* the black son of a bitch."

Bodine quickly became a fixture in the store, and pretty soon he began to show up in the mornings to ride with Langston James in his truck while he went his rounds delivering the papers. The black man steadfastly refused all offers of a job, and finally Langston James stopped bringing it up for fear he would drive him away. Beyond all the other considerations promoting the relationship, Bodine presented him with his first and only genuine opportunity to practice noblesse oblige. But that was only the half of it. The other half was that he liked the grotesqueness of accepting something like charity from a black man.

Though he was not working for Langston James according to a contract, Bodine rolled and threw papers the way a hired helper would have done. Doing this earned him the right to ride in the cab of the truck on the paper route. At other times, especially in broad daylight and around town, he sat in the bed, facing backwards and perched on a lyre-backed drugstore chair, which he placed against the cab. Alone, the two of them, in the cab of the truck during the early morning hours, with the countryside and the town asleep and the dash lights glowing on their faces, the radio tuned to wheezing out-of-town stations, Langston James talked and talked, unravelling his sad history matter-of-factly, telling his story without complaint.

Langston James made frequent loans to Bodine, loans which he instigated himself for the most part, though the black man would occasionally make a modest request. In the aggregate they amounted to a salary, because both of them understood that they would never be repaid. In fact they amounted to something *more* than a fair salary would have come to under more formal terms of employment. Langston James realized this, but he wrote it off as part of the price to him of the noblesse oblige. It was an arrangement that was fragile enough to satisfy them both.

Cowie and Halstead accepted Bodine at face value. There were plenty of working relationships between white men and black with the same surface quality. The bus boycott in Montgomery and the Supreme Court decision had not been felt in Whippet. Langston James never talked to Cowie about the feeling he had, because there was no way to do it at that time. Eventually Bodine became one of the family, as the concept went in 1956. Langston James put a small table and a stool on the back porch, and Cowie fed him there out of the kitchen. In good weather he took his meals sitting on the back steps.

* * *

During the recession of 1958 several of the newspaper customers cancelled their subscriptions. The actual loss in money didn't amount to much, but Langston James read in it dire portents for their future.

"I knew it was too good to last," he said, wringing his hands. "We've got to cut back, Cowie, honey."

"Stand over there, Eljay," she said. "You blocking the teevy. Gumby's my favorite."

"Are you listening to me, honey?" he said, moving aside and looking at the screen. "What *is* that thing?"

"Ain't he cute? That little feller goes straight to my heart."

"It ain't a turd, is it?"

She looked at him but didn't reply.

"It looks like a turd." He turned to Halstead. "Don't it look like a turd, Halstead?"

"Don't you answer him, Halstead," she said. "He's just looking for trouble. I told you already. That there's my favorite. Don't get your bowels in an uproar. We're not going broke in the next thirty minutes."

Langston James looked at the screen. "That there's your *favorite*?" he said. "I paid three hundred and forty-nine dollars for that teevy."

"You got your heart closed up with a dollar sign, Eljay. If you can't understand about lovely things, you can just run along and leave us alone."

"Listen here," he said. "You got you a short memory, friend. I remember eating grits three times a day."

"You were lucky. I remember beans."

"What?"

"Grits're good for you."

"Three times a day?"

"Whatever."

"We didn't even have no fatback."

"Mmmmmmmmmm," she said. "Grits with fatback is good eating."

"We didn't *HAVE* no fatback."

"Well," she said, waving her hand. "Step thattaway, Eljay. You blocking the teevy again."

He looked at her for a minute then stalked out of the room.

"I'll remember when the time comes," she said, calling after him.

Langston James did not trust her to comprehend the seriousness of their situation, so he sneaked in economy measures on the sly. He turned down the pilot light on the hot water tank, put burned out bulbs in half the lamps, and turned off the water at the meter from nine in the morning until three in the afternoon. All of those economy measures were reasonable in their conception. At least they all had a faint glow of logic behind them. His decision to rinse out and reuse a single condom for three weeks running was made in pure desperation.

"What?" he said.

"I said turn on the water. I'm pregnant."

"Oh Lordy," he said. "Are you sure?"

She nodded her head. "Ain't it wonderful?" she said, giving him her serene smile of gestation. Langston James looked at the expression on her face and recognized it as confirmation beyond anything a rabbit could provide.

"Oh Lordy, Lordy, Lordy," he said.

Their second son, Gabriel, was born in the summer of 1959. By then the economy was back to normal, they were throwing more papers than ever, and Langston James was sure his troubles were over.

In fact, his troubles were just beginning.

Gabriel was named for the angel.

Five

GABRIEL WAS A GENETIC BACKFIRE, a statistical improbability of the same magnitude as the sun doing figure eights in the sky. Langston James knew something was up when he went to the viewing window and saw that his son's crib had been placed right up front where everybody could see it. When Halstead had been born, the nurses had kept his crib well sequestered, far in the back where no beam reached. The ugliest nurse on the floor had been assigned to look after him.

Gabriel — though he was an affront to the laws of probability — was a beautiful baby. In fact, he was the most beautiful baby that had ever been born in the Braxton County Memorial Hospital, if not in the world. He smiled and recognized faces and looked people in the eye. He never cried or was fretful. He never drooled. If he had stood up in his crib and recited poetry and played the accordion, he would have excited comment, but not surprise. He was uncalibrated, definitive perfection — the ultimate, all-time ur-baby, who made the one on the Gerber label look like Porky Pig.

Langston James was appalled.

He kept his dismay to himself until Cowie came home from the hospital, then he tried to talk to her about it.

"What're we gonna do, Cowie?" he whined.

"Do about *what*, Eljay?"

"Just look at them regular features, honey. That's what I'm talking about."

Cowie was constitutionally serene, but maternity lowered her metabolism to invertebrate proportions. "Yes," she said. "Ain't he beautiful?"

"That's what I mean. That's exactly what I mean." Langston James's voice went so high a dog outside the house started to whine.

"Well?" she said.

"Are you listening to me?"

"Not especially," she said, tucking the swaddling around Gabriel's chin.

"You think he belongs in this family?"

As well as she could, Cowie cocked an eye at him. Two eyes really. Trying to meet her gaze made his bad eye wall more than ever. "You think I've been playing around?"

Langston James looked first into one eye, then the other. Tender glances were hard to come by in their relationship. Finally he shook his head slowly. "You're not listening to me, Cowie," he said. "I mean what're we going to do about that there child, honey?"

"He's our natural born offspring, Eljay."

"I never said he wasn't." He nodded his head. "Listen, you're a good woman, darlin'. What I meant was what're we going to *do*?"

She looked at him for a minute. "I can tell you got *something* on your mind, Eljay, but I be damned if I can tell what it is. Can't you come out and say it?"

Langston James stood wringing his hands and sawing his head from side to side.

"Listen," he said. "Let me put it this way. He's...*pretty*."

Cowie nodded and looked at the baby. "No," she said. "What he is is *beautiful*."

"All right," he said, as if the question had been settled.

She thought a minute, sucking on her lip. "Was there anything else?" she said at last. "Is that it?"

"Look at the rest of us, Cowie. You and me and Halstead. That child don't fit the pattern, honey. He ain't, you know, one of *us*."

"What're you talking about, Eljay? He's as one of us as your sperms can provide."

"Well, you can't make no sow's purse out of a silk ear."

She looked at him for a long minute. "You're not talking sense, Eljay. Let's go into this later. I'm going to give him the breast now. Would you mind stepping outside for awhile?"

"What?" he said.

"I'd like a little privacy, if you don't mind."

"I seen your tiddy before. Lots of times. This here is serious, honey. You've got to listen to me."

"You don't understand motherhood," she said. "You got no idea about motherhood at all and everything it means."

"He's too pretty to be a *girl*, let alone a boy. How you think that looks?"

Cowie's eyes, which were not much good for seeing far off, were just about right for near focussing with a child at her breast. "He's an angel child," she said, guiding her nipple to the mouth of the infant.

Langston James stood wringing his hands. "Take that child off your breast and listen to me, Cowie."

"That's exactly what he is. An angel child."

"All right," he said. He walked to the door. "We've got to talk about this, Cowie. As of now we ain't spoke the last word."

She nodded her head, not listening. "Close the door gentle when you go out," she said.

"The last word ain't been spoke on this," he said. "Not by a long shot." When he went out of the door, she couldn't hear the click of the latch as he pulled it softly to.

In the kitchen, Halstead was standing at the sink washing dishes.

"He's something, ain't he, Daddy?"

"What?"

"Gabriel. He something, ain't he?"

"It's a worry to me, Halstead. He ain't in accordance with this here family. He ain't in accordance at all."

"What you mean?"

Langston James stood shaking his head. "I mean just look at him." He hugged himself and leaned against the counter. "It makes me draw up inside."

"You rather he looked like a frog?"

"What?"

"Everybody thinks he's really something, Daddy."

"I'd rather he's one of *us*, Halstead. That's what I'd rather he was." He frowned. "What's wrong with a frog?" he asked. "What kind of a frog?"

"Well," said Halstead, swishing his hands in the water of the sink. "Ain't no help for it. There he is. He sure ain't no frog. I reckon we'll get used to the idea."

"Lordy, oh Lordy," said Langston James, shaking his head. He looked at Halstead working his hands in the sink. "What's the matter?"

"Seems like it's stopped up."

"Let me see." He plunged his hand into the soapy water and jabbed his fingers into the drain. The water sloshed greasily in the sink. "It's stopped up," he said. There was a pained expression on his face. He sounded like he was going to cry.

"Yessir," said Halstead. "That's what I figured."

Langston James put his head down on his arm. When he

spoke his voice sounded broken and weary. "See what I mean, Halstead? Our luck's done gone bad already."

"Cause the sink's stopped up?"

"It's a sign, Halstead. What we got here ain't only just the beginning." He paused. "There's other things."

"Such as?"

"I been having trouble with the truck lately."

"Daddy, that truck's nineteen years old. You're *always* having trouble with it."

"Well. I been having *more* trouble with it."

"You ought to get you a new one."

Langston James jabbed his fingers at the sink. "That ain't all. I got me a carbuncle."

"You think Gabriel give you a carbuncle?"

"All I know is I ain't had me no carbuncle in twenty years. What you got to say to *that*?"

"I ain't got nothing to say."

"Signs is signs, Halstead."

"You sure it ain't just a boil?"

Langston James looked at him in a hurt way. Then he took his hand out of the sink and undid his belt.

"What you going to do?" said Halstead.

"I know a goddamn carbuncle when I see it," he said. He began to unbutton his fly.

"Daddy," said Halstead, holding out his hand, "don't show me your carbuncle. I don't want to see it. A son's got no right to question his father."

"A carbuncle ain't no laughing matter, son," he said, beginning to refasten his fly. "I known a man die from a carbuncle."

"Daddy," said Halstead, "I ain't laughing." He patted his father's shoulder. "Don't take it so hard. He ain't but two weeks old. We got time. We got plenty of time."

"I know bad news when I see it, son. I got me a *Di-rect* line when it comes to bad news." He collected himself and stood up. "Go get the plunger. We've got to take things as they come."

"That's right, Daddy," said Halstead. "Why don't you get you a new truck?"

* * *

"Whyn't you get you a new truck?" Bodine spoke with his whiney voice. "Way this one runnin' give me palpitations."

"Roll the papers, Bodine, roll the papers. I'll worry about this truck when the time comes. Real trouble—that's what I got on my mind just now. Real trouble." He winged a paper out of the window.

"Mizres Wilson on vacation. You wasn't supposed to throw her no paper."

"I forgot."

Bodine rolled papers in silence for awhile. "Nothing you going to do about that child," he said at last. "Miss Cowie ain't going to stand for nothing like that."

"Oh Lordy, Lordy." He flung another paper out the window.

"That one gone in the ditch. You better stop and let me put it in the drive. Mister Dekle want it right on *THE* spot."

Langston James stopped the truck and backed down the highway. "Don't hunt for it, Bodine. Just throw him another one."

"You keep this up, you going to be carrying your brain around in a paper sack."

"What?" Langston James put the truck into first.

"This here's Bible stuff. I mean *serious*. How come you ain't talked to your preacher? Maybe he could set you right on it."

Langston James drove for awhile in silence. "You got any children, Bodine?" he said at last.

Bodine rolled two or three papers before he answered. "I got me a couple."

"You don't never talk about them."

"Nothing to talk about. They just chirruns."

"What they look like?"

"Mostly they look like they mommas. What you mean... 'What they look like?'"

"You say 'Mommas'? How many women you got?"

"Several."

"All at once? Or one at the time?"

"All at *once*? What you take me for? I be a baptized Christian. Anyway, I couldn't hardly handle them *one* at the time."

"You a rascal, Bodine. You know that?"

Bodine nodded. "Ain't had but few complaints. I got a certain *style*."

"You love your children?"

"Course I do. I'm they daddy, ain't I?"

Langston James nodded. For awhile he didn't speak. "It's eating on me, Bodine. I feel like I need to shoot myself in the foot or something. Put my hand in a fire."

"Well, now, that'd be a *heap* of help."

"You really think it'd do some good to talk to Brother Moates?"

"Preachers sposed to be good for talking trouble at."

"I don't know. Them sermons he preaches don't speak a lot for his judgment. Last one I heard was on David and Goliath and the consecrated nature of *projectiles*. Nearabout every one gets worked around to how the Lord loves him to shoot things. He's hipped on the subject."

"Well," said Bodine.

"I heard him preach sermons on the Thompson submachine gun and the M-1 rifle. *Two* sermons on the M-1 rifle. He said God ordained the invention of it to show He was on our side."

"You don't have to pay him no mind if he puts crazy talk on you."

Langston James drove for awhile in silence. "I don't reckon it could hurt none. He hits the nail on the head every *once* in awhile. A man'll go for anything when he's desperate, Bodine."

"Uh huh," said Bodine. Then he added, "Think about you a new truck as well."

* * *

Langston James found Brother Moates in his back yard shooting at tin cans with his new H&R twenty-two pistol.

"I got me a problem, Brother Moates."

Brother Moates squeezed off a round at a Heinz Pork and Beans can. The can leapt into the air spinning. "You know anything about pistol shooting, Eljay?"

"No."

"It ain't like no rifle. You got to pull down on your mark." He went through the motion to illustrate. "Keep it moving, else you ain't going to hit nothing."

"I see," said Langston James.

"If it's more'n twenty-five feet you ain't hardly going to hit it anyways."

"Is that a fact?"

"You ain't even likely to hit a *man* if it's over twenty-five feet. Not so it'll do you any *good*."

"Listen," said Langston James, "I need to talk to you about something."

"You got a problem, Eljay? That's what I'm here for. Burdens of the heart and daily woe."

"I'm glad to hear it, Brother Moates."

"Step thisaway." He walked off towards the can, picked it up and examined it. "Went in at the 'H.' I'm pulling a little to the left. What I was aiming at was the 'I.'" He held the can up for Langston James to see.

"You hit the 'H' all right." There was a huge starburst of metal on the back side of the can where the bullet had come out.

"Them holler points do the job all right." Brother Moates set the can back down on the ground. "I'm just getting used to it." He held the pistol at arm's length and sighted at the back fence. "When I get the feel of it, I'll work on shooting from the hip."

"I see," said Langston James.

"You catch a prowler, you ain't got time to set and take aim. Usually."

"I reckon not."

"You got to get it off fast." He went through a quick-draw motion to illustrate. "Course I'd hate to shoot a man, you understand. But somebody breaks in your domicile in the middle of the night you ain't going to sit around and have no discussion."

Langston James thought a minute. "I don't reckon I'd shoot nobody. I ain't even got a gun."

"What?" Brother Moates lurched and gave him a surprised look. "What you going to do when somebody breaks in your house?"

"I reckon I ain't going to shoot him."

"You ain't even got no weapon in that truck? You driving around in the dark hours throwing them papers, Eljay. That's a dangerous time."

"I got me a piece of pipe I keep under the seat."

"Well, yes. That's all right. But think how close you got to get to use a piece of pipe."

"I wouldn't want to shoot nobody anyway. That don't seem like no Christian act to me."

Brother Moates gave him a serious look. "You think it's Christian to let some tee-twat just walk in your house and steal your treasures and rape your wife? I don't recollect nowhere in the Bible says you got to put up with that kind of activity. 'Eye for eye, tooth for tooth, life for life.' Exodus . . . Chapter twenty-one:

verse twenty-four. *Life for life*, Eljay. *That's* the way I read the scriptures."

"Don't it say 'Vengeance is *Mine*, saith the Lord?'"

"Not quite. 'Vengeance is mine; *I will repay*, saith the Lord.' That's the whole of it. Romans...Chapter twelve: verse nineteen." Brother Moates nodded at Langston James. "Far as the *next* world's concerned, that's his business for sure. Long as we're talking about *this* one, I reckon 'The Lord helps those as helps themselves.'" He nodded again. "That ain't scripture, but it ought to be."

"Listen," said Langston James, "I didn't come here to argue with you. I got me a problem."

"You ain't a big feller, Eljay. Let's face it. You got to get awful close to make use of that pipe of yours. If he comes at you on your left side, it ain't going to do no good at all."

"Yes," said Langston James. "Well, let me tell you about this problem I got."

"Feller your size needs all the equalizer he can find. Get 'em while they's still off a ways."

"Listen. I come to tell you about this problem."

"Okay, Eljay. Let's hear it."

"Well," he hesitated, thinking of the best way to get into it. "Me and Cowie been having a disagreement lately."

"Ah, yes." Brother Moates smiled and nodded his head. "The ladies. We can't get along with them, and we can't get along without them. Don't I know it."

"Yes, well. This argument we been having...she's got her head set against me."

Brother Moates looked at Langston James and frowned. "'The contentions of a wife are a continual dropping.'"

"What?"

"That's what the Bible says, Brother McHenry. Proverbs... Chapter nineteen: verse thirteen. 'The contentions of a wife are a continual dropping.' And don't you forget it."

"Dropping?"

"Strange days, Eljay. Strange days is upon us. Women wearing pants and smoking cigarettes. She thinks she got to have her way, but you let her have it and you ain't going to see the end of it. Take a strong hand. 'Wives, submit yourselves unto your own husbands, as unto the Lord. For the husband is the head of the wife, even as Christ is the head of the Church.' That's advice comes straight from the Lord. Ephesians...Chapter five: verses twenty-two and twenty-three. Look it up."

"Seems like you got you a lot of Bible verses worked up on this subject."

"I made me a *point* of it, Eljay. You got to arm yourself for the times."

"Yes, but, well, this ain't no simple problem I'm talking about."

"The home where the woman rules is a sink of iniquity and an abomination. You go ahead and let her have her way and you going to see what I'm talking about."

"Cowie's a good woman, Brother Moates."

"I never said she wasn't. All I'm saying is don't you let her get the upper hand. You do and you'll be living an abomination in the sight of the Lord." He nodded to emphasize his words. "I don't mean nothing physical, here. I never did hold with beating up on a woman." He stopped and thought for a minute. "Maybe a little slapping around. You know, just with your open hand. Long as you don't close your fist on her. Anyway, a rod of hickory is preferable to an abomination in the sight of the Lord." He held the revolver in both of his hands. "You oughtn't let her do it. For her own sake you oughtn't let her do it."

Langston James looked at him for a while without saying anything. "Much obliged," he said at last. "You given me the slant I was looking for."

"What she really wants, Eljay, is a firm hand. Firm but gentle. It ain't going to make her happy for you to give in. One thing leads to another."

"Yes," said Langston James, "I appreciate it."

Brother Moates held out the pistol to him. "Take a shot before you leave. You ought to give it a try."

"I reckon not. I never cared much for firearms."

Brother Moates shook his head. "I really worry about you, Eljay. Riding around in the dark of the night with just that colored boy and you. I'd feel a whole lot better in my heart if I knew you had some substantial protection close to hand."

"I'd end up shooting myself. Anyway, they cost too much."

"This little H&R goes for twenty-five dollars," he said, holding up the pistol and turning it this way and that. "Twenty-five dollars ain't going to break you. It's an investment really."

"I reckon not."

"I got a little Baretta twenty-five caliber in the house. I'd let you have it for ten dollars." He thought a minute. "Course a twenty-five ain't much good for personal protection. You got to put it up side a man's head to hit him. A good thick leather jacket'll turn it aside. Just the same, it's better than nothing."

"Is it better than prayer?"

"What?" Brother Moates looked surprised.

"I pray every night the Lord will keep me safe."

Brother Moates looked at him thoughtfully. "Well, yes. Of course. I go into the closet several times a day myself." He looked at the pistol, then put it into his belt. "Prayer is, you know, good *basic* protection, but you can't always count on it to handle the specific case."

"You can't count on it?"

Brother Moates thought a minute, nodding is head. "I think that's a fair way to put it. You can't leave *everything* up to the Lord. He got a right to expect you going to do your part too."

"And my part is to carry a gun?"

"I think you ought to consider it."

"I see."

"Would you like me to offer up a few words just now?"

"Don't sound like you put much stock in it."

"Don't be ironical, Eljay. You got to deal with the world the way it is." Brother Moates kneeled and clasped his hands. He looked up at Langston James. "You care to join me?"

Langston James kneeled facing him.

"Oh, Lord!" said Brother Moates, in the loud, nasal voice he used for serious, public supplication. "Oh, Lord, as you can see, this small cripple sheep stands in need of Your shield and guidance. Help him to remember his wife and children and their dependence on him and how he got to protect himself for their sake. Make him mindful of what all evil there be lurking in the dark shadders of the world. Guard and keep him as he goes about his newspaper delivery business in the dangerous hours of darkness." Brother Moates paused. A minute went by in silence.

"That it?" said Langston James, without raising his head.

"Just a minute." Brother Moates went on. "Help him, oh Lord, to cherish the wife of his bosom, and not to let her get the upper hand on him in their domestic matters. Help him, oh Lord, to keep her in line." He paused again. "All this we pray in the name of Jesus Christ, your only son, who shed his blood for us and suffered at Calvary. Amen."

They stood up. "Remember, Eljay...a *firm* hand. Firm but gentle."

"I'll keep it in mind."

"By the way," said Brother Moates, "what was you and Cowie arguing *about*?"

"Something to do with the children. Not much to it really. Much obliged for the advice," he said, backing out of the yard.

* * *

"Well, Bodine," he said, "so much for that. He told me . . . well, as *much* as told me . . . to beat up on Cowie. How you like that advice? You think that's going to solve my problem?"

Bodine finished rolling a paper before he answered. "You can't never tell about preachers. *Sometimes* they talks pretty good sense."

"The odds ain't with you when it comes to Brother Moates. I figured it was a waste of time, only I'm really desperate."

"I could see you was. I hope you wouldn't do nothing crazy."

For awhile Langston James drove in silence. "I need to tell somebody what it was I had in mind," he said at last. "You know, get it out in the open so I could see what it sounds like."

Bodine didn't answer him.

"I was thinking." He spoke slowly and calmly. "Well, you know. I could maybe put a twist in his leg." He waited for Bodine to react. Bodine didn't say anything, so he went on. "Just a *little* one. I mean, now's the time to do it. You don't wait for a pup to get growed before you bob his tail."

"Uh huh," said Bodine. "I thought it was going to be something crazy. You feel like you just *got* to tell me about it, I reckon?"

"I ain't talking about nothing *big* here. Just a little twist in his leg. Look at Halstead."

"You never put no twist in Halstead's leg."

"Halstead didn't need no twist. Halstead's okay just the way he is."

Bodine rolled a couple of papers before he spoke. "I hope you ain't found no need to mention this to Miss Cowie."

"I said it was *driving* me crazy, Bodine. I didn't say I was done drove."

"You want advice, or you just going to talk awhile?"

"Well, you could say what you think."

"Let me hold the pipe."

"What?"

"I want the pipe over here on my side if you going to hear any advice from me."

"Listen. I don't mean nothing drastic. Just a little break so his foot would turn in noticeable. Maybe a little twist in his arm to make it even."

"You getting any of this from Preacher Moates?"

"No. I never did go into details with him. I reckon he'd have me shoot Gabriel, you know, here and there."

"I'd say ain't none of this getting to the bottom of your problem."

"What you mean?"

"How you going to fix his face? That the real place you got trouble."

Langston James thought for a minute. "I couldn't do nothing to his *face*. You think I want to hurt the child?"

Bodine shook his head. "Ain't no little limp going to fix him up to suit you. Maybe you could get you some lye and dip him in it. Or set him out on a ant hill for a while." He creased and rolled a paper. "I knowed a child fell in a turpentine vat once. Hot turpentine. After they fished him out he looked something like what you got in mind." He sent a paper winging into the darkness. "Course the child died." He began to roll another. "That the risk you got to take." He looked at Langston James. "Long as he got that angel face you ain't going to be happy with him."

Langston James sat looking out the windshield of the truck, not saying anything.

"You see what I be saying, don't you?"

"You ain't understood a word I said, Bodine. You know that?"

"What it is . . . you can't stand him being different."

Langston James looked at him in surprise. "Different is what I want him to be, Bodine. You missing the point. You missing the point altogether. He ain't different enough."

"What you mean is, he ain't different the way you want."

"What?"

"He mighty different from you."

Langston James put an Old Gold in his mouth and punched in the lighter.

"You want him just like you and he ain't. Who else you think he so much like? That child don't resemble no child I ever seen before."

Langston James took several drags on his cigarette. "I should have known I wasn't going to get no satisfaction out of talking to you, Bodine. I don't think you got no idea what I'm talking about."

"Trouble with you, Mister Eljay, you can't see they's more'n one way to be different."

Part 2

Late Summer 1959

Six

SCHEMING WAS A WAY OF LIFE for Langston James, but thinking wore him out. It made deep breathing come upon him and choked him in the throat with strange vibrations. The more he thought about a problem, the more it spread and tangled on him until finally his mind thickened and stopped. He found himself unable to make even the simplest choices—as between putting on his pants before his socks or his socks before his pants. When he finally reached the point where he had to wake up Cowie and get her to help him decide, he knew it was time to do something.

"I'm going to take me a trip tomorrow," he said. "Just a little one." It was Thursday evening and Cowie was clearing away the supper dishes.

"Where you going?"

"I thought I might run up to Savannah. For the day. I need to get outside Whippet so I can think things over. Whippet ain't much of a town for thinking in."

"Savannah is?"

"I always liked Savannah."

"I always *liked* Savannah too. I don't recall I ever had any big ideas in the vicinity." She pursed her lips and nodded. "Of course I never had any big ideas in *this* vicinity either." She looked at him. "I guess it's worth a try. You want me to go with you?"

"I wouldn't be back till after dark. You got your papers."

She didn't say anything. The expression on her face was neutral.

"Bodine can ride with me. For company."

She nodded her head without speaking.

"You wouldn't take it hard?" he said. "I'll give you a trip another time."

"I reckon we could both use a rest."

"You want to go see your folks? I could carry you over to see your folks on Sunday."

"Daddy's not much fun on Sunday." She stopped and thought a minute. "Daddy's not much fun *any* time. He's *really* hard to take on Sundays. I'd about as soon stay home and sit on a tack, if it's all the same with you." She thought for a minute. "What I'd *really* like to do is go down to Waycross and get me a hamburger."

"Whatever you say."

"There's a place in Waycross makes really good hamburgers."

"I'll get you a hamburger in Waycross on Sunday."

"That will be nice," she said. They nodded at each other. "And, Eljay," she said, "try to get this out of your system, honey."

"That's what I've got in mind."

"It's wearing me out."

"I know what you mean. It's wearing me out as well."

* * *

When he picked up his papers at the drugstore on Friday morning, Langston James went in and got four packs of Old Golds
and two Dr Peppers. "You want to go to Savannah, Bodine? I got
to unclog my mind."

Bodine thought about it. "How far it be to Savannah?"

"Hundred miles. Hundred-twenty maybe."

"I mean how *long*?"

"Three hours—three and a half. Truck won't do more'n
forty-five."

"This a *working* trip?"

"Not exactly. You can ride in the cab if that's what's bothering
you. Most of the way anyhow."

"How much of the way be *most*?"

"I ain't going to have you sitting up front with me in the *middle* of Savannah, Bodine. You can put that in your pipe and
smoke it." He thought about it for a minute. "You got you a
hardon for disaster?"

Bodine developed a superior look. "It be something special
about Savannah?"

"You can't see from one end of it to the other all at once like
them little towns you're used to. That's for one thing." He began
to sound exasperated. "How come you got to drag your feet every
time I make a suggestion?"

"I be havin' to listen to you go on about the child all the way
there and back. Ain't I? Ain't that what you got in mind?"

Langston James didn't say anything.

"Old Gold cigarettes and a Dr Pepper don't dollar out on that
deal. I done heard me enough on that subject already. I need
something to boot."

"Get in." Langston James leaned over and opened the door on
the passenger side. "Get in and have you a Dr Pepper." He put
the pack of cigarettes on the dash. "Have you an Old Gold as
well. Have you *TWO* Old Golds."

Bodine thought a minute. "I wants me *three* Dr Peppers and a hot dog and a special keepsake for the trip."

"Keepsake? What kind of a keepsake?"

"Somethin' I can't get around here. You know, so I can remember about Savannah and all."

"*Three* Dr Peppers?"

"Three."

"Get in," said Langston James.

Bodine climbed into the truck, moving in his slow, ethnic protest manner.

Langston James drummed his fingers on the steering wheel. "I wonder could you maybe move a little faster, Bodine? You got dead flies dropping off you."

"Savannah gonna stay put till we gets there."

"I mean this to be a pleasure trip. You going to ruin it for us?"

Bodine slammed the door. "Some pleasure," he said.

After they finished delivering the papers, and were heading down the road to Waycross, Langston James turned reflective in his thoughts and manner of speaking. "You ever have any dreams, Bodine?" he asked.

"I don't reckon I got time to have no dreams."

"Bullshit, Bodine. You always got to let me know what a hard life you living. You got time to *sleep*, don't you? Just answer the question."

Bodine didn't say anything.

"Anyway," Langston James paused and looked at the speedometer, "I never had dreams all that much." The pointer was whacking and jumping around forty-five. "I been having one lately. The same one over and over." He shifted his foot and tapped the steering wheel with his finger. "When you're having the same one over and over they say it *means* something. That's what they say."

"You got more time than me," said Bodine.

"What?"

"Get on with it."

"Listen, Bodine," he looked at him lit up by the dash lights, "I want you paying attention to this."

Bodine didn't say anything.

"What they say is sometimes it'll help if you tell somebody what all it is you been dreaming about. I read that somewheres." He paused. "This ain't no recreational dreaming I'm talking about. This here is *serious*."

Bodine pursed his lips and waited.

"I want you to know that."

Bodine nodded.

"I been having this same one for about a week now. It's a scary dream." He paused. "Well, in a way it is. Mostly I worry about having it over and over for such a long time. Anything gets at you if it goes on too long."

"I reckon *hearing* about dreams could get you down if you got too much of it."

"Listen. You got you a pack of Old Golds and a Dr Pepper. Now give me some undivided attention, goddamn it. I'm *paying* for this."

Bodine upended his Dr Pepper and took an elaborate swallow. "Well, you ain't payin' much." He smacked his lips several times for emphasis. "You going to tell it, you better get started. We ain't headed for *Chicago*."

Langston James tapped the steering wheel with his finger. "In this one . . . I'm talking about getting myself killed." His voice went flat.

Bodine looked out the window on his side of the cab. "Killed? Like . . . dead?"

"Yes. It starts out in a western town. Like Texas. In a bar. Like a cowboy picture show. But they fixed the bar up into some kind of a court. Something—you know—official. Maybe a place I would go to get a license of some kind. It's like it was my idea to come there."

"Excuse me," said Bodine, looking at him. "You say *killed*?"

"Just let me tell it, Bodine. I want to get it out in the open."

"I just need to get myself straight on it. Sound like a *serious* kind of a dream."

"*That's* what I been trying to tell you."

"But what you said was '*killed*'?"

"That's what I said. Okay?" Langston James waited a minute then went on. "There's this fella who's like a judge. That's not what he is exactly, but he decides things for you, and maybe would give you a license to do them. Something like that."

"I don't never have no dreams my ownself you know. We working outside my range right here."

Langston James looked at Bodine for a minute. "Well, get it *in* range." He turned back to the road. "He's foreign looking. Mexican, maybe. He's got dark hair and his eyes don't follow me all the time, but I feel like he's taking everything in. He's smoking one of those long, thin cigars—a Crook. A black one. Twisted. And he's got a black leather strap on his wrist. There's something about him I like. I think right away he's a nice fella. That he would always know what he's talking about . . . no bullshit." Langston James paused and pursed his mouth before he went on. "But I know too that he'd kill a man if he had to."

"Nice fella, eh?"

"You can be both."

"Must be a white man."

"What? I *told* you. He's a Mexican."

"Sound like a white man I knows. . . . Sound like *lotsa* white mens I know."

For a minute Langston James didn't say anything. "You know what, Bodine? Talking to you's like pissing up a rope. Sometimes it is."

"Nice fella...gets people kilt? Sound like twisty thinkin' to me."

"Uh huh. Tell you what. Let's us go into that another time. Okay? Right now I want to get this out. No need you puttin' your two cents in *every* word I say. Okay?"

Bodine didn't say anything.

"If this wasn't a private conversation, wouldn't nobody believe it. Way you contradicting me like that."

"You ax me."

"No, I didn't. I *told* you."

"What you want me to do?"

"Use your ears awhile. Give that mouth of yours a rest."

Bodine shifted in the seat and made a sucking noise.

Langston James went on. "He looks like he'd be a big man with the ladies, but—you know—men would like him too."

"*Now* he sound like a colored man."

"What?"

"Sound just like a colored man I know."

"I told you. He's a Mexican. Mexicans ain't colored, Bodine. Not exactly."

"Except for that."

"Except for *what*?"

"I know Mexicans ain't colored."

"This ain't a colored man I'm talking about, Bodine. All right?"

"Okay."

"It's somebody I've seen before though." He looked at Bodine. "You think Mexicans're colored?"

"I ain't never seen no Mexican. I know they ain't American. Is they?"

"Good for you, Bodine." Langston James tapped the steering wheel. "Mexicans got moustaches mostly. Sometimes they act sneaky. In the picture show. Only not this fella I'm talking about.

He don't act sneaky at all. He's very, you know, on top of things."

"Colored people got moustaches. I knowed plenty of colored people got moustaches."

"This one ain't colored. Believe me. Now let it go. I known plenty colored people got moustaches too. Wasn't all of them men." Langston James waited a minute. "Okay?"

Bodine didn't say anything.

"I don't remember any talking, but I would have done it. And there must have been some, because we come to a decision. He sits there holding that cigar very dainty in his hand, the way a foreigner would. Kind of upside down. Every now and then he'll take a pull on it—he holds it in his teeth with his lips pulled back. He's got very white teeth." Langston James thought for a minute before he went on. "Finally I figure out that what I'm doing is setting things up to have myself killed."

Bodine gave him a serious look, then frowned. "We coming to the killing part?"

Langston James nodded. "Sort of."

"You was *sort of* killed?"

"That's right."

"You going to be *sort of* dead when it over?"

"Just listen to me, Bodine. I'm getting to it. Not much more to go."

"I reckon not if you having to do with that kind of activity."

"Just listen. Okay? I need to get this out."

Bodine threw away a half-smoked Old Gold, then took another one out of the pack and lit it.

Langston James went on. "There's some kind of a machine in the town that will do it for you, and this foreign looking man is the one you have to see about it."

"The Mexican?"

"Yes."

"He boss of a killing machine?"

"That's what I'm trying to tell you."

"Nice fella, you say?"

"I told you he was." Langston James paused. "I don't need that tone, Bodine. Lighten up."

"Just sayin' what *you* said."

"I'm going to get this out one way or the other, Bodine. You're making it take longer than need be."

"I don't know about any of this."

"Just *listen*, goddamn it."

Bodine took several quick drags on his cigarette. After the last one he held his breath. "Okay," he said.

"He listens to me, but he's not trying to talk me into anything. It's kind of like a business proposition with him. But he's taking me serious." Langston James stopped and thought for a minute. "I don't remember that there was any money involved."

"Colored man I know smokes that way too. Them twisty cigars—all black."

"Crooks."

"What?"

"They call them 'Crooks.'" He held up his index finger and curled it down very slowly and elaborately into a hook. "Crook . . . crook . . . crook. Got it?"

Bodine looked out the window without answering.

"I'm telling it, and it ain't no colored man I'm talking about. It's a goddamn *Mexican*. All right?"

Bodine made a humming noise in his throat, but he didn't say anything.

"I promise you it wasn't no colored man. If I ever have me a dream about a colored man, I swear to God you going to be the first to know. Okay?"

"You *said* you wanted me to pay attention."

"See can't you do it, you know, to yourself. I want to get this over with."

"That'll suit me fine."

"Okay . . . okay?"

Bodine nodded. "Okay," he said. He lit another Old Gold.

"After awhile it gets decided. And I'm going to get into the machine. But not right away."

"This sure getting to be a *long* dream."

"It sounds long when I tell it. When you're *having* it, it moves right along. Ain't nobody there to interrupt you every five minutes when you dreaming it."

"*I* ain't having it."

"Be thankful, Bodine."

"I be more thankful if you didn't have it too."

"You the one slowing things up."

"I never have me no dreams."

"If you ever do, I'll be glad to listen to you tell all about it. That's a promise. Next time you have you a dream, you come straight to me and tell me about it."

"I never have no dreams."

"Well, that ain't my goddamn fault. If you *do* I want to hear about it. I really do. I want to hear about it right away. Now be quiet and let me get this over with."

Bodine lit another cigarette.

"Open you another Dr Pepper. It'll give you something to do." Langston James drove for a minute or two in silence, collecting his thoughts. "I know who it is, but I can't think of it right now. The Mexican fella. It was somebody I seen in the picture show. Maybe I'll think of his name directly."

"I be lookin' forward to that."

"We go out in the street. It's a street like the cowboy streets in the picture show. Got board sidewalks roofed over. High-front buildings. All the buildings seem to be bars. It's bright out in the street, and the street is bare dirt."

"Never seen no picture show. They wouldn't let us in when I

was little. When I got big I wadn't interested."

"That's the way the streets are in the picture show. You take my word . . . if you don't mind."

Bodine took a sip of the Dr Pepper, then a drag on the cigarette.

"We're out in the street. We stand there in the middle where it's sunshiney. And then some people bring this machine out, roll it up where we're standing. It's about as big as a wagon, but it's made out of iron. It looks like it was made a long time ago. Not a hundred years ago. Not that long. But it's put together with bolts. And everything about it is heavy, the way they used to make things. I can't remember exactly what it looked like, but that's something like what it was. It's boxy and heavy. Not up-to-date. In the middle there's this part that goes straight up like some kind of hopper. It looks like something that should be pulled by a horse. I mean the whole machine. But I remember it was a bunch of people pushed it into the street.

"We're standing there looking at it, and this other bunch of people comes up. It's like a family, with women and children and some men. About a dozen of them altogether. They're all dressed up the way people would be dressed up in a cowboy picture show if they was going to church. Some of them're carrying flowers."

"I *told* you. I never did see the picture show. No use you talking about what it was like in the picture show. Picture show don't mean nothing far as I'm concerned."

"It's like a funeral. You know what a funeral's like? You got to go along with me here, Bodine."

"I know what a funeral's like."

"When they get to where we are, standing by the machine, a man who's walking in front of the people stops and turns around. He goes from one to the other—shaking hands with the men, kissing the women on the cheek. He does that for all of them. Finally he gets to the last person. She's a woman too—the prettiest one of the bunch—and he gives her a very big kiss on the mouth, then he picks up one of the children and holds him for a minute. After that the Mexican—the one I take to be the judge—he opens a door in the side of the machine, and the man crawls in. He looks awkward doing it, and he don't take off his hat. It takes him a minute. Then they shut the door and bolt it closed.

"The people stand around looking at the machine, and the judge pulls a lever and something starts to move down the hopper on the top of the thing. I don't remember seeing it, but I know it's moving, and I know what it is. It's like a big, square cutter that goes down on a ram—like a cookie cutter . . . but *Big*."

"A *cookie* cutter?"

"That's the closest I can come, Bodine. A big, square cookie cutter. The motion ain't slow, but it ain't fast neither. It goes down . . . steady. That's the only way I know to tell about it. Just real steady."

Langston James stopped and looked at Bodine. "You ever make root beer, Bodine?"

"What?"

"When I was little, momma used to make root beer out on the back porch. When she got her batch made, she'd pour it off in bottles I'd picked up for her around town. I used to go out with my wagon and bring it back full of bottles, and mother'd scald them out in the kitchen. When she had all the bottles filled, she'd put caps on them with a capper she'd bought somewhere.

"The thing I'm talking about had the same motion as that capper. Slow and steady, with a kind of extra, setting shove at the bottom of the stroke."

Bodine held up the Dr Pepper bottle and looked at it for a minute. Then he threw it out the window.

"I can't see inside the machine in my dream. And nobody ever tells me what's going on. But I know. That cutter—it's square—about a foot square—goes right through the chest of the man that's inside the machine. It cuts a plug out of him. Right in the middle of his chest where his heart is. I can't hear it doing that. And, like I said, he's shut up inside the thing, so I can't see in it. But I *know* what's happening.

"After it's over, the people that came with him don't stand around. They throw down bunches of flowers in the street where the man got in the machine, then they leave. The flowers're just laying there in the street after they're gone.

"Then we go back inside the bar—me and the Mexican, the foreign fella who's the judge. There's some other people with us too, but I don't remember them. The machine stays out there in the middle of the street, with the flowers all around the place where the man got in. It's over, and nobody rolls it away, or tries to open it up to take out the body.

"When we get back inside the bar, I begin to think about how it's going to be for me after I crawl inside that thing and they shut the door. *That's* when I start to sweat. I'm thinking I don't really want to go through with it, and I wonder why I ever came around to make these arrangements in the first place."

"It cross *my* mind as well," said Bodine.

"I don't know what it was, Bodine. I tell the judge that I've changed my mind. That I don't want to go through with it any more. He frowns and takes a couple of pulls on the cigar, but he don't tell me I *have* to go through with it. It's very peculiar the way he acts. It's like he didn't care one way or the other until I brought it up, but now the fat's in the fire, and it will be—well—an *inconvenience* to have to change the plans. Everybody in the room seems to have the same feeling—like they're disappointed. And now I know that my family is there too." Langston James paused and looked at Bodine. "You're there as well."

"I 'speck I would be." Bodine thought a minute. "I be disappointed too?"

Langston James thought a minute. "I guess so. *Everybody* is disappointed. Like I said." He went on. "For a long time the judge don't say nothing. He just sits there smoking the cigar, holding it in his dainty way, putting it in his mouth between his teeth pulled back. Squinting because of the smoke. He don't look at me. Just kind of looks at the smoke. For a long time I don't know whether or not I'm going to have to go through with it anyway. He's the one that has to decide.

"Finally he looks at me and says, 'Okay.' That's all he says. Just, 'Okay.' And then I know it was *my* choice all along. The only thing he was worried about was I changed my mind. He didn't like that much. And it's not a court at all. The whole thing was up to me. Only he was taking my decisions really serious."

"I'd say gettin' yourself killed was a right serious decision."

Langston James didn't look at Bodine.

"Is that it?" Bodine spoke softly.

"I think so. That's about all I can remember. The whole time it was up to me."

Bodine shook his head. "I wouldn't think you'd have *time* to dream nothing that complicated."

"It takes longer to tell it. Everything happens pretty fast in a dream."

"That's a lot to happen in a *night*. I never heard a dream that long before."

"It sounds long because of the way I had to tell it. It wouldn't take long to dream it. When you dream it, you understand a lot of things I had to tell about."

"That's a pretty crazy dream."

"You reckon it means something?"

"I reckon it got to mean *something*. I hope you ain't looking for me to figure out what it is."

"It scares me. That's the thing about this one."

"I can see how it would be."

For awhile they didn't say anything. Finally Bodine spoke. "I wonder how come I never have me no dreams."

"I don't enjoy them. That ain't what I meant. Especially not this one."

"It seem like I'd have me a dream *sometimes*. I mean, I ain't got much time for foolishness—but I ain't never had no dream in my *life*."

"I always had them. Maybe it runs in the family."

"Maybe white folks got more time on they hands."

"Listen," said Langston James. "What you reckon it might mean?"

"How would I know that? I told you wasn't no use you askin'. I ain't no Mexican."

"What?"

"You know. One of them people tells you fortune and things."

"Mexicans don't tell no fortunes."

"You know what I mean. Anyway. I done told you. I ain't never had no dreams my ownself. How I be going to make sense out of something crazy like that?"

"You know what a Mexican is, Bodine? I mean *really*?"

"Somethin' foreign."

"Gypsies're the ones tells fortunes. Reads your hand and looks in the future. Don't no Mexican do that kind of a thing. You get out once in awhile and you learn about Mexicans and Gypsies—things like that. See 'em on the television as well. Look how much good this here trip to Savannah's done you already." For a minute Langston James didn't say anything. "Never mind," he said at last. "I feel better now. Just unloading it was a help."

"I thought you would. Feel better." Bodine hesitated for a minute. "Was I really there too?"

"I didn't see no faces exactly. But I'd say you was. Cowie and

Halstead as well."

Bodine shook his head. For awhile they rode in silence. Finally Bodine spoke again. "Listen," he said. "Can I get me a Dr Pepper? That dream of yours give me something of a thirst."

"We'll be hitting U.S. 82 shortly. I'll get you a Dr Pepper when we hit 82. Have you an Old Gold."

Bodine took the pack off the dash and shook out a cigarette. He looked at it a minute, then put it back. "I already over my limit." He worked his mouth. "Feel like I been suckin' on a dry hole."

"Talkin' it out made me feel a lot better."

"Well," said Bodine, taking a dip out of his Tube Rose can, "I glad you got some good out of it." He paused. "Leastways the child wadn't in it."

Langston James narrowed his eyes. "You know what?"

"What?"

"What you just said." His voice sounded dry and thin. "I just seen his face." He paused. "The one got in the machine...it was Gabriel."

"Oh Lordy," said Bodine.

Seven

OUTSIDE OF WAYCROSS, Langston James pulled into an all-night filling station to get a Dr Pepper for Bodine and a couple of packs of Old Golds for himself. There was a Confederate flag on a staff at one end of the pump island and an American flag at the other end. A large "Impeach Earl Warren" sign covered the window of the station, and smaller, gum-backed "Impeach Earl Warren" stickers were plastered on the pumps and the drink cooler, and even on individual cans of oil and brake fluid on a rack by the door.

The man who came out to pump gas for them looked at first glance like the kind of creature the mob of townspeople was always trying to beat to death with rakes and hoes in a Franken-stein movie. As he came closer, that first impression shifted a lit-tle, and he took on the look of a man who had long been engaged in a fierce battle with life's malign forces, and was generally getting the short end of it. The first and third fingers on his right hand were missing, as well as his thumb. A huge, white scar bisected his face diagonally. The sewing job on it bespoke lack of attention and general ineptitude, and looked like it might have been done with seine twine and a ten-penny nail. The suture lines were very noticeable, so that it pretty much resembled the way the Union Pacific looks going through the Medicine Bow Range on a topographical map of Wyoming. A similar scar—only red—disappeared up his arm under the rolled-up sleeve of his shirt. As he moved, various parts of him progressed at different rates of speed. It was a dark night, and in spite of the natural affinity Langston James had for that kind of thing, he didn't much like the sort of violent activity the markings suggested. Until he heard the man actually speaking words, he hesitated to get out of the truck. There was an embroidered patch over the pocket of his shirt which read "Dunk."

"Filler up, mister?"

"That's right."

"Reg'lar?"

"I put high-test in this thing, it'd blow the head right off her. Better save it for a Buick. Only place I'm going is Savannah. Ain't headed for the moon."

While the man pumped the gasoline, Langston James went to the cooler and got two Dr Peppers. Back at the truck he handed one in to Bodine and took a loud swallow off his own. "This your main line of work?" he asked the man.

"Done some lumberin'. I like this better."

"Looks like you taken right smart punishment somewheres or another."

"Yeah. I didn't have the head for lumberin'. Them saws was always takin pieces off me. Vola-Shirl finally made me quit. She said it wasn't but a matter of time till I lost something *really* important, and when I did she was going to wash her hands of me." He choked the filler on the tank before he hung up the hose. "Vola-Shirl's my wife. She's some kind of woman. I couldn't stand to hang around her just lookin' on. If you know what I mean. She sort of invites participation."

"How'd it happen?"

"Just kind of now and then. You know—here and there. Wasn't all at once. I got an abstract side to me, so I'd get to thinking about one thing or another, and 'fore you knew it there went a piece." He held up his hand with the missing fingers. "Can't keep that up but so long. Thing is, you ain't seein' but the half of it. Just what shows out here in the public eye." He took hold of a button on the front of his shirt and pumped it in and out. "You wouldn't *believe* what all there is underneath these here clothes." He looked at Langston James in a narrow way. "What kind of work *you* in, mister? Looks like you dropped a thing or two your ownself."

"Well," Langston James spoke reflectively. "I ain't actually *lost* anything yet. Not the way you have."

"Maybe not. You sure look like you been rearranged some."

Langston James thought a minute. "You know, that's not a bad way to put it."

A small animal came out of the lubrication bay. At first Langston James thought it was a white rat, but its manner was too confident and proprietary for that.

"That a *dog*?"

"Don't she look awful? Vola-Shirl's the one let it happen. That there's a full-blooded miniature poodle. Come'ere, Francine." The dog bared its teeth and growled. "She's a feisty little thing. Never took to me much. Vola-Shirl sets right much stock in her though. I go along." Francine turned and walked back into the bay in a disdainful manner. "We got the papers on her."

"Looks like a white rat."

"Vola-Shirl took her to a jackleg dog trimmer over in Blackshear. He's the one skinned her like that. Mister, don't never do business with no jackleg dog trimmer. Let that be a lesson to you. You get what you pay for in this world. I'm mighty glad she's the one let it happen and not me."

"She stood there and watched him do it?"

"No. Not exactly. He wouldn't let her in the salon. Called his place a 'salon.' Generally that'd be a good sign, but you can't always tell. When he brought her out that's what he done to her. Said he tried and tried only he just couldn't get it to come out even. He wanted to charge her five dollars for it anyway. I got to admire his guts. It's a wonder Vola-Shirl didn't square his circle with a four-by-four. We had to pull her off the mailman just for talking mean to that animal." He thought a minute. "Vola-Shirl's a little on the feisty side her ownself. Handsome women's like that sometimes. You got to take the rough with the smooth." He hooked his thumb toward the hood of the truck. "Check 'at oil?"

"Go ahead. It might take a quart."

The man wrestled with the lever on the hood, trying to turn it the wrong way. Before Langston James could step up to show him how to do it, his hand slipped and he tore a gash in his finger. He put it into his mouth and sucked on it while he groped around with his other hand looking for the dipstick. Before he found it, he burned himself once each on the manifold and the head, and raised sparks fooling around with the battery terminals. Finally he unscrewed the radiator cap to check the water. It came loose with a loud hissing sound, shooting a geyser of hot water and steam into his face. "You got to be careful around automobiles," he said, taking out a greasy rag and wiping his face. He rubbed the cut finger against his pants' leg. "Any piece of machinery is liable to get you if you don't watch out."

"You ever think about working in a mattress factory?" Langston James moved a step or two away from him. "Don't look like you going to last too long in this here job."

"I couldn't stand bein' cooped up. I need to be out in the fresh air. Confinement don't accord with my nature."

"Well, I reckon you know better'n me...," Langston James leaned toward him, reading the name patch, "Dunk."

The man looked down at the patch. "No," he said. "My name's Monroe." He put the accent on the *Mon*. "This here's Duncan Crowther's shirt. He's the one owns the station. My shirt got et up by a fan belt. That's how I got this here one." He held out his scarred arm for Langston James to see.

Langston James shook his head. "How long you reckon you can keep this up?"

"Listen, mister. I figure when it come time for me to die I'm gone *know* what all I done in my life. I can put my finger on ever mark I got and add 'em up. I'm gone know what I *been*."

"I reckon that's a comfort to you, is it?"

"Some life's a waste. You get cut down, and you don't never know *what* happened."

"Couldn't you cut notches in a stick?"

"Don't make light of it, mister. I've thought into it pretty deep."

"Well," said Langston James. "How much I owe you for the gas?"

Monroe looked at the pump. "Three seventy-five with the oil."

"I got two Dr Peppers as well."

"Three eighty-five."

"And two packs of Old Golds."

"We got Luckies, Camels, Chesterfields, and Philip Morris. Dunk won't stock no outlaw brands."

"You think Old Gold is an outlaw brand? They advertise in *Life* magazine."

"It ain't *my* fault. Dunk's the one makes up his mind about that kind of thing."

"Never mind the Old Golds."

"I roll my own mostly. For a treat I like me a Herbert Tareyton now and then." He thought a minute. "Dunk'd wear a dress to church 'fore he'd stock Herbert Tareytons."

"Old Gold's got 'Apple Honey.' Says so right there on the pack." Langston James took out his pack and showed Monroe.

"That's what Dunk wouldn't like about Old Golds. He wants straight out, pure nicotine. He don't go for mixtures. Dunk won't put gravy on his mashed potatoes."

Langston James handed him a five-dollar bill.

Monroe went into the station to make change. When he came back out he handed Langston James a dollar bill and fifteen cents change. He also gave him a plate with a picture of Woody Woodpecker on it. "Plate goes with a fill-up."

"Well," said Langston James. "How about that?"

Monroe hesitated for a minute, then he stepped up close and lowered his voice. "I ain't one to tell a man his business, mister, but you think it's a good idea riding around with a nigger in your cab like that?"

"What?"

"I couldn't help but notice. That ain't exactly the way we do things around here. Good thing I was the one on duty. Dunk wouldn't let me pump gas for a truck with no nigger in it. Not sittin' up there in front like a white man."

"He *works* for me. You think I'd ride around like that for pleasure?"

"It ain't nothing to me, mister. I'm just telling you for your own good."

Langston James held out the plate. "Why don't you keep the plate?"

Monroe shook his head. "Plate goes with a fill-up. Just friendly advice, mister. That's all I meant."

"Uh huh," said Langston James. He got into the truck and

cranked the motor, then he gave the plate to Bodine. "Hold this, Bodine. When we get down the road a ways, I want you to throw it out the window."

"What's wrong with it? Gabriel, he'd like that plate."

"Give it to me," said Langston James. "*I'll* throw it out myself."

Bodine gave him the plate. "When we get out on the highway a ways, I need to take a pee."

"How come you didn't do that back at the station?"

"You think Dunk fixed up a place for a colored man to take a leak? I wouldn't want to take it out in that vicinity."

"You could of pissed on one of them 'Impeach Earl Warren' signs he got stuck up all over the place."

"'Long here be okay. I can walk off in them trees yonder."

Langston James pulled onto the shoulder. He turned the lights off but left the motor running while they went into the pine scrub together.

Back in the truck, they drove for awhile in silence. When Langston James spoke, he didn't look at Bodine. "How much you hear?"

"Most of it."

Langston James didn't say anything.

"Don't tell me you surprised to find out what they think of colored folks in Waycross, Georgia."

"I don't know, Bodine. I reckon it wasn't his fault. I just been telling you about my dream and all. Sometimes I don't think about you like a colored man. We spend a lot of time together." He sounded like he was apologizing.

For awhile neither of them said anything. Finally Bodine spoke. "What you think about that man gettin' all tore up like he was?"

"What you mean?"

"Seem like he *like* it."

Langston James thought about that for awhile. "He's *used* to it. That's the impression I got."

"Kind of remind me the way you talk about Gabriel. Cuttin' up on him and all. Kind of remind me of your ownself as well."

"What way?"

"Like it *good* for you or somethin'."

"I knew what he was talking about, if that's what you mean. Hurtin' ain't all that bad. Not when you get right down to it. *Thinkin'* about hurtin', that's the bad part."

"How about hurtin' somebody else?"

Langston James nodded. "That too. It's a hard thing, Bodine. It can be a good thing as well."

"Like when you seen Gabriel's face on the man got in the machine?"

"You talking about my dream?"

"Uh huh."

Langston James nodded. "That dream was a troubling thing before I saw that face. It's something else now. It's a whole lot bigger than it used to be. Terrible hard . . . terrible hard."

"Let me hold the plate."

"What?"

"Breakin' that plate won't do nobody no good. Gabriel, he'd like that plate a whole lot."

Langston James let him take the Woody Woodpecker plate out of his lap.

"I hope I talked it out. What I told you about that dream. Maybe I won't be having it no more. I don't think I could stand it now. Not since I seen his face." He lit an Old Gold and offered the pack to Bodine. Bodine took one and lit it. He rolled down his window all the way to let out the smoke. The air was cool and damp, and the sky over the tops of the pine trees was graying out into first light. "Leastways we missed Old Dunk."

"Look like we got luck on our side." Bodine wrapped a paper around the plate and slid it under the seat.

"How about what he said about Old Golds? You can't buy a better smoke than Old Golds."

"You worried about that, are you?"

"It's just something else to think about." Langston James drummed on the steering wheel. "I got to be careful. I don't know what come over me back there. Just sometimes I forget who it is you really are, you know?"

Bodine didn't say anything.

"Don't nobody around here know us. We're a long ways from home."

"Long ways," said Bodine. He flipped his cigarette out the window.

"Ain't it a funny thing?"

"What?"

"Sometimes I don't think of you like you was a colored man at all. It's just, you know, you ain't nothing but just plain Bodine. Not no different from anybody else." He turned the thought around in his head for a minute. "You ever see it that way?"

Bodine shook his head. "No," he said flatly.

"Tell me something, Bodine. How you think about me? I mean really. You ever think about me like I was, well, colored too? Be truthful with me now."

"Never did."

"How about *one* time?"

"Not one time."

"Why you reckon that is?"

"I don't think about that neither."

"Well, think about it now. We're out here in the middle of nowhere. Sun's not even up yet."

"We ain't *that* far from home."

"I'm asking you, Bodine. Who you think I am?"

"You be Mister Eljay."

"That's it?"

"That all it *can* be."

Langston James drove for awhile without saying anything. When he could read the Burma Shave signs, he turned off the headlights.

"You know what, Bodine?" he said at last.

"No."

"It's a sad goddamn world."

Bodine looked straight ahead out the windshield of the truck. "How about that?" he said at last.

As the sun came up, the mood in the cab of the truck shifted onto more normal and astringent lines. When Langston James spoke he sounded irritated. "Sometimes I talk too goddamn much."

Bodine didn't comment.

"I'm glad I got it out. The dream. I'm glad about that all right. Only thing is, I don't want none of this coming back to me. *Ever.* You hear? I got me a business to look out for. Whatever I said last night was confidential. You understand?"

Bodine looked out the window on his side. "I wouldn't want to tell nobody anyways."

"Well. See that you don't."

Bodine turned and looked at him. "Who you think I be going to tell? Dunk back there?"

Langston James shook his head. "You know what, Bodine? There's times I don't know what in the *hell* I'm doin'."

"*This* be one of them times?"

"What?"

"I just be tryin' to keep up."

Langston James's voice sounded weary. "I don't know. I don't even know that."

"Well," said Bodine, "tell me when you find out."

Eight

THE SUN WAS UP OVER the pines and was shining full in Langston James's eyes until they turned north on U.S. 17 at Midway. "It won't be long now," he said, rubbing his eyes. "Look at them signs, Bodine. Big mothers. You can tell we're getting close to something worth your time. I wouldn't even be surprised if there's a Stuckey's around here somewheres.

Bodine ran his tongue around his cheek, readjusting his pinch of Tube Rose, then he spit out the window. "Hooray," he said flatly.

Roadside advertising, especially billboards, became something of a cause when Lady Bird Johnson took up beautification in the middle sixties, but they weren't all that much of an issue in 1959. From Savannah to the Florida line, the signs on the Georgia section of U.S. 17 looked to be more a settled feature of the landscape than the highway did — as if they were there first, and the road had worked its way out between them, like a stream in a gully.

SILVER SPRINGS — MARINELAND — ST. AUGUSTINE

Going south was like riding a flume of many-colored promises straight to the heart's desire. It would have been distracting, except that there were so many of them they cancelled each other out, and flowed together into a kind of strident and gaudy monotony. On the outskirts of towns they bunched and clustered together, overlapping each other, and could hardly be read at all.

Most of the signs advertised Florida tourist attractions, so they faced northward on both sides of the highway to catch the eyes of drivers coming down from the states above Virginia. Going north on that highway—well, it was pretty much over by then, though looking at the backs of all those billboards was also good for the tourist business in a retroactive way. It certainly put into travellers' minds that they were leaving the place where the good times were.

Set in among the big, professional signs, there were other, smaller ones—a lot of them hand lettered. A good many of those faced north *and* south. Some of them were very small, with things like "JESUS SAVES" and "FLEE FROM THE WRATH TO COME," and quotations from the Bible with chapter and verse citations. Also there were slightly larger ones advertising strictly local tourist courts and restaurants. The places they proclaimed were marginal operations that needed to hawk their attractions going as well as coming.

From Midway north, Langston James began to notice a particular series of those smaller signs. They were only about as big as a sheet of plywood, but there were a lot of them, spaced at intervals down the highway, and their simplicity and persistence and bright, pure colors caught his eye.

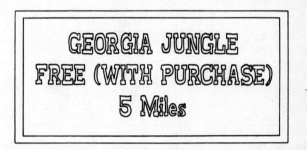

The background was red, with yellow letters outlined in black and a white border around the whole thing. They didn't look like they had been done by a professional, but they looked like they had been done with care.

The drawings of the animals were crude and childlike, and some of them needed dwelling on to make out just what animal had been intended.

The racoon showed the best likeness.

"You want to see the funny monkeys, Bodine?"

"That monkey don't look funny."

"My treat, Bodine. *That* monkey don't look like nothing."

"Let's us see how funny that there monkey is going to be."

As they drove north, the signs moved closer together. Finally they left off the pictures and messages, and just concentrated on the distance.

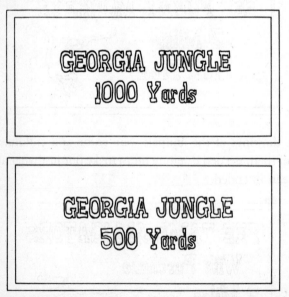

At the end there was a burst of signs — MONKEYS — ALLI-GATORS — RACOONS. So close together they got in each

other's way. Then, finally—

And a double-size sign—

"He spent him a fortune on plywood alone," said Langston James as he pulled the truck off the road.

There was a low frame building, with a bamboo palisade leading off to the right and left of the entrance, blocking the view of the cages. There was also a Standard Oil gasoline pump, with a hand lever.

Langston James stopped and opened his door. Bodine didn't move to get out of the truck. "You better see do they let colored folks in to see them funny monkeys," he said.

Langston James nodded. "Right. Smoke you a cigarette. I'll go see about the lay of the land."

Inside, the building was low and dark, with rows of trestle tables and a counter at one end. It looked like a fishing camp, with unfinished walls, showing the studs and the inside of the siding. Around the walls were various trophies—a rattlesnake skin, tacked onto a board. A deer head. A fish with its glass eye missing, mounted and painted in glary, metallic colors more reminiscent of a Messerschmidt, or the rocket ship Buck Rogers went to Mars in, than anything owed to the artful hand of nature. There weren't many windows, and the bamboo palisade blocked the ones on the front, so it was very dark.

Langston James could see a head above the counter at the end of the room, but he couldn't tell whether it was a man or a woman. Except for that the room was empty.

"Howdy," said the head behind the counter. The voice didn't give away the sex any more than the head had. It sounded more like a woman than a man.

"That you?" said Langston James.

"Ain't nobody else," said the voice.

As he shuffled toward the counter, he could see that the face was melancholy and wrinkled, like a stepped-on basketball with most of the air let out—the same orange-brown color. It barely topped the counter. When he got close enough, he could tell it was a woman, with eyes that were very pale blue, and black hair parted in the middle and pulled back like an Indian's.

"Lord God, mister," she said. "What in the *world* happened to you?"

"Natural causes, lady. It's a long story. Where's the funny monkeys at?"

"No offense meant, friend. I got deep respect for the sorely afflicted. This here's a Christian woman you're looking at."

"Glad to hear it. I got me a colored feller out in my truck. You Christian enough so's he can come in and see the funny monkeys too?"

She looked at him for a long minute. "He work for you or something?"

"Yes, ma'm."

She nodded her head and pursed her lips. "Long as he's with you and you buy him something," she said at last. "He can take it outside."

"Certainly."

"What'll you have?"

"How much?"

"A purchase." The woman sighed. "That's what the sign says. Cokes is the cheapest we got. They're a dime. We don't sell no penny candy. Be as much of a sport as you can afford."

"You don't make breakfast?"

"No," she said. "I don't eat it myself."

"Let me have two Cokes and a couple packs of them peanuts." He put a dollar bill on the counter. "I'll be back in a minute." He went out to the truck and got Bodine. "No problem, Bodine," he said, smiling as hard as he could. "She says she's a Christian woman."

"What *that* mean?"

"It means don't look no goddamn gift horse in the mouth. Now come on."

When they came back, the woman was standing by the cooler at the side of the room. Out in the open she looked even smaller than she had behind the counter. She had on a denim skirt, a red-and-orange checkered shirt, a black shoestring tie with a silver longhorn slide, and a two-inch tooled leather belt with silver studs. She slid back the cover of the cooler and took out two Coca-Cola bottles, holding them by the necks in one hand while she opened them with an opener on a key chain hanging from her belt.

"Thirty cents," she said, handing them the drinks. "The peanuts is in the jar on the counter." She gave Langston James his change out of a pocket in her skirt. "You can take it outside," she said, speaking to Bodine, and pointing to a screen door at the back of the room.

"Yes, ma'm," he said, and left.

Langston James got two packages of peanuts from the glass jar on the counter. "Now where's the monkeys?" he said, looking around the room.

"He's out back," she said, pointing to the screen door. "Follow your boy."

"He? Like...*one* he?"

"Monkeys can't live in this climate," she said. "Summer's okay. The cold weather, that's what gets them."

"How about the one?"

"We brought him in last winter—I'm *sorry* to say. In the house." She held her nose between her thumb and forefinger, elaborately. "He ain't getting inside *this* winter. I'll guarantee you he ain't."

"I'd think a monkey like that'd represent right smart of an investment."

She looked at him for a minute without speaking. "I don't care," she said finally. "I ain't sharing my house and home with no monkey this winter. Once is enough. You ever *smelt* a monkey?" She fanned her face and screwed up her nose. "Whooooo."

Langston James shook his head. "Lady," he said, "I ain't often *seen* a monkey, much less smelt one."

"Count your blessings, mister. A monkey is...," she thought for a minute, "*vile*."

"I never noticed."

"Spend the winter with one, friend. It'll come to your attention."

"I guess so."

"I wouldn't do it again for all the tea in China. I don't care how much he cost."

Langston James looked for Bodine, then back at the woman. "We going to get to see him?"

The woman pointed to the screen door leading out to the back from the room. "Walk on through, friend."

Outside, Langston James gave one of the packages of peanuts to Bodine. Then he took a swallow of his Coke, bit off the top of the cellophane packet and poured the peanuts into the bottle. Bodine stood holding his Coke and peanuts in his hands.

"It's okay, Bodine," said Langston James. He turned to the woman, who was looking at Bodine. "It's okay for him to eat them out here, ain't it?"

She waited a minute before answering. "Why don't you take them over there?" She pointed to a bench set against the back wall of the building.

"He wants to see the monkey too," said Langston James. "I bought him a Co-Cola."

"Well...," she hesitated. "Okay."

Bodine put the peanuts into his pocket and took a swallow of his Coke. He made a face.

"Give me your trash when you're through," she said.

Behind the building there was a compound, a series of cages, with sandy walks between. Most of the cages were made of chicken wire. One of them had a low, wooden fence around it.

The monkey was in the first cage, sitting on a trapeze and picking at his leg for fleas. The sign on the cage said, "Genuine Spider Monkey." At first they didn't see him, he was so small. About the size of a squirrel, with greenish yellow fur, thin and patchy, the pink skin underneath showing through.

"Something *does* smell bad," said Langston James. He looked around at the other cages.

"No need to look around, mister. That's it right there."

"You mean you lay it *all* on that there monkey?"

She gave him a vigorous nod. "That's *all* Ajax. Racoons is clean animals."

"What about the others?"

"There ain't no others," said the woman. "Only Old Doc, the alligator. Old Doc ain't clean, but he don't smell like no abattoir."

"Ajax?" Langston James looked at the monkey.

"Arkwright named him. You wouldn't think nothing that little could smell so bad."

"He don't look much like the picture," said Langston James. Then added, "On the billboard."

"Animals come and go, mister. Signs is *permanent*. We had us a monkey looked that way when Arkwright made the sign. He smelt worse than a spider monkey. They's more *of* 'em. Only he was too mean to bring in the house."

"You do a pretty good business?"

Without answering him, she leaped forward and banged the cage with her hand. "Stop it!" she yelled. Ajax had a huge erection and was stroking it in a moody way. She struck the cage again. Ajax gave her a sad look and turned his back to her. "Why Arkwright couldn't get us a lady monkey I'll never know. All that one does is play with himself and make pee pee."

"Well," said Langston James. He didn't want to look in the cage with the lady there.

"I can't wait for the cold weather," she said. "It'll kill the smell."

"How about the monkey?"

"Him too."

"Cold gets 'em, eh?"

"Fifty-eight degrees," she said. "Fifty-eight degrees and they contract pneumonia. I'm watching the thermometer." She looked at Ajax for a minute. "That sounds hard-hearted, for a witnessing Christian woman. But I feel like I owe something to my nose. Ain't nothing in the Bible about having to put up with monkeys in your house."

"You're right about that. I don't recall nothing about monkeys in the Bible."

Bodine walked away. Langston James and the woman followed, looking in the empty cages while she told him what they *used* to contain — in the good times.

"There's a bird!" Langston James pointed. It was a blue jay. When he spoke, it flew away.

"I told you. We got Ajax and Old Doc and Poo-Coon," she ticked them off on her fingers. "Animals don't live long in cages anyway, and Arkwright can't get around like he used to. Used to he'd keep them cages full. It's better in the spring."

Langston James looked at her.

"They die off as the summer wears on," she said. "They *all* do. Like I said, animals don't live long in cages. The sadness gets them . . . whatever."

They came to the cage with the racoon.

"We take care of Poo-Coon," she said. "He's four years old."

The coon shuffled back and forth, from one end of the cage to the other.

"Can we see him dance?"

She looked in the cage. "You're seeing him," she said.

Langston James looked at the coon. "He's just walking, lady."

"Arkwright thought it looked like he was dancing."

"He did?"

"You got to use your imagination," she said. Then she added, "It ain't cost you but thirty cents, mister — and you *drinking* the Co-Cola. I never said we was no Silver Springs."

"I see what you mean. No offense."

Old Doc, the alligator, was plainly visible in his pen, but he was so immobile it took a little time to get him into focus.

"Does he move much?" asked Langston James.

"I ain't sure he moves at *all*. Especially not in the summertime. He twitched a little coming out of the winter. That's the last time I *seen* him. He might be dead. It's hard to tell with a alligator. Especially a *old* alligator. I wouldn't stick my leg in there to find out if I was you."

Langston James looked around. "Them's all the animals you got, eh?"

"That's about it."

"Well, Bodine," he said, upending the Coca-Cola bottle and tapping it to shake out the last of the peanuts, "that's right educational, wadn't it?" Bodine didn't reply.

"We used to have us a lot of different things," she said, speaking to Langston James. "Arkwright can't keep up with it no more."

Langston James looked around. "Tell me the truth," he said. "How much money you make on a thing like this?"

"It ain't all that much your business, I reckon." She thought a minute. "We don't see five hundred dollars a year, mister. Not cash money. Arkwright shoots the meat—most of it anyway. No trouble about that, even if he can't get them *live* no more. We got a garden. I put up things for the winter." She paused. "I buy salt, sugar, and white bread. We stock cigarettes in the store. That's it."

"How long you been here?"

"You can't just add it up like that, you know? We don't have to take orders from nobody. That's the main idea."

"I see," said Langston James.

"Arkwright bought the place in 1937. We come up from Darien to get it going."

"You ain't never had no good years?"

She looked at him. "I don't recall we ever had any *bad* ones, mister. Not the way we figure it. Things were really lively during the war. The soldier boys going back and to Camp Stewart used to stop by pretty regular. We had some good times during the war.

She thought a minute. "Used to be we had a bobcat and a

black bear—things people would really be interested in. Old Doc had more life in him back then too." She sighed. "You can't keep up with the times."

Bodine finished his Coke and gave the bottle and peanut wrapper to Langston James to give to the woman. Langston James passed them over to her. "I guess we better be getting along," he said.

They went back through the screen door into the room.

By the counter was a gnomelike man, his face one degree more wrinkled than the woman's, and tanned a darker brown. "Inez!" He spoke in a loud, generalized way, as if the room were empty.

"That's Arkwright now," she said, speaking to Langston James.

The clothes Arkwright wore were identical to hers, except that he had denim pants instead of a skirt, and a gray felt hat with wooden kitchen matches stuck in the band. His hands were behind his back.

"Which hand you take?" he said.

"We got us a customer," she said. "What you got?"

"Guess which hand?"

"He caught him something," she said, talking to Langston James. "Can't be too big and him hold it behind of his back with one hand. It's always something new every day with Arkwright."

"Which hand? Come on." He looked at Langston James and winked.

She pointed to his right hand. When he took it out from behind his back, there was a large blacksnake in it. He was holding it behind the neck, but it had coiled around his forearm. There were three loops around the arm and the snake was moving for a further purchase.

"It ain't poison?" she said, drawing back.

"It's a blacksnake," he said. "You think I'd be whipping a cottonmouth around like that?"

She turned to Langston James. "You never know with Arkwright. Ain't nothing he's ascaird of."

With the other hand he flopped four squirrels onto the counter. "Supper," he said.

She made a face. "They ain't hardly worth the price of the shells," she said. "I ain't much on squirrels. Too much cleaning for the meat you get. Anyway, when you get the skin off them, they put me in mind of a rat."

Her voice when she talked to her husband had a different sound. It was softer—more unmistakably a woman's.

"We got a customer, Arkwright."

"I see we have." He looked at Bodine, then back at Langston James. "What'd you think of the animal jungle, mister?" Bodine walked to the front door, opened it, and went outside. None of them watched him leave.

"Your wife said you used to have a bunch of animals," said Langston James. He paused. "I just bought a Co-Cola and some peanuts."

"It ain't hardly worth no T-bone steak," he said. "Used to be it was worth your money."

"It ain't no cheat," said Inez. "You don't see no spider monkey every day." She thought a minute. "Smell one neither."

"Not for no Co-Cola it ain't," said Arkwright. While he was talking, he kept unwinding the snake from his arm, trying to stretch it out, so they could see how big it was.

"Six foot," he said.

"We ain't got no place to keep snakes," she said.

"I'll put him in with Doc."

"Put him in with Poo-Coon," she said. "He'll have it for supper."

"I'm going to let it go," said Arkwright. "I just wanted to bring it home so you could see it. He's a big one."

"Get it off from the house," she said. "I don't want it coming up my leg at the clothesline."

Arkwright went out through the screen door with the snake.

"Arkwright knows I'm trembly about snakes. I gritted my teeth and offered to let him put in some cages. Snakes is something the customers would be interested in. But he knows snakes put me in a tizzy...and I ain't the tizzying kind."

For a minute she didn't speak. "You from Savannah?" she said.

Langston James shook his head. "Going there. I'm from Whippet myself."

"Last time we was in Savannah was spring before last. I reckon it's changed a good bit since then."

"Probably," he said. "I hadn't been there in ten years."

"We bought Ajax on that trip," she said. "Arkwright never did like big towns noway."

"I see," said Langston James. "About how far is it to Savannah?"

"Nineteen mile."

"I see."

"We got everthing we need right here." She swung her arm around, taking in the room.

"How long you been married? If you don't mind."

"Thirty-six years. Arkwright was in the lumbering business down to Darien. One day he just up and quit. 'Inez,' he said, 'I'm tired of eating sawdust.'" She thought a minute. "That's the way it is with Arkwright. Something new ever day. You can't keep up."

"Thirty-six years," said Langston James.

"Sawdust can kill you, mister—you breathe enough of it. It'll clog you right up."

"I could believe it," he said, thinking about Monroe. "Saws'll get you too."

"You can stay out the way of a saw. That sort of thing's up

to you. Ain't nothing you can do about the sawdust."

"I see what you mean."

"We come up the road in 1937 and gone into business for our-selfs." She thought a minute. "It don't pay to work for the other fella. We'd never had nothing if Arkwright didn't have the backbone."

Langston James looked around the room. "I guess not," he said.

Arkwright came back in through the screen door. "I put him out at the edge of the woods," he said. "He won't be back." He looked at Langston James. "Snakes won't stay around where they's people. They's mostly cowards really."

Langston James nodded. For a minute they stood there in silence.

"That colored boy works for you, I reckon?" Arkwright looked at him when he spoke. His eyes were a lighter blue than his wife's.

"I don't get around too good," said Langston James. "He helps me out. I got a paper route."

"You have an accident or something?"

"Partly. Some's natural."

"I see."

For a minute they stood there in silence. "You know what?" said Langston James. "I'd like me a souvenir."

"What?" said Inez.

"I don't get out of Whippet all that much. I thought it would be nice to take back a souvenir for my wife."

Inez looked at Arkwright. "Well," she said, drawing it out, "Weelllll . . ."

"We used to have some tourist items," said Arkwright. "When we first gone into the business. We wasn't never no Stuckey's." He looked at Inez. "What happened to them things, Inez?"

"Just a minute," she said. She went through a door behind

the counter into the part of the building where they lived. In a minute she came back with a cardboard box. "Nobody ever bought nothing anyway," she said. She put the box on a stool at the counter. It was full of coconuts with scowling faces carved on them. "This is about all we got left." She pulled one out and held it up to look at it. "Ugly thing, ain't it? You say you getting this for your wife?"

"For a souvenir."

"I reckon she'd be just thrilled to death if you taken her one of these." She put the coconut back into the box. "You ought to give consideration to a string of pearls."

"It's just for a souvenir. I'll take her a *real* present as well." Langston James picked up the head and looked at it. "What you think?" he said.

"I think it's an ugly sucker," she said. "Kind of looks like your friend out there." She swung her head towards the door. "Tell you the truth, mister. I don't know if I'd like to see you come marching in with nothing like that if I was your wife."

Arkwright smiled. "She's a born salesman. You can tell."

"I ain't going to lie to the man."

"It's just a thought. I wouldn't give it to her in no serious way. How much is it?"

Inez looked at Arkwright. "I forget," she said.

"I bought those in '49," he said. "They'd be a dollar."

"A dollar?"

"Seventy-five cents," said Arkwright. "I'd be glad to get rid of it to tell the truth. Personally, they always given me the creeps."

Langston James looked at the snakeskin on the wall. "How much for the snakeskin?" he said.

"It ain't for sale," said Inez quickly.

"That rattler bit me," said Arkwright. "My hand swole up till it looked like a hornet's nest. I got him where I want him right there."

Langston James took out his wallet and gave them a dollar. "A dollar's fair," he said. "For the head. Don't worry, lady," he said, speaking to Inez. "I ain't only just buying it for the notion. I'll get her something more substantial in Savannah."

"A dollar was the original price," said Arkwright. He handed the bill to Inez, who rolled it up in her handkerchief. "Would there be anything else? I'm sorry about the snakeskin."

Langston James held up the scowling coconut, like it was a severed head, looking at it eye to eye. "I guess not," he said. "This here is enough ugly to last me awhile."

"You want me to put it in a paper bag?" said Inez.

"No need."

"Much obliged," said Arkwright. "Drop by next spring. Spring's the best time for the animals."

"He catches them over the winter," said Inez.

"Maybe I will," said Langston James. "I got me a boy at home. It ought to be right educational for a boy."

Nine

"WHAT YOU THINK, BODINE?" Langston James held up the coconut head for Bodine to see. Bodine looked at it for a minute, then turned and looked out the window without saying anything.

"Don't you get pouty on me, Bodine. This here's a pleasure trip." He turned the coconut and looked at it himself for a minute. "You reckonize one of your relatives or something?"

Bodine continued to stare out the window on his side. "Looks more like your fambly than mine," he said flatly.

Langston James frowned. "Well," he said, turning the coconut this way and that, "I suppose you're right. Halstead got the same bushwhacked look on his face. Same color hair as well." He put the coconut on the seat between them. Don't you go telling Halstead I said that." He thought a minute. "Don't you tell Cowie neither. It's wrong of us to say it anyways."

"I wadn't thinking of Halstead."

Langston James put the truck into gear and jerked it out onto the highway. For awhile they rode in a thickening silence.

"All right, goddamn it. I don't have to put up with this, Bodine. You want me to turn this truck around and take you back to Whippet? I ain't going to have you spoiling my trip."

"I wanted me a Dr Pepper," Bodine spoke in a measured way. "Co-Colas gives me gas." He put his fist to his mouth and belched to emphasize the point.

"Have you a cigarette." Langston James tossed the pack into Bodine's lap. "It'll settle your stomach." Bodine laid the pack carefully on the dash, then took out his can of Tube Rose and put a pinch under his lip.

"I'll get you a goddamn Dr Pepper in Savannah."

"You *knows* I don't drink Co-Colas," Bodine said at last. He rolled down the window and spit. "Never did."

"Listen, Bodine. I'll turn this goddamn truck around faster'n you can say 'Jack, Roberson.'"

"I want me a Dr Pepper," said Bodine. He was sitting up very straight and looking down his nose at the hood of the truck. "And a hot dog as well...no onions."

"This ain't slavery, Bodine. I never said I was going to *buy* you."

Bodine didn't comment.

"Anyway. It ain't my goddamn fault. They let you *in*, didn't they? They was good people really."

Bodine spoke with his head turned away. "I know they was," he said. "That's the worst part."

On the outskirts of Savannah, Langston James pulled the truck over for Bodine to get out of the cab and into the bed.

"It's broad daylight, Bodine. No tellin' how many 'Dunks' there might be in Savannah."

"No tellin' how many they is in *Waycross* neither."

In town they drove the length of Broughton Street and back

again, looking at the stores. They parked on a side street by the Kress five-and-ten-cent store and went in. It was big as a cathedral inside, with gritty wooden floors and fans turning slowly up against the high ceilings.

"It cool enough to butcher a hog," said Bodine, looking up at the fans.

"That's the air condition, Bodine. Don't act like a cracker."

"A *cracker*?"

"Just act natural. I'll meet you back here directly."

They went their separate ways, drifting up and down the aisles, looking at the items in the glass-divided compartments on the counters. Langston James considered the toys at the children's counter, thinking of a present for Halstead. Toys weren't Halstead's style, but Langston James thought getting one would be good for him. "Halstead needs to lighten up," he thought. Finally he bought a Buck Rogers ray pistol made out of stamped tin. Pulling the trigger cranked a small siren inside, and when he tried it out several nearby customers quick-stepped away. The counter lady frowned at him. He handed the pistol to her with the money. "Loud, ain't it?" he said. The lady took the bill and examined it closely, as if she suspected it might be counterfeit, then rang up the purchase and put the pistol into a paper bag without saying anything. Her manner changed from distrustful to sullen.

"It's a long way to Whippet," he said, making conversation.

"No," said the counter lady. There was an unpleasant and very superior looking smile on her face. "It's a long way to *Tipperary*."

"What?" said Langston James.

"Didn't catch it, did you?"

"Catch *what*? I'm trying to tell you." He took the Buck Rogers pistol out of the bag and held it up. "You wouldn't find an item like that in Whippet."

The sullen look came back over her face. "You going to buy

something else?"

"I wouldn't want to put you out."

She folded her arms across her flat chest and walked to the other end of the counter.

* * *

"DO YOU LOVE YOUR WIFE?"

Langston James flinched at the sound of the voice. It came from a tall man with oily hair and a gold tooth. He was standing at a card table that had been set up in the aisle. The table was covered with a cloth and there was a cutting board in the middle of it. Beside the table was a trash can half full of various kinds of peelings.

"You talking to me?" Langston James looked around.

"How many hours a month does your wife spend peeling potatoes? You ever think about that?" The man was wearing a white shirt and a green tie with a palm tree painted on it. While he was talking, he stuffed the tie into the pocket of his shirt out of his way. There was a long brown stain down one leg of his seersucker trousers. In his hand he held a large butcher knife.

"Not hardly," said Langston James, looking at the knife and taking a step backward.

"Does your wife bend her knife like this when she peels potatoes?" The man bowed the blade of the knife as he spoke. The hand holding the blade had bandaids on two of the fingers.

"I don't know what she does, mister. How would I know a thing like that?"

"I'll tell you what, friend. I'll bet you she don't. And you know what that means?"

Langston James tried to think what it meant.

The man went on. "It means she's wasting a lot of potatoes. She's cutting off the best part. You'd be surprised how it mounts up." The man seemed to be angry at something.

"Is that a fact?" said Langston James.

The man put the knife on the table with a flourish and picked up a small, odd-looking instrument. "This here's a Jiffy Peeler," he said. He moved it this way and that to display it from different angles. There was a serious look on his face. "They's more important things in life than peeling potatoes, mister." He thought about what he'd said, then added, "I mean you need time to do the things you really want."

Langston James bobbed his head, following the movements of the peeler in the man's hand. "Hold still," he said. "You making me dizzy."

"This here's a genuine labor-saving miracle, friend. I ain't telling you no lie." He picked up a potato and began to attack it. His movements were rapid and precise, too quick for Langston James to follow. A stream of potato peelings flew in an arc away from the man's hand and into a pile on the table. When he had finished with the potato, he picked up a carrot and repeated the performance. "Works with all kinds of vegetables," he said. "Fruit as well." He peeled and cored an apple, then did a fancy cut on an orange. "You want her to spend her life in drudgery?"

"Is there some kind of a trick to it?"

"No trick." The man ran the peeler across the palm of his hand. "No trick all. No danger to it neither. A five-year-old can use this implement. Science done done it again."

"How much is that thing?"

"Twenty-nine cents. You believe that, friend? You're putting years on her life for twenty-nine cents." He held out a card with a Jiffy Peeler stapled to it.

Langston James took the card and looked at it.

"It'll last a lifetime, friend," said the man. "And smooth the connubial waters."

"What?"

"It'll put ease in the heart of the little woman."

"I could use me some heart's ease just now," said Langston James, opening his snap purse. "I reckon I couldn't go wrong for twenty-nine cents." He gave the man three dimes.

"That's the best investment you ever made, mister," said the man, taking the money. "Have an apple?" He held out the peeled and cored apple from the demonstration.

"You owe me a penny."

"Penny tax," said the man.

Langston James took the apple. "You got an interesting line of work there, mister," he said. "How much you make in a year?"

The man looked at his watch. "Time for my break," he said. He took his tie out of his pocket and left.

For a long time Langston James stood chewing on his apple and wandering around the store. At the counter that contained things for small children, he finished his apple while he looked over the rattles and sucking toys and other baby items. Finally he bought a rubber duck for Gabriel. The saleslady was small and fluttery. She had a kind face and a fluty voice.

"He loves his bath," he said to her as he handed her the money.

She squeezed a honk out of the duck. "He'll love his daddy for this," she said.

Langston James contemplated the kind face of the woman for a minute, then he stepped up close to the counter and lowered his voice. "Could you tell me something, ma'm?"

"What's that?"

"You ever hear of a place called Tipperary?"

* * *

He met Bodine at the front of the store.

"What you got, Bodine?"

Bodine reached into his bag and pulled out a bottle of strawberry-scented lamp oil. Langston James sniffed the bottle. "Smells like strawberries."

"Hope so," said Bodine. "I paid thirty-nine cent for it."

Langston James handed him back the bottle. "See what I mean, Bodine? You can't get you an item like that in Whippet. Some ways a city's got it all over little bitty towns."

"What you got?" Bodine looked at his packages.

"Man said it was a miracle. I only paid *twenty*-nine cent for mine."

"We'll see did you get your money worth," said Bodine.

Langston James gave him his packages. "Listen. You go on back to the truck. I'll get us some hot dogs."

"Get me a Dr Pepper too," said Bodine. "Co-Colas gives me gas."

"Bodine," said Langston James, "you say that one more time and I'm going to kick your ass." A lady who was passing at the moment gave him an upswept look. Langston James tipped his hat to her. "No offense, ma'm. This here's a private conversation." The woman put up her nose and walked out of the store. "See what you made me do?"

Bodine turned to go. "Don't put me no onions on that there hot dog. Onions gives me gas as well."

"Why don't you give me a list? No way I'm going to keep what all you can't eat in my *head*."

"Co-Colas and onions on my hot dog. Two things is all. If that be too much for you I can get you a pencil to write it down."

"Get on to the truck."

"Much obliged," said Bodine, tipping his hat.

At the lunch counter Langston James bought two hot dogs and two Dr Peppers. He and Bodine ate them standing by the truck on the sidewalk, then they leaned against the tail-gate and smoked two cigarettes apiece while they watched the people passing by.

Langston James nodded in a thoughtful way. "I love the passing parade," he said. He took a couple more drags on his cigarette, then dropped it into the gutter and stepped on it. "But we ain't got a whole lot of time. Let's go on down to Tybee Beach."

"They's a heap of colored folks in that there store." Bodine spoke reflectively. "White folks as well. All mixed up together."

"Don't get too worked up, Bodine. They was all spending money."

"The saleslady treated me nice."

"You had better luck than I did." Langston James thought a minute. "The lady sold me the duck was all right."

For awhile they watched the people. "That's enough of the passing parade. Let's us go on down to Tybee. We come this far, might as well see what the ocean looks like."

"What ocean?"

"*Atlantic* Ocean. Lord God, Bodine."

"Ain't nothin' but water is it?"

Langston James looked at him for a minute. "And the Grand Canyon ain't nothing but a goddamn hole in the ground, right?"

Bodine picked his teeth with the nail of his little finger. "I think I done seen it already."

"Oh? That right? Seems like you'd remember a thing like the Atlantic Ocean."

"Same one in Florida, ain't it?"

Langston James narrowed his eyes. "Which side?"

"What you mean 'which side'?"

"Which side of Florida you talking about? East or West?"

"What difference it make?"

"Oh, well. Only one side got Atlantic Ocean on it. Other side got Gulf of Mexico."

"Big difference?"

"A Gulf ain't no ocean."

"Anyway, I seen it. Lotsa water. I'd ruther go back in the ten-cent store. Heaps of inneresting things in a ten-cent store."

"Get in the back, Bodine. I don't want to discuss it no more."

"If you done made your mind up, what you ax me for?"

"Get in the back."

"It hard on my piles, sittin' flat down back there. How come we ain't brought the chair?"

"Piles? You ain't never said nothing about no piles before. Where you get piles?"

"Got 'em on my rear end. Where you *think* I got 'em, on my elbow?"

"How come you never said nothing before now?"

"You ain't never ax me."

"Why would I ask you if you got piles? That ain't even a civil question. You think *ever*thing's up to me?"

"You the *boss*."

"Nevermind. It ain't but a little ways. You can stand it."

"If I got to be tuckin' 'em in my socks when we get through, you be the one to blame."

"I'll be the one to blame anyways. Get in the back."

Bodine climbed into the bed, moving in an elaborate manner. "Some pleasure," he said.

Langston James rapped on the window. "You stay with me, Bodine. I'm going to make you broad."

"What part you got in mind?"

"Make your mind broad."

"Maybe I better stand on my head."

"Sit on your thumb. And don't tell me no more about it."

"Don't hit no bumps. It be slappin' on my behind something fierce back here."

"Just till we get out of town, Bodine. City driving ain't going to hurt you none."

"Some pleasure," said Bodine.

Tybee Beach was twenty miles out of town at the end of U.S. 80. The last ten miles stretched across open marsh and was lined with palm trees and oleander bushes. Once they were well out on the causeway, Langston James pulled over and let Bodine back into the cab. He held out an Old Gold to him as a peace offering. "How's your piles doing?"

"Gonna' need repackin' when this is over." He took the cigarette and waited for Langston James to light it. "It's a funny smell," he said, puffing a cloud of smoke into the cab.

"That's the Atlantic Ocean. You don't smell the Atlantic Ocean every day."

"Smell like feets to me."

"You know what, Bodine?" Langston James looked at him. "Sometimes you got a piss poor attitude. Goddamn if you ain't."

"Puttin' my butt in a soft place'd help heaps."

After they crossed the last bridge onto Tybee Island, Langston James pulled over again and told Bodine to get into the back.

"Ain't you got something soft I could sit on? I gone feel like I been passin' porkeypines after all this."

"Rumple you up some newspapers and sit on 'em. It ain't but a little piece now."

"This better be a awful good ocean."

"Trust me, Bodine. It's the best ocean there is."

* * *

Tybee Beach had seen better days, though even in the best of times it had never been much more than a local attraction. Back around the First World War there had been an elegant dance pavillion where big name bands like Jan Garber and Blue Steele had played. In those days the only way to get down there was by a narrow gauge railroad, and riding it was a social event in itself. Young people packed onto it after work on Saturday—a straw hat and picnic basket crowd—hanging out the windows and singing Tin Pan Alley songs. After the bandstand on the pavillion closed down at eleven-thirty, there was always a rush and scurry to make the last train of the day, which left at midnight. The old railroad bed still ran parallel to the highway. Where the tracks had been on the island itself, down the center of Butler Avenue, there was a median with palm trees growing on it.

War always seemed to bring out the best in Tybee, as it did in Savannah itself. Patriotism has always been a big item there, which is a fortunate thing, since the city is more or less surrounded by military installations of one kind or another. The Marine boot camp at Parris Island is just forty miles north at Beaufort, South Carolina, and Camp Stewart, a big Army training camp, is thirty miles south at Hinesville, Georgia. National emergencies filled them up, and the weekend overflow gravitated south and north looking for good times. Until the end of the Second World War there was a coastal defense unit in Fort Screven at the north end of the island, and Navy ships came up the river from time to time. The Marines and the soldiers from Stewart were fresh out of training—which meant that they were in the best physical condition of their lives and jacked up to the point of combustion—thirsty and horny and sorely in need of calming down. Savannah wasn't very good for that, since it inclines pretty sharply towards combustion in its own right. Tybee was better. Especially in broad daylight.

Nine-tenths of the island was a place for families. There was the Fort at the north end, and a trapline of bars and souvenir shops and the pavillion and the Tybreeza Hotel at the south end—which cranked up after the sun went down. But the mile and a half stretching between those two points was all frame houses, most of them built around the time of the First World War. They weren't identical, but there was a definite style to them. Mostly they were white, with green shutters and trim, set up on pilings, with screened porches wrapping them around on three sides. Some had widow's walks on top, and most had names. From May to September they were occupied by three—sometimes four—generations at a time. All those grandmothers watching all those children created a kind of generalized atmosphere of supervision, which had a calming effect on beach activities. So even in war times it was a pretty quiet place.

Whenever a war *wasn't* going on, things slowed down even more. Mostly there were just local people in evidence, with now and then a family from Augusta or Macon, or a honeymoon couple from some little town in South Georgia. Since it was eighteen miles out of Savannah and off to the side of U.S. 17—the main north-south highway—it wasn't a place people were likely to stumble on by accident. Northern tourists on their way to Florida didn't know it was there to begin with. And most people from Georgia, if they lived more than fifty miles away, generally went ahead and made a real trip of it—following the signs until they ended up in St. Augustine, or Daytona, or Fort Lauderdale. If they did come that way, by the time they got to Savannah, they were only four hours away from Jacksonville and the alligator farms and glass-bottomed boat rides. So getting to Tybee just about had to be the result of a deliberate act.

Still, south Georgia *did* surround it, so you could count on a small but noticeably unstylish element walking the beach on any given day. Men and woman in rented wool bathing suits—long after Latex had come in—some of the men even wearing tops, and nearly all of them in street shoes with the laces untied and no socks. They had fire-red faces and necks and hands, but the rest of their bodies had the color and texture of hairy mayonnaise. The women, what was showing of them, were about as red as the men were, but not many of them put on bathing suits anyway. Mostly they reclined fully clothed on chenille spreads or bedsheets, their legs in brown cotton hose stretched out in front of them with their ankles crossed. They leaned back on their propped arms, gazing intently at the horizon as if they expected ships that would come and carry them away.

In the summer of 1959, with no war going on, it was a friendly, local sort of place, and there was only one thing about it that posed a problem for a pair like Langston James and Bodine: dogs were welcome on the beach, but Negroes weren't. It was an arrangement which didn't get amended until the late sixties, at which time it was reversed, so that Negroes were allowed on the beach but not dogs. Langston James hadn't counted on that particular feature.

Ten

LANGSTON JAMES DROVE DOWN Butler Avenue toward the south end of the island. They were only one block away from the ocean, and were able to catch glimpses of it down the numbered access roads on their left. "That's it, Bodine," Langston James inclined his head to indicate the direction, and when Bodine didn't respond, he tapped on the rear window to attract his attention. "Atlantic Ocean, Bodine. Thattaway." He made a jabbing motion with his finger. Bodine turned his head briefly, then squared and fixed his glance over the tailgate of the truck.

At Sixteenth Street, Langston James turned off Butler Avenue and drove down to the beachfront, then turned parallel to the seawall along the line of souvenir shops and bars, driving slowly. After two blocks, he turned off and came around again. He did that loop twice. After the second pass, he pulled into an alley and stopped the truck. For a minute he sat in the cab, drumming his fingers on the steering wheel and thinking. When he got out of the truck, he turned his head this way and that, as if trying to catch the direction of a distant sound. Then he folded his arms and rested them on the window sill of the open door.

"You know what, Bodine?" he said at last.

"Yeah," said Bodine. "Ain't no colored people."

"Not a single, solitary one."

"Looks like a white folks' ocean to me."

"I hadn't thought about it."

"*Now* can we go back to that ten-cent store?"

"Don't talk for a minute, Bodine. I got to think this out."

"What do it be to think *about*? You got eyes in your head same as me."

Langston James stood up and looked at him. "I hadn't come all this way so we can sit around and *listen* to that ocean. Gimmie a minute. I can figure this out."

Bodine took off his cap and wiped his forehead, then squinted up at the sun. "It hot out here."

Langston James pursed his mouth, then drew it into a thin, tight line. "I got niggered out in Waycross *and* that funny monkey place. I be *God*-damned if I'll be niggered out of the Atlantic Ocean." After he spoke, he looked up quickly at Bodine. There was a faint smile on Bodine's face. "I don't mean *you*, Bodine."

"Words is a comfort, isn't they?"

"No," he said. He paused. "Well, yes. Sometimes they are." He didn't look at Bodine when he spoke. "I don't use that word much in private. Hardly ever. I'm sorry it came out the way it did. I'm about run out of patience."

"You the one ax me to come."

"It ain't you I'm out of patience with. I'm out of patience with the goddamn *world*."

"Ain't a thing new about this. No reason you got to take on so just this minute."

"Well, I hadn't noticed it so much up to now. Somehow it came to me all at once."

Bodine stood up and fanned himself with his cap. "Well," he said, "what we going to do?"

"Sit down." Langston James got back into the truck and slammed the door. "I'm going to drive around while I think it over. I think better when I'm movin'."

For awhile he drove aimlessly, crawling the streets of the south end of the island. Wherever they went, eventually they came back to Butler Avenue. On one of his passes, Langston James noticed a hardware store with a rack of garden implements next to the entrance. He gave them a thoughtful look as they drove past, then he circled the block and pulled in to the curb. "Hmmmmmmmm..." he said.

"What you 'hmmmmmmmmin' about?"

"Trust me, Bodine. I got it figured out." He turned off the motor and opened the door. "You wait here. I'll be back in a minute."

Bodine looked up at the sun, then took off his cap and fanned himself with it. "It's mighty hot at this here ocean."

"I wouldn't be but a couple of minutes. I'll get you a Dr Pepper when I come back."

He went into the store. When he came out he took a shovel from the rack by the door and walked over to the truck. "Lookey here." He held up the shovel. "This here's your *Disguise.*"

Bodine looked at the shovel and frowned. "What you want me to do—*hide* behind of it?"

"All you got to do is carry it. Long as they think you're working it'll be okay." He took the price tag off the shovel and banged it on the curb a couple of times. "Put a little use on it, don't you see?" He put it into the bed of the truck, then got into the cab. He put his head out the window. "You know what?"

"I don't reckon I know nothing."

"There's a Chinaman runs that store."

Bodine craned his neck around. "What kind of a Chinaman? How you know?"

"I know a Chinaman when I see one. How you think I'd know?"

"Was he yaller?"

"No. He wasn't exactly yaller. I could tell though." He paused. "What you *mean*, 'What kind of a Chinaman'? How many kinds you think there is?"

"They's all kinds of white people...Georgia white people...Florida white people...Italian white people."

"Listen. If you don't know what you're talking about, why don't you be quiet? It was just a plain, everyday Chinaman. Running the store. I told you we was going to see us some unusual things."

"I ain't seen no Chinaman."

"You seen the Atlantic Ocean."

"Smelt it as well. Whyn't we go on back to the ten-cent store?"

"You *seen* the Atlantic Ocean, but you ain't *experienced* it yet. I paid three dollars for that shovel."

"You can always use a shovel."

"Trust me, Bodine. Long as you don't look like you enjoying yourself, it'll be okay."

"Some pleasure."

Langston James drew his head into the cab and started the motor. Before he pulled out into the street, he tapped on the window.

"What?" said Bodine.

"Hold that shovel up where people can see it."

Bodine raised the shovel over his head.

"Don't play games with me, Bodine. We're almost there."

"Some pleasure," said Bodine, lowering the shovel.

"And, Bodine," said Langston James, "Italians ain't white

people. Where'd you get an idea like that? Italians're Catholics."
He shook his head. "I don't know about you, Bodine. I just don't
know."

* * *

At the ocean end of Sixteenth Street was a parking lot that
fronted on the boardwalk. At the entrance to the parking lot was
a small, white stucco building with "POLICE STATION"
painted on it in large, black letters. As they pulled up to it, a
policeman stepped out of the door. He was a large, soft-looking
man, with a round baby face and pouty lips like a cupid. His
uniform was too small for him, and the hat he wore fitted him
like a party favor. The way it sat on his head it looked like it had
dropped there by accident, and he didn't know about it yet. He
rested his right hand on the butt of his pistol and held up his
other hand for them to stop.

Langston James smiled at him like a man sitting on a hot-
plate. "What is it, officer?" The guilt in his voice could have gotten him twenty years all by itself.

The policeman waved his free hand. "Pull over there." He
indicated a space next to the building outlined in yellow paint.

"It's a yaller curb."

"Pull over."

"Was it anything wrong?"

"Right there," said the policeman, pointing. He had a high
voice with a trace of a lisp in it.

Langston James pulled the truck into the space.

The policeman walked over in a John Wayne manner and
stood for a minute looking out at the ocean. When he spoke,
he didn't look at Langston James. "Don't you know that's dangerous, mister?"

Langston James looked around inside the cab, trying to see

what he was talking about. "It is?" he said at last.

"It ain't actually against the *law*. But it's dangerous just the same." Since the policeman was looking out at the horizon, Langston James had the impression he was talking about the ocean. "You hit a bump and you might could throw him out on the highway."

Langston James thought about what he'd said for a minute. Finally he turned his head and looked through the window at Bodine. "You talking about *him*?"

"What if you had a wreck? You didn't think about that, did you?"

"You mean you want him to ride..." he hooked his thumb toward Bodine, "*inside* the truck?"

While they were talking, a second policeman came out of the building. He was a smaller man, older, with a clipped grey moustache. He was holding a copy of *True Detective* with his finger inside to mark his place. The badge he wore said "Chief."

"What is it, Flatt?" His voice sounded weary. He looked down at the large policeman's right hand on the butt of his pistol. "Keep that thing in your holster, Flatt. No need to have it out and waving around." He looked at Bodine, then stepped up to the door of the truck. "You got business here, friend?"

Langston James hadn't thought out his lie ahead of time, and he faltered badly. "We come to dig some..." he paused. "worms."

"*Worms*?" Both men spoke at once. Flatt started to draw his pistol.

"You take it out and I'm locking it in the safe, Flatt. I'm tired of worrying about you and that gun." The Chief gazed over the top of the cab for a minute, then he leaned down and looked Langston James in the eye. "You come to the beach to dig worms? What kind of worms was you planning to dig?"

"See," said Langston James, pointing over his shoulder at

Bodine. "He got the shovel."

"That's right. He certainly has got the shovel."

Langston James thought for a minute. "You act like you didn't believe me."

"You got that impression, did you?" The Chief looked out at the ocean, then back at Langston James. "We got people come down here to dig all kinds of things. Sand dollars. Turtle eggs. Some people even come down here to dig for buried treasure. You're the first one ever came to dig for worms."

"First one?"

"*Very* first."

Flatt stepped up. "Want me to run them in, Chief?"

"For digging worms? Stand over there, Flatt. You make me nervous." He pointed back toward the station.

"I ain't too good when it comes to making up lies," said Langston James.

"I'd have to agree."

Langston James looked at the Chief for a minute. "Can I trust you, mister?"

"Where you from?"

"Whippet, Georgia."

"Whippet? Where's Whippet at?"

"Up country. About a hundred and twenty miles."

"Anybody tells a lie as sorry as you do could stand a little trust." He added. "You can trust me."

"What I'm going to tell you is the straight-out truth."

"It couldn't be any worse than what you've told me already. Why don't you give it a try?"

Langston James looked him in the eye. "We didn't see no colored people. I figured if you thought we was working it'd be all right for him to take a look." He pointed back at Bodine. "He ain't never seen the Atlantic Ocean."

"I see," said the Chief.

"We had a couple of bad experiences back up the road. I thought it might be against the law."

"It ain't against the law." The Chief looked at him for a minute. "I see you got a right inventive mind after all." He paused. "In some respects."

"It ain't against the law?"

"Well. There isn't anything written down. Not in that way it isn't."

"You mean it's okay for him to look around?"

"Well," said the Chief, "not exactly."

"I don't quite know what you're saying."

The Chief thought a minute. "Tell you what. Leave your truck here. Anybody stops you, tell them you're looking for a leak in a water line."

"That'll be okay?"

"You came a hundred and twenty miles to see the ocean." He looked at Bodine. "It'll be okay as long as I don't see him in a bathing suit. Keep him carrying that shovel where everybody can see it."

Langston James got out of the truck. "See, Bodine. I told you it was going to work." Bodine didn't say anything.

"Anybody desperate enough to tell a lie big as you did ought to get some consideration." The Chief started back into the station. He stopped and turned back to Langston James. "Don't make a day of it. I'll give you two hours, then I'm ticketing your truck."

"Much obliged," said Langston James. "Two hours'll be fine."

"Promise me something," said the Chief.

"What's that?"

"If you do find some worms, let me know about it."

"What kind of worms?" said Langston James.

* * *

For a while they walked along the seawall, Langston James trying to put on the look and stride of a man with a purpose, Bodine dragging behind in a workman's slump with the shovel over his shoulder, his lips pooched out and his eyes cast down.

"Look!" Langston James stopped abruptly and Bodine walked into him from behind.

"Whatwhatwhat?"

"Act natural, Bodine. You doing fine."

"Some pleasure."

"You hungry? I could use me a corn dog."

"What's a corn dog?"

"Right there." Langston James pointed to a small glassed-in stand. Attached to it was a red-and-white striped awning with trestle tables set out beneath it. "Step over thataway, to the side there, and lean on your shovel." Langston James pointed to the side of the corn dog stand. "I'll get us a couple. You getting broader by the minute."

The man behind the glass was small and swarthy. He spoke with a foreign accent that was high and nasal. Langston James held up two fingers. "Two corn dogs," he said. "All the way." Then he added, "One without onions."

The man looked at him for a minute, darting his eyes over to where Bodine was standing leaning on the handle of the shovel, then back again to Langston James. "Purchasing both for your personal self?" he said at last.

"What?" Langston James drew his mouth tight and narrowed his eyes. "You selling or *dis*-patching?"

"What?" said the man, stepping back from the counter.

"How long you think you got to keep up with them?"

"I am the responsible person, sir."

Langston James made an "O" with his mouth, then pointed to it elaborately with the index finger of his right hand. "This is where it goes in," he said. "You want me to show you where it comes out?"

The man darted his eyes at Bodine again, then licked his lips. "You will consume them somewhere else?" he said, looking back at Langston James.

"Listen," said Langston James. "We're working people. It ain't even your goddamn country, is it?"

The man twitched his mouth several times, drawing his features toward the center of his face. "I am learning the ways of doing things," he said at last. "This is the best job I am having. I will be keeping it if you don't mind."

Langston James slapped the money down on the counter. "Listen, buddy," he said. "This is America."

"America," said the man. "For sure."

"In America the goddamn customer is always right."

"Certainly," said the man.

"Certainly?"

"The customer is always right."

Langston James drew his head back and gave the man his good eye. "You ain't even big as I am, buddy. You oughtn't be mocking me like that."

The man looked at him in a puzzled way. "You are the one who is saying it."

Langston James looked at Bodine. Bodine had taken his chin off the handle of the shovel and was standing up with an intense look on his face.

The man put his head through the window at the counter and yelled to Bodine. "Nothing of a personal nature, sir. It is altogether accountable to the custom." Bodine put the shovel over his shoulder and walked off toward the back of the corn dog stand with a disgusted look on his face.

"You needn't call attention to him, mister," said Langston James, lowering his voice. "He ain't much blacker than you are."

"It is something I am entirely aware of," said the man. "I am indeed a colored person myself." He took the money off the counter in a dignified way and began preparing the corn dogs.

"Well," said Langston James, "You probably from a whole nigger country. It ain't the same thing."

"Quite similar," said the man, still very dignified. He handed Langston James the corn dogs. "Do not be sitting in the proximity, please."

Langston James took the corn dogs and stood looking at the man for a minute. "Listen," he said at last. "I'm going to tell him you said you was sorry."

The man nodded. "That will be quite proper," he said. "It is indeed the fact. My desire is not in accordance with the custom."

"I hate to see him get his feelings hurt."

"He will be understanding my position."

Langston James nodded. "It'll take the edge off. He's a good man. I hate to see him, you know, get his feelings hurt."

The man nodded. "Truly," he said, "you are somewhat different yourself."

"Listen," said Langston James, hiking up his shoulder, "I ain't different, I'm *unique.*"

"Well," said the man, looking him up and down, "that is so as well." He nodded again. "Nevertheless, I am referring to the circumstance of your friendliness with a colored person."

"Ah," said Langston James.

The man shook his head slowly. "I do not believe I am yet understanding the custom so totally. America is a difficult place."

Langston James nodded. "I see what you mean," he said.

"Nevertheless," said the man, "God bless America. As it were."

Langston James thought about this for a minute. "I reckon," he said at last.

"I hope you will be relishing your corn dog."

Langston James nodded.

"Your friend as well."

Langston James looked at him and nodded again. "Which one don't have the onions?"

"Corn dogs are not having onions in any event," said the man.

Bodine was leaning against the back of the corn dog stand with his arms crossed over his chest, hugging the handle of the shovel. Langston James held out the corn dog to him. "He said he's sorry, Bodine. He hopes you enjoy your corn dog. He's a colored man his ownself. I didn't ask where he came from, but you could tell he wasn't no American colored person. Whatever it was. The way he talked would of given him away anyhow."

Bodine hugged the shovel handle tighter and looked away. "I ain't hungry," he said.

"He *said* he was sorry. It ain't his fault."

"I know whose fault it is."

Langston James stood holding out the corn dog. "Listen," he said. "I'm sorry too, goddamn it. That's it. Now take the corn dog. I done paid for it."

Bodine looked at him. "Why you got to make such a fuss? That man just doing his job."

Langston James looked at the corn dog in his outstretched hand. "It ain't going to make no difference whether you eat the corn dog or not. It ain't going to be no worse of a place one way or the other. I done bought it. You might as well enjoy it."

Bodine took the corn dog without saying anything. They leaned against the back of the stand while they ate.

"How you like your corn dog?"

"It's okay."

Langston James nodded. "What you reckon he is? I wouldn't exactly call him a colored man."

"Well. He ain't white."

"That's right." Langston James licked his corn dog stick. "Reckon how many varieties there is?"

"More than there is of Chinamen." Bodine slid the last of his corn dog off the stick with his fingers and put it into his mouth. "According to you."

Langston James looked down at the ground for a minute, thinking. He shook his head. "This is wearing me out."

"Some pleasure."

"You know what, Bodine? Sometimes this world just ain't worth a shit. I be goddamned if it ain't."

"You commencing to get broad your ownself."

Langston James nodded, looking at the ground. "I figured limping and twitching and seeing everthing twict done that for me already." He looked at Bodine. "Okay," he said, "I reckon I'm spreading out *some*."

Bodine nodded and licked his corn dog stick.

"How'd you like your corn dog?"

"It wadn't bad. I think I tasted onions."

"They ain't got any, Bodine. Don't tell me about no onions." There was a pause. "Well," he said, trying to sound cheerful, "You can say you seen the Atlantic Ocean."

"I could of *said* that before."

"What would I have to do to make you grateful, Bodine? I ain't going to outright kiss your ass." Bodine didn't answer. "Gimme your corn dog stick." He wrapped it in his napkin with his own, then put them into his pocket. "Nice sticks," he said. He wiped his mouth with the sleeve of his short-sleeved shirt. "I reckon we can go now. Keep a grip on that shovel."

Eleven

LANGSTON JAMES AND BODINE walked off away from the boardwalk toward the back side of the amusement park. Behind the ferris wheel and merry-go-round there was a small tent with a sign on it that read, *"Zola The Snake Lady."*

"Look, Bodine," Langston James pointed to the sign.

"You going to pay money to see you a *snake?*"

"Snake *Lady*, Bodine. Snake *Lady*."

"Hmmmmm...," said Bodine. "How you going to get me in this one? Tell 'em I be a snake handler?"

"Don't go hummmmin' me, Bodine. We'll have to cross that bridge when we come to it. Our luck's running pretty good. Hang on."

At the side of the tent there was a loudspeaker. Out of it came a tape-recorded spiel, not a very long one, but repeated over and over—"Zola the Snake Lady. She was captured in South America. She is here and she is alive." The voice was nasal and distinct in its pronunciation, but the accent was Southern — and slightly enfeebled, as of an elderly person. After the spiel there were two long, indistinct gutteral sounds — sounds more gastric than vocal. They certainly didn't evoke anything that ever came out of a snake.

In front of the tent a man was sitting on an aluminum folding chair. He was wearing a dirty seersucker suit and a Panama hat. In his ear was a hearing aid that was supposed to be flesh colored, but looked like a wad of bubble gum, or some kind of growth gone out of control. The cable connecting it to the battery pack on his belt was the same vibrating color of pink and thick enough to feed an arc welding wand. On his lap the man was holding the top of a cardboard Tootsie Roll box. He was cutting little "V's" out of the edge of it with a pocket knife. The way he worked at it was slow and deliberate, and there was an expression of great concentration on his face. If he had been carving angels to go on the pulpit of a church he couldn't have been more serious about it.

Langston James and Bodine stood watching him for a minute or two. Bodine took the shovel off his shoulder and put it point down, then rested his chin on the handle. "Reckon he got it turned off?" he said at last.

Langston James took a step closer, then leaned down to speak into the man's ear. The man stopped sawing at the "v" he was working on and rolled his eyes up at Langston James without moving his head. His face was knobby and sad, like a melancholy bag full of golf balls. He had a dapper pencil-line moustache that was mostly grey, and a stubble of grey beard.

Langston James rocked on his heels, then smiled and said, "Howdy."

The expression on the man's face didn't change, but he put down the box lid to the side of his chair, closed the blade of the knife and dropped it into the lid. Then he took the battery pack off his belt and stood up. He was tall and thin and the stoop in his shoulders matched the melancholy expression on his face. He fiddled with the knob on the battery pack for a minute. "A quarter," he said tonelessly. His eyes were on Langston James, and in the silence after he spoke his features tightened two or three notches deeper into sadness. He glanced at Bodine.

"Two for fifty cents?" Langston James said, looking him in the eye.

The man didn't answer right away. There was a red handkerchief lapping out of the breast pocket of his coat like an inflamed tongue. He pulled it out with a flourish and wiped his face.

"You think he's going to scare the snake lady? She's from South America, ain't she?" Langston James drew himself up as he spoke.

"You take things personal, don't you, Mister?" The man put the handkerchief into his pocket, arranging it to suit him and looking down at it while he talked. "Personally I don't give a damn. Wait till you're hurt before you start to holler."

Langston James looked around. "You think we going to scare off all these customers you got piling up on you? This here's 1959, mister. The law says he's got rights."

"I know it," said the man. "You're not too good at listening are you? I *said* I don't give a damn." He fluffed the handkerchief. "You know, the crazy thing is, ten years ago it wouldn't have made any difference. I wouldn't of given it a second thought. It's a nervous time just now."

Langston James shook his head. "We got Gunga Din selling corn dogs over thisaway, and some kind of slanty-eyed pissant owns a department store over thattaway. But I can't get an honest *American* colored man in to see a freak show with hard cash."

"Listen," said the man. "Zola's not no freak. She handles snakes. Freaks're something else. I know all there is to know about freaks." He gave Langston James a squinty-eyed stare and his face tightened for a moment, then sank another degree deeper into melancholy. "No need to go bad-mouthing freaks. Freaks are okay." There was a watery look in his eyes. "Seems like a man in your condition ought to know better."

"What you mean? What you *mean*? You calling me a freak?"

The man shook his head. "No," he said. "There's lots worse things I could call you, mister. But, no. I'm not calling you no freak." He contemplated Langston James for a minute. "I don't know what your trouble is exactly, but you're not all that—you know—*interesting*." He nodded his head when he spoke, then his voice softened. "No offense meant. I mean freaks're *really* different. Special. You got you another category altogether when you're talking about freaks."

"Just because a man's different don't mean he's no freak." Langston James drew himself up as high as he could.

"There you go. You're absolutely right about that. And just because a person's a freak don't mean he's all that different." He nodded and tapped his chest. "You know...as a *person*."

For a minute neither of them spoke. Finally the man unscrewed his face a notch or two and put out his hand. "My name's Garvin Treecastle," he said. "You've caught me at kind of a low point just now. I've seen better times."

Langston James hesitated and looked at Bodine, then he put out his hand. "Langston James McHenry," he said. "Eljay for short." He gestured toward Bodine. "Bodine Polite."

Treecastle put out his hand to Bodine. "Your friend here got ahead of himself. I go by the law of the land, friend. Your money's good as anybody's."

Bodine raised his chin off the shovel handle and looked at Treecastle's hand for a long minute. Then he put out his own and let Treecastle take it. "Yessir," he said.

"I've worked with colored men before," said Treecastle. "Never had any complaints." He looked around over their heads at the ferris wheel and the merry-go-round, then he turned and looked at his tent. When he turned back to them his face was melancholy again. "I had the best ten-in-one on the circuit," he said. "And that ain't no lie."

"Is that a fact?" said Langston James, thoughtfully. "What's a ten-in-one?"

"We don't like to call them a freak show. 'Ten-in-one' is the term we use in the trade."

"I see," said Langston James. He gave Bodine a significant look.

"I had a ten-booth tent. Alligator Lady, Midget, Giant, Sword Swallower, Fire Eater..." He turned to Bodine. "The Fire Eater was a colored man...Allie Babba."

Bodine nodded. "What?" he said.

"His name was 'Fred' really, but he got to wanting us to call him Allie Babba for spiritual reasons. You a Muslim?"

Bodine looked at Langston James then back at Treecastle. "Not that I knows of," he said.

"Fred converted. After he turned into a Black Muslim, he wouldn't let us call him 'Fred' no more. He said he was a new man and we had to call him by his new name. 'Flamo' was his professional name." Treecastle thought for a minute. "You couldn't call a Fire Eater 'Fred' anyway. If you get right down to it, 'Allie Babba' was a better name than 'Flamo.' It showed more imagination. But old Fred didn't hang around much after that. He lit out for Detroit or Chicago for the sake of his conscience. I hated to see him go. But you've got to respect a man for his honest beliefs."

"And you say they was all good people?" Langston James asked. "You know—the freaks?"

"Well, Tiny—that's the midget—he could be a pain in the ass. But on the whole I'd have to say they were a pretty agreeable bunch." He thought for a minute. "Last fat lady I had was trouble, but Florine wasn't all there in the head. One I had before her was as sweet a woman as you'd ever care to meet."

"She was?"

"Absolutely."

"What happened to her?"

"She died. That's the trouble with fat ladies. They don't live too long. But Dolly was a sweet woman."

"What about Zola?"

Treecastle thought a minute before answering. "She can be sweet herself. Only thing about Zola is she likes her snakes."

"Well," said Langston James, "she *is* a snake lady. What you expect?"

"I know. I just never got used to it is all. Snakes're all right, you know, from a distance. I don't care to get real intimate with them."

"And she ain't no freak?"

"Zola? Not to look at, if that's what you mean. She's natural as you or me." He thought about what he'd said. "I mean you wouldn't notice her if you was to meet her walking down the street...if she didn't have her snakes with her. Which I don't reckon she would."

"And she ain't no freak?"

"Not the way you're thinking about it. Not like the Alligator Lady or the Thin Man was a freak. It's just in her head, you know. Not even *all* of it—just a little, bitty part of her head. Really unusual people are hard to come by. It's my business. I know what I'm talking about."

"You wouldn't call me no freak, eh?"

Treecastle looked at him closely for a minute. "What happened to you? Accident?"

"I was little. I don't remember. *Some* of it's natural." Langston James thought for a minute. "My head got mashed. I *do* remember that."

"That was an accident I reckon."

"Yes, well. It made me to draw up. Everthing else is the work of the good Lord."

"'Good' ain't maybe quite the word."

For awhile they stood without speaking. Finally Treecastle took out his red handkerchief and wiped his face. "The public is interested in unusual people. I always figured it was an object lesson for them."

"You did?"

"Yes. Most people don't have all that much to put up with in their lives. Not really they don't. Not like yourself for instance. It's a good thing for them to get reminded what *could* of been. You know— just a little bad luck is all it takes. It can be a terrible world out there."

Langston James nodded and looked at Bodine. "Tell me about it," he said.

"Well, not always." Treecastle looked thoughtful.

"What?"

"It's not always bad luck. Sometimes it's just plain desperation." He sucked on his lips for awhile. "Back in the Depression. I've known people do things to themselves just to get a job." He frowned.

"What kind of things?"

"It makes my skin crawl just to think about it. I never did go in for geeks."

Langston James looked at him. "You got a wide range of experience, mister. I lived all my life in Whippet, Georgia. What exactly is a *geek*?"

"Excuse me. He's the fella eats the live chicken."

Langston James looked at Bodine, then back at Treecastle. "A *LIVE* chicken?"

"Just bites the head off and chews it up and swallows it."

Langston James made a face. "*SWALLOWS* it? What's he want

to do that for?"

"I never would have one in my ten-in-one." Treecastle put the handkerchief back into his breast pocket. "Did it for the money, I guess. Most of them were likker heads...or worse."

"You mean...*LIVE*? Like, with feathers and all?"

"That's what I mean. Makes you sick, don't it?" Treecastle thought for a minute. "Of course, cutting off your feet's not quite the same thing. But the two got *something* in common. Even a carnival's got a moral side to it. That's the way I always looked at it."

"You mean the geek cut his feet off too?"

"Thirty-five...thirty-six...somewhere around there. This guy comes in...well, *rolled* in. He had him a little platform out of a board with skate wheels nailed on it, like a veteran. He told me how he did it. He tied strings around his legs—you know, his ankles—and kept pulling them tighter every day. He said it took him six weeks. After that he just broke them off—broke off his feet at the ankles."

"Lord God!"

"You're right about that. He had them with him too. His feet. Hanging around his neck on a string. He offered to get his ears cut off too. Then he asked for suggestions about what all he could do to get me interested. I hate to think what I could of taken off him. He was a desperate son of a bitch. When I wouldn't put him in the show, he tried to sell them to me."

"What?"

"His feet. He tried to sell them to me. He said I could put them in a jar with alcohol and get people to pay to see them." Treecastle looked at Langston James. "You know what he wanted for them?"

Langston James shook his head.

"Five dollars. At first he said five dollars apiece. I didn't want to talk to him about it. It made my skin crawl just standing there looking at him. I wanted to get him the hell out. When I wouldn't talk to him, he said he'd take five dollars for the pair. Sweet Jesus!" Treecastle shook his head. "I got Tiny to roll him out."

"*BROKE* them off?"

"That's what he said. He said they didn't have any feeling in them by then. The first two weeks were the worst." Treecastle looked at Langston James. "There's some desperate people in this world, mister. I've known a father cut off his own child's nose and ears then hold his head down on a stove eye to stop the bleeding. Things you wouldn't believe."

Langston James looked at Bodine without saying anything. Bodine stared back.

"This ain't just for meanness I'm talking about. I'm talking about pure desperation and crazy love. He put that child out on a street corner with a tin cup. I swear to God he thought he'd done the boy a favor—given him a way to support himself you see."

"I see what you're talking about." Langston James looked at Bodine again. Bodine shook his head.

"Desperation can put a kink in your brain. I don't know what to think about it really." Treecastle shook his head. "Don't *want* to think about it at all, to tell the truth. A midget is straight-forward—you know—honest. You figure the Lord knew what he was doing there and maybe there's a lesson in it. A six hundred-pound fat lady—that's a mystery you can live with. There ain't nothing *they* had to do with it, so you can lay it off on the Lord, and that's your explanation. But eating a live chicken and cut-ting up on yourself . . . I don't reckon I want to see the hand of God in something like that." He paused. "Maybe I *could* under-stand it. Everything's got to have *some* reason behind it. Only I just don't want to have it around me—you know—every day. Some lesson're just too much to take in."

Langston James had a serious look on his face. When Tree-castle stopped talking, he let out a long breath. "I reckon God was telling him what to do."

"What?" Treecastle furrowed his brows.

"You know, 'The Lord moves in mysterious ways'." Langston James paused. "Complicated ways as well."

"Too goddamn complicated for me," said Treecastle. "I don't like to think about it. A ten-in-one don't need to be morbid. I always thought it was educational."

For awhile they stood there without speaking, each working at his own private vision of the thing. "You know," Treecastle unscrewed his features several notches, "I talk too much. No need to get down in the mouth and dreary." He looked around. The music from the merry-go-round and the ferris wheel came to them as popping, rhythmic sounds—a strong beat, but wash-ing together and converging until they became tuneless and idi-otic. In the backwater behind the rides where the tent was located, there was no one else to be seen. "Two for fifty cents," Treecastle said at last. He spoke to Bodine. "You run a ten-in-one for a few years and colored people don't seem like any novelty. We quit segregating in '57. No sense losing money." He nodded his head and put an expression on his face that came close to being a smile. "I wasn't turning them *away* in '38."

Bodine looked as though he didn't know whether to take the remark as a compliment or not.

"Tell Zola it's all right," he said. "She ought to know, but sometimes you've got to remind her." He pursed his lips. "Maybe it's the snakes or something. She's got lapses." He nodded. "She's my wife to tell the truth. All I got left from the ten-in-one." He paused. "And her name's not 'Zola.' That's just for the show. Her real name's Dolores." He thought about what he'd said. "Don't call her that. And don't let her know I told you. Jesus. I don't know what's the matter with me. We ain't been doing enough business lately to keep me on my toes." He gave Langston James two small slips of paper with "ADMIT ONE" printed on them in a flourished hand. Treecastle shook his head. "I mean I don't know why I been telling you all this. I guess I'm getting old and crazy...something." He paused. "Every now and then I need to get those things out in the open and think about what all they mean. I hate to do it by myself. Goddamn if I don't." He pointed to the flap of the tent. "Step that way, if you don't mind."

"Tell me something," said Langston James. "Did you capture her in South America?"

"Pretty close," said Treecastle. "I got her out of a bar in Fort Myers, Florida. But she claims she went through the Panama Canal once. I think she probably did. She's a pretty truthful woman on the whole. That's one of the things I admire about her." He looked at Bodine. "You can leave your shovel outside."

Inside, the snake show was pretty much of a disappointment. The space was small and dim, lit by a bare electric light bulb hanging from the ceiling. It had the feel of a pawnshop, or maybe an Army-Navy store. Everything looked used and forlorn, but with a kind of anticipation hanging in the air, like maybe something really interesting would turn up. Around the walls was a shelf and on it were crudely built boxes—like orange crates, with screened fronts—insubstantial looking and not very reassuring. There wasn't much activity going on in them, as far as Langston James could tell, and, in fact, a good many of them seemed to be empty. But he thought that estimate wasn't to be trusted. He was sure he could hear furtive movements— menacing, slithery sounds—coming out of them. On top of one of the cases a big, grey tomcat was sleeping. When they came into the tent, he raised his head halfway and squinted one eye open at them. It was one of those perfunctory gestures that cats are so good at, and the condescension in it made Langston James angry. The cat obviously wasn't interested or threatened by them, and he put his head back down and went to sleep again.

The biggest disappointment of all was Zola herself—a thin, plain looking woman of about sixty in a nondescript blue dress and a purple cardigan sweater. Her hair was a grey-washed ginger color, and it stood out from her head like she had been testing electric light sockets with her finger. She was asleep on an aluminum folding chair with her mouth open and her arms crossed on her chest. Her dentures had slipped, and her mouth flapped in and out with her breathing, making clacking sounds that were distinct and nerve-wracking in the small space of the tent. Langston James had to shake her several times to wake her up.

"Excuse me, Miss Zola," he said. "We come to see the show."

For a minute she stared around in a panic-stricken sort of way, then she got up, straightened her dress and sucked her mouth into shape. On her feet, Zola was an imposing figure of a woman. She was taller than Langston James by at least a head, and was able to look Bodine himself in the eye.

"I declare," she said, touching the back of her head, a gesture that had an angular, giraffe-like grace about it. "I must have dropped off for a minute there. We don't do much business in the middle of the afternoon."

"Yes, ma'm."

"Listen," she said. "Would you gentlemen mind turning around for a minute?"

"What?" Langston James had the beginning of a protest in his voice.

"These here aren't exactly my Snake Lady working clothes. Garvin generally gives me a sign when customers're on the way. I don't know what's the matter with him lately. He's been sleeping at the switch. What I mean is...you caught me off guard. I'd like to slip into something more appropriate for the occasion."

"I see." Langston James looked at Bodine and the two of them turned around. They seemed apprehensive at the idea of turning their backs on a snake lady—as if they were afraid she might drop a cottonmouth down their shirt collars while she had them off guard. There was a creaking sound, then a lid slamming, followed by several minutes of rustling and heavy breathing.

"All right," she said at last. When they turned around they flinched in unison at the transformation in her appearance. Zola had put on a turban of sky blue silk with a huge red stone in the center of it, and was wrapped in a wine red velvet cape with gold trim. She had also managed to powder her face white and put on blood red lipstick and dark blue eye shadow. In the dim light of the tent her presence loomed and menaced them. The two men took a step backward with their shoulders touching.

And then she spoke . . . the sinister effect of her appearance was broken as soon as she opened her mouth. Her South Georgia twang didn't go with the outfit she had on, but it was very reassuring.

"There," she said. It came out "thuh-ai-yuh." Three syllables, mostly through her nose, with her lips hardly moving at all. "Ain't that better? You pay for a Snake Lady—a Snake Lady is what you ought to get."

"Is that you?" Langston James hunched forward and narrowed his eyes.

"In the flesh."

"Well," said Langston James, looking at Bodine, then back at Zola, "I'll swan."

"Yes, ma'm," said Bodine.

She looked at Bodine. "Don't get many colored folks here."

"Mister Treecastle said it was all right."

"Of course it is. We go by the law. Tybee Beach isn't what you'd call up-to-date. Now is it?"

"We noticed," said Langston James. "It's all right long as you ain't no American."

"What?"

"If you're not white, it's all right if you come out of a jungle somewheres."

"I don't know exactly what you're talking about, mister. You mean he's some kind of a jungle bunny?" She looked at Bodine. "He talks all right."

"No. I mean he's a hundred percent American."

She nodded. "That's what I thought. He looks okay to me." She looked Bodine up and down.

"What I mean is, they got a Chinaman runs the department store and some dark-complexioned fella making corn dogs. We ain't seen hide nor hair of a real *American* colored man."

"Yes," she said. "I been in the jungle myself some."

"Is that a fact?"

"Listen. I can take your tickets. I guess I expect what you come to see is the show."

"That's right." Langston James handed her the slips of paper. She tore them in half and dropped the pieces into a shoebox with a slit cut in the top. "This here is basically a educational type show," she said. "People don't understand about snakes and what all good they do."

Langston James nodded.

Zola looked at him closely. "I bet you don't care much for snakes, do you?"

Langston James hesitated. "Well," he said, "I don't mind them so much, you know, long as it's an abstract proposition we're talking about. I wouldn't say they was one of my favorite animals to associate with in person." He held up his hand. "No offense meant, ma'm. Mister Treecastle told us you're pretty high on reptiles."

"What about you?" She said, speaking to Bodine.

"Ma'm?" Bodine lurched when she spoke.

"How do you stand on snakes?"

"I could do without them."

"That's what *YOU* think!" Her voice was startling in its volume, even for such an imposing woman. It filled the small space inside the tent. Things seemed to begin coming to life inside the cages at the sound of it. Even the cat opened one eye. Langston James and Bodine stepped closer to each other. "Snakes do a heap of good. Snakes eat rats and things. Some snakes even eat other snakes."

"And they bite people." Langston James spoke in a small voice.

"There you go," she said. "Not all that much really." She sucked on her dentures while she thought—a rapid, in-and-out motion with a clicking sound. "Not unless you go fooling around with them they don't. Any animal is going to protect itself."

She looked from one to the other. "Either of you been bit by a snake? I mean *personally?*"

Langston James and Bodine looked at each other. Langston James shook his head. "Not that I recall. How about you, Bodine?"

"I don't remember I ever give one the chance."

"Uh huh. Either one of you ever *known* anybody be bit by a snake?"

"You mean firsthand?"

"That's right. Firsthand is just what I'm talking about."

"Weelllll..." he said, drawing it out, "now that you pin me down, I don't reckon I have."

"See what I mean? Snakes've got an awful bad reputation, but they don't do that much damage when you get right down to it. More people die getting stung by wasps and the like."

"Is that a fact? I can't hardly believe that."

"I don't care to associate with wasps neither," said Bodine.

"You can look it up. Don't hardly anybody really die from a snake bite. Course you wouldn't want to let one at you for the fun of it."

"Wait a minute! I do too know somebody got bit by a rattle-snake." He turned to Bodine. "Fella at the funny monkey place, Bodine. Remember?" He turned back to Zola. "He got the skin on the wall in his store to prove it."

"How did it happen? Was he bothering the snake?"

"I wadn't there, lady. He killed it."

"I'd say that'd come under the heading of bothering it." She paused. "Of course if you go sticking your hand in one of 'em's mouth you're going to get what's coming to you. If he'd of let that snake alone, he wouldn't of had no trouble. You got to go out of your way to get bit by a snake. Did he die?"

"I reckon not. I talked to him this morning."

"See?"

"Yes, well. That don't mean I want to keep one for a house pet."

"Listen. You could do a whole lot worse, mister. You ruther have you something like that no good cat there?" She gave the grey tom a hostile look. "I can't stand cats. Feels like they got electricity in their fur." She gave an involuntary shudder.

"But snakes're okay?"

"Cats look so *satisfied*. I know I shouldn't let it bother me, but it chafes me something awful." She looked at the tom. "They eat snakes. Did you know that?"

"I'm not surprised. Roaches too. I've seen that with my own eyes. Cats are way overrated."

"I've lost stock to that one. He'd put me out of business if I let him."

"He eats *your* snakes?"

"Four I'm sure of. Three garters and a hognose. He's got his eye on that blacksnake over there." She pointed. "Only Willard's too big for him. I wish he'd take a crack at Charles the Fourth," she indicated a box with a sign that said "King snake." "That'd solve the problem. Charles wouldn't fool around with him.

A kingsnake can handle himself."

The tom twitched his tail a time or two, then opened his mouth in a jawbreaking yawn. He didn't look at them.

"See," she said. "He knows we're taking about him. It's hard to get the goods on him. Garvin won't believe it lest I catch him with one sticking out of his mouth."

Langston James nodded.

"Mister, would you do me a favor?" she said.

He hesitated. "Does it have anything to do with snakes?" he asked.

"No."

"Probably," he said.

"Would you pick him up and get him out the way? He just loves to rub up against me." She gave another shudder. "That's something else about cats. They know how to get your goat. And they *like* to do it. When we get to that box he's on he's going to get up and show me how much he loves me. Don't tell me he don't know what he's doing."

Langston James nodded, then went over to where the tom was stretched out and picked him up by the scruff of the neck. "What'll I do with him, lady?" he said, holding the tom at arm's length. The tom was taking it pretty well.

"Get rid of him."

Langston James started for the door of the tent.

"Not *that* way. That's Garvin's cat. He don't like to see this kind of thing." She made a face. "Here," she said. "Give him to me." She took the tom from Langston James, an awkward maneuver during which the cat hung there making a humming sound deep in his throat. While she was getting a grip on him, Zola pulled down the corners of her mouth and gritted her teeth. Once she got her purchase, she turned and without hesitating gave a looping, underarm swing that flung him up onto the back wall of the tent. It was a firm and definite move that bespoke a good deal of practice. The tom splatted up against the canvas, spreadeagled and hanging by his claws. For a long minute the cat didn't move. There was a contemplative and philosophical air about him.

"Look at him," said Zola. "He's acting like that's *just* the place he wanted to be all the time. No way you can get satisfaction out of a cat. I don't know what Garvin sees in them."

Langston James and Bodine watched as the cat started to slide downward, making ripping noises on the canvas. "I reckon he feels the same way when it comes to snakes," he said.

"Yes," Zola nodded. "He's a good man, except for that." She sighed. "We've all got to put up with each other I reckon." She wrapped the cape around her. "Step thisaway," she said. "I got something to show you." She led them over to a large chest. The chest was crudely made, but elaborate—painted gold and silver with a random but enthusiastic pattern of brass upholstery nails decorating most of the available space on it. She opened the box and lifted out a huge coiled snake, hefting it like a piece of furniture. Langston James and Bodine took a step backward together.

"This here's Jupiter. You needn't be afraid. Jupiter's dead." She whacked it a time or two on the lid of the chest, raising a cloud of dust and shaking off a few scales. One of the glass eyes popped out, and Zola had to retrieve it from the floor. She licked it before she put it back into the socket. "Makes it stick," she said. She adjusted the position of the snake a couple of times before she stepped back to admire it. "Garvin—that's Mister Treecastle out there—Garvin had him stuffed for me for our anniversary." She adjusted the snake again on the lid of the chest. "I used to do an act with Jupiter. Mister Treecastle had a freak show. I was the snake lady."

"Mister Treecastle calls it a ten-in-one."

"I don't care *what* he calls it. They were freaks, mister. You got another name for a full grown man thirty-two inches tall?"

"Well. You were *in* it. I reckon you ought to know."

"That's right." She adjusted the snake more precisely. "I thought so much of Jupiter...Garvin had him fixed for our anniversary."

"He looks real."

"He *is* real, mister." She thought for a minute. "I mean, he's dead and all, but far as the outside goes, he's just about the way he used to be."

"You got you a first-class job there, lady."

Her face softened as she looked at Jupiter. "Isn't he lovely?"

"Lovely?"

"Lovely."

"I'll go for *impressive*. I don't believe I can handle *lovely*. He's still a snake, ma'm."

"You don't know him like I did."

"You're right about that. How long he been dead?"

"Four years."

"I'd say he's holding up pretty good." He dusted a few scales from his shoulder.

"Yes," she said, speaking in a solemn manner. "Snakes live a long time, but they can't live forever. I sure did hate to see Jupiter go. He was—you know—a *really* good snake."

Langston James stepped up for a closer look. "What I'd say is that's a really *big* snake."

"He's a python. They *get* big."

"Yes, ma'm. That's what I said."

"I couldn't do my act with nothing tee-ninecy. People aren't going to pay good money to look at something they could step on out their back door. Jupiter was ten feet, nine inches. That's actual measure. We got some roustabouts together one time and stretched him out to do it." She contemplated Jupiter. "He didn't like it much. Mostly he was a right even-tempered snake—especially towards the last. But he didn't like strangers laying hands on him."

"I wouldn't think it would be no problem."

"There're plenty of smartalecks in this world, mister. You'd be surprised."

"I already am."

"Listen. You've come to see the show. Maybe we better get on with it." She stood with her hand on Jupiter's head and began to speak in a formal manner, as if she were addressing a large group. "Like I said, this here's more an educational type thing. Snakes get bad mouthed enough anyway. Let me take you around." She walked from cage to cage, lifting out the snakes and giving a little talk about the special points of each one—all of which were good ones. The way she told it, dogs and cats were vain and useless creatures when you compared them to snakes. In her view, people could learn a thing or two from snakes when it came to the way to behave. As she went on, she lost herself more and more in the message she was conveying. Her voice became softer and gentler, and before it was over she was talking baby talk to them. It made Langston James's skin creep and bristled up his back hair. Zola offered to let them handle several of the snakes themselves. "Their skin's not a bit slimy. Feel it." Both declined. The recital was strange enough, but it became more and more educational as it went along, relentlessly so, and except for the times she flashed the snakes around in their faces it got to be a pretty sleepy business. The insistent note of instruction wore on them badly. Before the show was over they were wishing that it was. Outside the tent afterwards, Langston James confided to Mr. Treecastle, "Lots of education going on in there, mister. More than we could handle really. Wouldn't you say, Bodine?"

Bodine looked at him in a pained way, then went to get his shovel.

"What?" said Treecastle, turning up his hearing aid.

"She's hipped on that education business, ain't she?"

"I told you. She's got this thing about snakes. Anyway, she always was a thorough woman...you know, in general."

"I'll have to say we got our money's worth. Lordy." He looked at Bodine. "Come on, Bodine. *Say* something."

Bodine nodded his head. "Much obliged," he said.

* * *

On the way home, Langston James wanted to talk about it. "Have you another cigarette, Bodine." He held out the pack to him. "What you think?"

Bodine took an Old Gold and lit it in a thoughtful way. After the second draw he spoke. "I reckon I got me a education of sorts. Don't know what *use* it going to be to me."

"You can't never tell. Anyway, knowing about things is good just by itself. You need to be broad."

"I like to know what *good* it going to do."

"Trust me, Bodine. Being broad's got a value just by its ownself."

For awhile they didn't speak. Finally, Langston James flipped his cigarette out the window. "How about that fella cut up on his child? What you think about that?"

"You *knows* what I thinks about that."

"Yes, well."

Bodine took a couple of drags on his cigarette. "Like the man said, it's some desperate folks in this world. Thing is, what did *you* think?"

"I know what he was talking about."

"I reckon *that's* the truth."

"You think I'm desperate, Bodine?"

"Well, you don't sound so much like you was just now. I reckon you got you some education out of this here trip your ownself."

"That's about the most of what was going on in that tent...she like to educated me right to sleep."

"I mean the whole thing."

Langston James thought for a minute before he answered. "Maybe so, Bodine. I ain't taken it all in yet."

"How about that dream? The killing machine? Still got that on your mind?"

"Not so much. I don't know what's going to happen about that. I don't feel it so much just now. Maybe I talked it out."

"You know, Mister Eljay, I figured it was *mostly* talk. What you said. You never can tell though. Like the man say, you get desperate, you can do some crazy things. I glad you got a calmer *sound* to you now anyway. Keep your mind on it and don't do nothing till you give it plenty thought."

"Uh huh," Langston James nodded. "Sometimes a man's got to get out of his rut and see what's going on in the world. Go see the beach and the Atlantic Ocean and have him a corn dog so it'll all come around for him. You know what I mean?"

"I know."

"I reckon it was crazy talk. Sounded crazy?"

"As a bedbug. If I'd taken it to heart. I figured it was talk mostly. You ain't a hard man, Mister Eljay." Bodine hesitated. "Never can tell for sure."

"Well. I couldn't tell my ownself. Sometimes you don't know what you've got in your mind. Nor what kind of a thing you might do if the time came."

"But you all right now?"

"Right now I feel pretty good."

"I feel pretty good as well."

Part 3

Spring 1962 - Spring 1963

Twelve

"THE DOCTOR DIDN'T SAY GABRIEL WAS CRAZY. He said he was *retarded*. It's not the same thing at all."

"I told you not to take him to no doctor anyway. He ain't but two and a half years old. You get doctors started on him now and they'll be passing him around till it's time to put him in the ground. Ain't you got no sense at all?"

"He didn't say he was retarded *bad*. Just a little bit. Couldn't you tell something was wrong?"

Gabriel had been fifteen months old before he took his first steps. He didn't speak his first words until after his second birthday—and only a heart full of love could make out what he was saying at that. They hadn't known how to read the signs, or didn't want to do it.

After the examination, there had been a note of mild exasperation in the doctor's voice. "He's not severely retarded, Mrs. McHenry. I'd say his I.Q. would be about seventy or seventy-five.

Of course, that's just an estimate. You'd need to have a full test run on him by a psychologist to get an exact figure."

They looked at Gabriel sitting at the testing table, trying to fit the square peg into the round hole.

"He's a beautiful child."

"Sweet child, too. His disposition is just as even."

"I expect he is," said the doctor. "He'll be able to look after himself. It's just going to take him more time to do things."

"We've got plenty of time."

"I expect you ought to bring him in to see me now and then."

"You can't make him well, can you?"

"It'd just be a good idea for me to keep up with him. No, I can't make him well."

"I'll speak to my husband about it. He's the one makes the decisions in the family. He doesn't hold with doctors much. No offense."

"Tell him it will be good for Gabriel."

"I sure will tell him that."

* * *

"Did the doctor tell you how good it was going to be for *him*? How much he charge to tell you Gabriel's crazy?"

"I told you. He never said Gabriel was crazy. *Retarded* is what he said, and he said it's not the same thing at all."

"How much?"

"Five dollars."

"Listen. If you think I'm going to put good money down that rat hole, you're crazy your ownself. And it's not going to cost you one red cent for me to tell you about it."

Eventually Langston James reached an accommodation with the condition of his son, but he couldn't decide whether the doctor's diagnosis was the answer to a prayer or a sentence of doom.

It seemed to him that it had to be one or the other. The difference was of a kind he hadn't anticipated. That was the shock of it. He thought about it and thought about it, and finally decided that he should be pleased really. Finding the flaw in his angel child brought Gabriel down to their level. But the mind of Langston James and the impulses of his body didn't work together. What Gabriel's condition did, after all, was make him more interesting—as a problem—than he had been as an example of perfection. None of this changed the child's looks, but it caused Langston James to see him in a different way.

For Gabriel's second birthday, Langston James had bought him a furry green frog with a red felt mouth and stuffing inside that crinkled. A hideous thing, really, but Gabriel loved it—dragging it around with him wherever he went. For his third birthday, he let Cowie get the child a kitten—an act of undiluted love, and a measure of the distance he had come since the trip to Tybee Beach. Langston James didn't care for animals in general, and, of course, he didn't like cats in particular.

"Animals think they've got it made. They don't have to *do* a goddamn thing."

But Gabriel had come close to learning to say the word, and Cowie thought it would be a good thing for him. The doctor thought so too, but she didn't tell Langston James about that.

"It's, you know, educational," she said. "We need to help him along."

"Let's get him a picture of a cat."

"It wouldn't be the same thing."

"It'll be *better.*"

"How about I get him a picture of a horse's ass?"

"What?"

"Then you can go live in the garage."

Delmer was the name they gave him, though no one could remember just where it had come from. The best Gabriel could do with it was "DeeDee." Langston James himself had to admit that Delmer was pretty good for a cat—even tempered and affectionate and abiding to a point that was almost doglike. But Langston James didn't like dogs either. And, even after he had admitted Delmer's good qualities, Langston James couldn't help looking on his tolerance as a sacrifice.

"Cat fur's got electricity in it. Slick-like—you know, snakey. Can't be healthy having one rub up against of you the way he's always doing. Saps my vital spirits is what it does. Makes me feel like I got artesian well water running up my spine... *down* it too."

"It's natural, Eljay. That's how cats show they like you."

"He *knows* it pisses me off. Don't tell me that animal don't know."

"Well, keep your hands off him. He belongs to Gabriel."

"He does it on purpose, goddamn it."

"Don't blaspheme in the house, Eljay."

"Goddamn it..." he said again.

"Hang it up, Eljay," she said.

Delmer grew up to be a big, black tom, who slept nineteen hours a day with his head on his paws and his tongue sticking out.

The tongue infuriated Langston James. "Look at that tongue, Cowie. And people think cats're smart." When he reached the point where he just couldn't stand the sight of it any longer, he would go and get the Tabasco bottle and shake out a few drops on it. The level of activity this produced was deeply pleasurable to Langston James.

The stupid way Delmer *acted* when he was awake irritated Langston James almost as much as the way he looked when he was asleep, though not quite. Since actions promised more in the way of consequences, he felt like they might turn out to be the solution to the problem. First of all, Delmer was clumsy. He was all the time crouching and making a leap for the table or a chair, but missing and banging his nose instead. Langston James thought that if he could get him to spend enough time climbing around up in the trees, he would be sure to fall eventually, and the way he fell would do the job. He thought this because of the way Delmer fell off the back porch. Delmer liked to sleep on the steps, but if anything made him wake up suddenly, he was sure to flinch the wrong way, and over he'd go. And the way he'd go was all of a heap—like a sack of potatoes or a sock full of sand. Never in the times Langston James had seen him do it had Delmer landed on his feet the way cats are supposed to do, so he figured it was just a question of getting him up into the live oaks often enough and waiting for his foot to slip.

Still, it was his activity away from the house that held out the most promise for Langston James. The few hours a day he was awake, Delmer moved through life with a wide-eyed and uncatlike stupidity, constantly making choices that were a major imposition on the workings of providence. Like trying, time after time, to become friends with the Doberman pinscher down the street, or the ten-pound tom who shared the neighborhood. When those didn't work out, he'd come home and rub himself against Langston James's leg. Somehow he got away with all of it.

"Delmer's a sweet cat. And, anyway, Gabriel likes him." It was Cowie's stock answer to his complaints. "You ought not to be selfish about it. You're setting an example. Think of it that way."

"*I'm* selfish? What about cats? Cats're the most selfishest animal there is. If it don't start at their nose and end at their asshole, they ain't interested in it. Just what kind of lesson is Gabriel going to learn from a cat?"

"*Some* cats're that way."

"*Most* cats're that way."

"Well. Delmer's not. You're blaming him according to the

category he's in."

"You can trust *some* categories. What if he was a snake? How about that one?"

"Well, now. *That's* crazy."

"I know a woman who likes snakes better'n cats."

"Listen," she said. "Hang it up, Eljay. That cat is here to stay."

He hesitated. "I know it," he said at last. "Talking about it helps me put up with him." He gave her a pinch on the bottom.

"I don't know about you, Eljay. I just don't know."

"I ain't as deep as a well," he said. "How about this?" He held up his finger. "I don't like cats. I don't like cats now and I didn't like cats yesterday and I never liked cats any time I can remember. Really and truly don't. And didn't. Including that one there." He pointed to Delmer where he was stretched out on the windowsill above the sink, sleeping with his tongue sticking out. "I'm letting it go for the sake of domestic tranquillity."

"You do that thing," said Cowie.

Talking about it was one way Langston James made bearable the feeling Delmer generated in him. But talking about it wasn't quite enough to do the trick. He also needed to *do* something to put the animal in his place . . . though this way of thinking certainly attributed more susceptibility to correction and improvement than Delmer ever showed any aptitude for. But when thoughts of Delmer spiralled down in his brain, Langston James forgot how stupid the cat was. One little trick that gave Langston James a lot of satisfaction was to take a rubber band and attach Delmer's tail to one of his back legs, then watch while he chased himself around trying to figure out what to do about it. Another one was to wrap his paws in little booties made out of newspaper. The crinkly, high-stepping, leg-shaking walk this produced was something even Cowie found funny to watch, though she admonished him about it after she'd had her laugh. Along about the hundredth time or so, Delmer finally violated his nature and got wary. After that, getting the things on him became a complicated business, and was finally more trouble than it was worth.

But by far his favorite trick was the one he called "*SLAMCAT.*" It involved luring Delmer up onto the screen door of the kitchen, using a sardine for bait to make him climb the screen on the outside. When he had him almost to the top, Langston James would kick the door open so that it slammed around against the side of the house. He liked to yell "*SLAMCAT!*" when he did it. There was enough give to the screen not to squash Delmer, and no serious damage was done. Also Langston James always gave him a sardine afterwards as a reward, so there was a kind of equation worked out in the event... Sardine (plus) equals Whack-on-the-Head (minus). Delmer kept coming back for it. He was so wild about sardines there wasn't anything else he could do. Probably he just took it for granted that getting whacked that way was the price you had to pay for the sardines you got.

The attention Langston James showed Delmer had unforeseen consequences. The attention may have been negative, but it was attention just the same, and more than anyone else in the family gave him. Delmer didn't have any kind of standard to make a comparison with, so he must have taken it at face value. In any event, Langston James became Delmer's favorite. Which certainly tended to prove what Langston James was always saying about him.

"That there is a *really* stupid cat."

Even with his little moments of triumph, sharing his home with Delmer was a sacrifice Langston James made, finally, for Gabriel's sake, and to keep peace in the house. At the time, he thought that making a sacrifice would put him on top of things—which it did, as far as Cowie and Gabriel were concerned. But that was before Mrs. Adelaide Fanshaw came into his

life for the second time. The damage she had done to him with
her Packard automobile in the summer of 1936 was minimal and
of no consequence compared to what she brought down on him
in the spring of 1962.

* * *

Mrs. Fanshaw and Earline Sweat were sitting at the front table
of Cantrell Poindexter's "On-The-Square" Rexall Drugstore
drinking their afternoon Coca-Colas and having a serious
moment. Earline was the wife of Elrod Sweat, the John Deere
dealer who had put Langston James on the road to respectability
in his car jumping days by running over him and sending him
to the hospital where he had time to think about the world and
other large things. Earline was also the program chairman of the
Mi Casa Garden Club. Mrs. Fanshaw was the president. Earline
was just getting to her point when Cowie walked by with
Gabriel, on her way to get him a stick of horehound candy at
Langston James's store. Mrs. Fanshaw watched them through the
window as they passed. Some movement she made caught
Gabriel's blue eye and the look he gave her pierced her to the
quick, starting vibrations in her brain and down her spinal
column and making her foot twitch. The palpitation she
experienced under her breast bone, was as of things shifting and
changing and rearranging themselves, like a shoebox half full of
marbles had tilted inside her. For a full minute after he had
gone, she fluttered her eyelids and tapped her foot, staring at the
spot where Gabriel had been. On her face there was an expression
of deep thought, verging on ecstasy. She stared and stared at the
spot on the sidewalk which had lately contained him. "Who *was*
that, Earline?" Before Earline could gather herself to answer,
Mrs. Fanshaw had gotten up and stepped out the door to get a
better look at the two as they disappeared around the corner.

"Who was that child?" she asked when she came back to the table.

"Cantrell..." Earline's voice was loud and straightforward, and there were points of irritation flickering in it just then. "Who was that passed by just now? The woman with the child?"

"Red-headed lady?"

"Don't you put words in my mouth, Cantrell. I said *woman*, not lady. And *red's* hardly the word for that mop. Lord. You'd think she'd put a hat over it out in public and all."

Cantrell waited to make sure Earline was through.

"Well...?" she said.

"That's Eljay McHenry's wife, Cowie."

"Langston James McHenry?" Mrs. Fanshaw had a naturally soft voice, but at the moment it had gone reedy and shrill—like it was coming out of her under pressure. "That couldn't be his child."

"Yes, ma'm." Cantrell adjusted his glasses and leaned on the prescription counter. "It's a strange world. I declare it is. Don't hardly seem possible, I know, but Gabriel's their natural issue. He was born in the Braxton County Memorial Hospital. Doctor Smoaks delivered him." Cantrell made an indefinite gesture with his left hand and adjusted his glasses again with his right. "He couldn't believe it neither."

"It's a strange world, Adelaide." Earline swirled her Coca-Cola glass. "I declare it is."

"That was a beautiful child, Earline." Mrs. Fanshaw said, speaking in an emphatic manner with a tear glistening in her eye. She was an emotional woman and easily tearful, especially where children were concerned. "A beautiful, beautiful child."

"Listen, Adelaide, honey..." said Earline. Earline was more colloquial in her form of address than Mrs. Fanshaw. She was four years younger and considered herself more up-to-date. "Listen, Adelaide, honey..." she said, "that child is out of this world."

"Oh, yes," said Mrs. Fanshaw. "That's *exactly* what I mean. He looks like an angel."

"I don't know how in the world it transpired..." Earline liked the sound of the word and repeated it, "*trans*-pired." She swirled her Coke glass and looked into it thoughtfully, as if she were reading a message in it. "With Eljay and Cowie McHenry for parents, I just don't know how..." Earline often didn't finish her sentences. Much of the time she didn't need to. Her devotion to the obvious was deep and abiding, and speaking it gave her the feeling that she was in touch with those things that were universal and permanent and truly worthwhile. As far as she was concerned, the only ideas worth bringing up in the first place were those that were already agreed on. She swirled her Coke glass again. "That child is *definitely* out of this world."

Cantrell spoke from the prescription counter. "She comes in here now and then." He paused and considered his words. "He's not all there in the head."

"What?" There was a stricken look on Mrs. Fanshaw's face.

"Oh, just a little off. He's a sweet child."

"Do you mean he's retarded?" The features of Mrs. Fanshaw's face softened. "How could he look like that and be retarded?"

"Well," said Earline. "He *is* a McHenry."

"Langston James is a strange looking man, but there isn't anything wrong with his brain." Mrs. Fanshaw looked out at the spot on the sidewalk. "I don't know his wife."

"Honey," said Earline, "you could see what she *looks* like."

Mrs. Fanshaw gazed into the depths of her fountain Coke. "Anyway," she said, "It just makes you want to love him all the more. That's what it does. If I had a grandchild like that I'd be on cloud nine."

"Honey," said Earline, "I know *exactly* what you mean."

* * *

Mrs. Fanshaw had no grandchildren.

Her daughter, Jennifer, had shaken the Whippet sand out of her shoes and hied herself off to New York City where she was living on an allowance from her parents, smoking dope, and practicing oral sex and other up-to-date intricacies with a Negro lover named Jed. She had given herself to him as an act of conscience, which was interesting, and might even have been admirable, except that her conscience, to tell the truth, was more active in the general than the particular. She accepted without a qualm the five hundred dollars a month her parents sent her. To her way of thinking, ingratitude was pretty much the equivalent of independence — at least it was close enough to work with. And, as long as she didn't thank her mother and father for the things they did to help her, her sense of moral superiority remained intact. That meant a great deal to her.

She paid them back, in a way, by sending home long, chatty letters detailing her activities with her lover. The letters all began, "Dear Adelaide," and were signed, "Jed's Woman." Just to be sure that her mother got the point, she included snapshots of herself and Jed twined around each other in poses which, while they weren't actually pornographic, were so intricate that they certainly went tiptoeing along the borders of bad taste. Mostly Mrs. Fanshaw just couldn't tell what was going on. In one of them she had the impression that Jennifer was wearing a sealskin coat.

Mrs. Fanshaw understood the miscegenation in a general way, but the sexual innuendos passed her by completely. She had a vague idea that her daughter was engaging in some kind of exotic Northern religious rites — maybe inspired by the Pope — possibly even Jewish — or worse. She had never been to New York herself, so she had no frame of reference for any of it. And she couldn't bring herself to talk to her husband about it either. The whole thing was beyond the grasp of a woman who had been

born in 1901 and had lived her entire life in Whippet, Georgia.
But if the Lord taketh away, the Lord also giveth. Since she didn't
understand what her daughter was doing, her heritage told her
that she didn't have to think about it.

Willard, her son, had married and stayed at home to go into
the bank. But in some ways that was even more of a trial for Mrs.
Fanshaw than Jennifer's absence. Willard was always there—or,
rather, Cleavis was. Cleavis was Willard's wife. She was from
Atlanta—a city girl, who found Whippet the utmost end of
piney woods hickdom, and regarded herself as toweringly
superior to all the forms of activity practiced and beloved by its
inhabitants.

Cleavis had a fine, tight derrière, and a lovely turn of calf and
ankle, and contemplating them made Willard go weak in the
knees. He thought about them at home, and at work, and going
back and forth between the two. He thought about them so
much because they were not so freely available to him as he
would have liked for them to be. The reason for this was that
during the medical examination which Cleavis had undergone
before her marriage, the doctor had remarked on the smallness
of her pelvic girdle, and had gone on to express the opinion that
she might have trouble in childbirth. The upside consequence
of that remark was that it had an aristocratic and refined ring to
it which made Cleavis feel proud of herself. The downside consequence was that it stayed with her, enlarging in her mind as she
turned it this way and that, until she had worked it up into a
nearly terminal dread of impregnation. She submitted to her
wifely duties—she even enjoyed them to a degree, as was man-
dated by her emancipated condition, not to mention her natural
inclination—but only after certain extensive preconditions had
been met. Before she would allow herself to be penetrated by the
conjugal member, her diaphragm had to be securely in place
and reinforced by double the prescribed amount of spermicidal

gel. She also insisted that Willard wear two condoms, and that
he practice premature withdrawal—at least to the extent that his
fortitude would permit.

Under those conditions, their lovemaking was so ethereal as
to be almost asexual. But Willard put up with it because he
loved her for herself as well as her fine derrière and calf, and also
because he was deeply convinced of his own rural inferiority. For
all of those reasons he was inclined to be grateful for small favors.
Her boredom and apprehension made him think she was more
than ever high class.

Mrs. Fanshaw's upbringing and circumstances—her people
had been in Whippet since before the Civil War, her husband's
had been there since just after—were the limiting truths of her
time and place. The net she could throw was not a wide one, but
it dragged deep. In wealth and family, she was the most promi-
nent woman in Whippet. She was also a sweet woman, and
thoughtful in all small ways, but on some topics she could have
been more persistent and single-minded only if she had done
her thinking through a tube. She wanted grandchildren. In
terms of her temperament, it could be said that she *needed*
them. It was a terrible cross for her to bear. If she had been less
refined or more inclined to ponder, she might have turned
mournful or waspish. She might even have gone in for a black
market arrangement of some kind. The times and her position
would have made that possible. Her husband could afford it,
and he loved to indulge her. As it was, all she could do was pine
and wait—a woman taken with maternity the way some people
are taken with hives—constantly and all over. In the meantime,
she hoped the past into the future—longing for the solace of a
child.

"Oh, how I wish I had a grandchild, Earline," she said.

"Well, all I can say is that Gabriel McHenry is out of this
world," said Earline. "Out of this *world.*" She held up her empty

Coca-Cola glass. "Two more dopes here, Cantrell," she said, ". . . if you don't mind."

* * *

From that day on, Mrs. Fanshaw seethed and boiled in the con-templation of what she might do to put herself in touch with Gabriel McHenry. It swelled inside her like a state of grace. She spent long nights thinking of the things she could do for him. The thought that she should not do anything crossed her mind, but she dismissed it out of the kindness of her heart. The pure existence of the child harried and vexed her, and she was too sweet-tempered a woman to have much will to resist. As with most things that touched her to the quick, she did not talk to her husband about it. Mr. Fanshaw was a naturally kind man who loved his wife, and she knew she could have her way with him in the end. But his work with figures at the bank made him a rational man—sometimes boringly so. And he always felt that he should give her advice. But advice was not what she wanted—especially advice that was calm and sensible. What she wanted was to follow her inclinations undiluted by suggestions of any kind. She trusted them to lead her close enough to Gabriel McHenry so that she might recover some of the lost function of motherhood, which was the better part of what she knew in this world, and the one thing she was sure of and happy with. When she reached the end of her capacity for estimating consequences, she called Cleavis's mother in Atlanta and asked her to buy a teddy bear for her at Rich's department store, and have it shipped to Gabriel. The package the bear came in could have held a refrigerator. The bear itself was taller than Langston James.

"What's she got in mind, Cowie? Sending Gabriel a thing like that? If he gets underneath it, it'll smother him to death."

"She's taken a liking to him, Eljay. No harm done. Gabriel likes it. It's cuddly."

"That's not the right word for it."

"Feel how soft."

"Put it in the box and send it back. We don't need charity from the Fanshaws."

"It's just Mizres Fanshaw. She's a lonesome woman. You don't want to hurt her feelings."

"All I want is just for you to send it back. You going to take sides about this?"

"No. She's a sweet, lonesome woman, Eljay. Nothing about taking sides to that."

Langston James fumed over it, but the bear stayed. Gabriel liked it—better than the frog. That was the thing that hurt him the most.

"Well..." said Cowie, "there's more *of* it."

When a note came from Cowie thanking her, Mrs. Fanshaw ordered more toys and finally a sailor suit. The sailor suit in particular outraged Langston James. "It's a hundred and fifty miles to the ocean. What's he need a sailor suit for?"

"Sailor suits're cute for little boys. Stylish as well. You don't need to have an ocean to wear it. Halstead's got an aviator cap. Where's his airplane?"

It took a month, but when the invitation to visit finally came, Mrs. Fanshaw was ready. Calloway, the chauffeur, had to make three trips carrying packages before he emptied the trunk and back seat of the Lincoln. She even brought presents for Cowie and Halstead and Langston James. Langston James took his and went out and sat on the back steps where he spent half an hour trying to tear up the hand-tooled leather wallet she'd brought him. But it was a good wallet, and he couldn't make much headway with it. Finally he went to the back fence and threw it over the garage into the alley. He kept the five-dollar bill she had put inside. In the house itself Mrs. Fanshaw got to hold Gabriel on her lap and stroke his fine yellow hair. It was not enough to soothe her—only enough to whet her appetite. One visit led to another, until finally she was coming by the house every day. On Sundays she brought presents, then took Gabriel off in the Lincoln to have Calloway drive them around the county while she sat with him under the checkered laprobe, feeling his warmth and answering his questions with the patience of love that knows no bounds.

Langston James fumed about that as well, but Cowie wouldn't let him have his way.

"It's only she's a good woman, Eljay. She likes to do for Gabriel is all."

Langston James was sitting at the kitchen table having his cup of coffee. Cowie was washing dishes at the sink.

"Money talks, Cowie. Don't nobody hear it better than little bitty children. She's trying to buy him away. What kind of business has she got hanging around with people like us?"

"She's not 'hanging around,' Eljay. That's not any way to put it. Mizres Fanshaw's a fine woman. She likes to do for Gabriel and see him happy. Where's the harm in that?"

"How come she don't feel like doing for Halstead?"

"Halstead's not her type."

"Halstead's ugly. That's all there is to that. *Ugly* ain't her type."

"Halstead's not ugly."

He looked at her and raised his eyebrows. "If Halstead worked at it, he might could get himself *up* to being ugly. Come *on*, Cowie."

She thought for a minute. "Halstead sets a mood," she said.

"Halstead's not ugly like you and me. He sure as hell ain't no goddamn Queen of the May."

"Don't blaspheme in the house, Eljay. You know how I feel

about it. Use dirty words if you've got to, but don't blaspheme."

"He ain't no *fucking* Queen of the May. That better?"

"No. Not really."

"None of us ain't her type, if you want to know the truth. We're poor people, honey." He thought a minute. "We're *from* poor people. That's what I mean."

"She's taken to Gabriel. If it comes to that, Gabriel's not hardly our type either."

"Gabriel's our natural child, Cowie. God's the one decided on that. Leastways that's what you always led me to believe."

"You know what I mean." She looked at him. "She's a good woman, Eljay. I don't care how many dirty words you think up to use."

For awhile Langston James didn't say anything. "I ain't never had nothing I had to protect from anybody. That's what I don't like about it. Anything I ever had, didn't nobody want it." He thought for a minute. "No big demand for crooked and broke and left-hand shit."

"Much obliged," she said flatly, turning back to the sink.

"Don't turn your back on me, Cowie. You know what I'm talking about. No cause to get your ass in a sling. Who'm I going to talk to about it if it ain't you? I got to talk to somebody." He slid his cup to one side. "You always did make an awful cup of coffee. That's another thing."

"We're good people, Eljay," she said, without turning around.

"I know that, honey. Only we're just ugly people is all. I'm not talking about qualities. What I'm talking about is lineaments. Your face and mine. Halstead's as well. Facts are facts."

She turned to face him. "Mizres Fanshaw's just being a good, kind, Christian woman. You going to protect Gabriel from good, kind, Christian people?"

"Cowie—them's the worst kind of all. A Christian'll shoot you dead for walking on their grass." He took another sip of coffee and made a face. "You know what I mean. It's the whole god-damn situation." He paused. "The whole—whatever the hell word you want to use...." He drummed his fingers on the table. "Mizres Fanshaw's okay," he said at last. "She's a good, kind woman—like you say." He puckered his mouth and drummed on the table again. "Kindness can kill you just as dead as spite, if you get in the way of it. Anyway—it's the whole goddamn situation." He thought for a minute. "I'm sorry, honey. Ain't another goddamn word I can think of has the right ring to it."

"She's got nothing to love for herself just now, Eljay. Only that daughter who ran away to New York, and that barren wife Willard married, spends all her time showing her butt on them tennis courts."

"I'll get her a lap dog."

She looked at him. He rested his elbows on the table and put his chin in his hands. "You know, Cowie. I always understood where I was at. You and me and Halstead. I had that figured out pretty good. I understood us. We was ugly. I could handle that. Everbody knows we're good people. Just nobody thinks about ugly folks. We was there, but we wasn't. I like it that way."

"Honey, you're not ugly. You're deformed."

"That's the voice of love talking, Cowie." He looked at her. "Love and them misplaced eyes of yours." He thought a minute. "I never *did* know if you could see what I looked like."

She smiled and reached across the table to take his hand

"I appreciate it, honey. But ain't you scared of pretty people? I mean when they get right up next to you?"

"You going to tell me you're scared of Gabriel?"

"Sometimes...sometimes I am." He pursed his lips and thought a minute. "Mostly I've got used to Gabriel, but some-times I am." He drummed his fingers on the table. "What about her taking him off in that big Lincoln every Sunday? What you reckon he thinks when she brings him back here? This house don't accord with no Lincoln automobile. Even Gabriel can figure that out for himself."

"Gabriel likes riding in that big car. You wouldn't deny him his pleasure, would you?"

"You're not making this easy, Cowie."

"He's just a little bitty child."

"What about *my* pleasure? I'm going to wind up with hate in my heart for my own son."

"Life's not always going to conform the way you want it to."

"Big news," he said flatly. His face looked weary. "Maybe we ought to move out of town."

"You think you're going to outrun it?"

"No. Maybe a little. Out of sight, out of mind. Maybe she'd forget about him." He looked at Cowie, then tilted his coffee cup and looked into it. "I reckon not. I can't afford to move us to China."

"What're you going to do somewhere else? We've got a roof over our heads."

"You know," he said, "it's hell to be poor *and* ugly."

"We're not poor."

"You know what I mean. I got to think of something."

"You drink too much coffee," she said, looking at the cup in an arch way. "It sets my nerves on edge."

"Ugly people got to do things for themselves. Handsome is as handsome looks."

"Well," said Cowie.

He picked up the cup, looked into it, then put it back down in the saucer. "You sure make a rotten cup of coffee," he said. "For a cross-eyed woman."

* * *

He was having the dream of the killing machine again, though he couldn't see Gabriel's face very clearly, and was less and less sure that's who it was. Sometimes he would find himself in the middle of the dream, and his eyes would be open, staring up at the ceiling of the bedroom. The thing that he was more and more afraid of was that he would be getting inside the machine himself. And that Mrs. Fanshaw would start turning up in the crowd. But, even so, talking about his troubles made them easier to bear, he thought.

For a while talking did.

Thirteen

BODINE DIED ON APRIL 1ST, 1963. And the way he died rattled Langston James as much as the fact itself. He read it as another item in the growing catalog of portents he was having to sort out and deal with. For two days Bodine didn't show up in the morning to help with the paper route. He just didn't show up. It wasn't Bodine's style, and Langston James knew it wasn't, but his thoughts had turned inward on him because Gabriel was going off with Mrs. Fanshaw, and he was losing his grip on things. He spent the first day smoking one cigarette after another and talking to himself—working at being angry and feeling betrayed—taking hold of the opportunity and getting all the good he could out of it. He enjoyed it. Life was giving him plenty of things to be mournful about, but bone white outrage was rare for him and a relief. The first day it was.

The second day his mind cleared a little, and he became worried. When he came in off the route, he went to seek out his friend and helper.

Though he had known Bodine for nearly seven years, he didn't know exactly where he lived, and had never been to visit him in his house. He found the place in Slabtown, the black section of Whippet, by asking directions from people he saw on the streets. They were furtive and sullen, but, pressed, they answered him, and he finally pulled the truck up in front of a shack covered with tarpaper in a brick pattern, and swept dirt for a front yard. He sat in the cab while he smoked a cigarette and looked at the house, contemplating the fact that this was the first time he had ever had occasion to visit Bodine in his own place.

Finally he got out of the truck and limped up the front steps. He knocked on the door, and waited. Through the cracks in the floorboards of the porch he could see a dog with a bright yellow eye looking up at him. The boards were spongy under his feet, and several had rotted through altogether.

There was no movement inside the house that he was aware of, but suddenly the door opened and a small black child was standing in the frame of the doorway with the darkness of the house behind her. Langston James caught the faint odor of strawberries with the strong tang of kerosene underneath it. There was also the day-old smell of fried fish and greens. They were not unpleasant to him, only insistent and odd and something he was aware of.

The child was eight or nine years old, thin, in a loose no-colored dress that was almost transparent. On the left side of her face there was a cream-colored splotch. It had the color and texture of buttermilk. Her left arm was held above her head by a brace, and a tube of skin looped down from her forearm and was attached to the splotch just below her left eye. At first he couldn't see that the arrangement of her limb was a medical one, and he thought that she was shading her eyes from the sun. When he did bring her into focus, her appearance startled him, and he took a step backward. If she had been larger, he might have run away.

The child didn't say anything. She only stood there looking at him from under the tube of skin with her runny eyes, sucking on the thumb of her right hand. It took a minute for Langston James to collect himself.

He swallowed hard. "I'm looking for Bodine Polite," he said at last. "Mister Bodine Polite."

The child took her thumb out of her mouth and pushed the heel of her right hand up her face, wiping her nose. For a minute she stood looking at him with big eyes while she put her thumb back into her mouth. The sucking noises struck Langston James as mournful and sad and they got on his nerves so that he wanted to ask her to stop. While he was thinking how to put it to her, she disappeared into the house. Langston James did not see her leave. One minute she was there, and the next the dark frame of the doorway was empty. He waited, shifting from one foot to another and breathing the strange odors of the house. Finally he heard scuffing footsteps and the languid movement of a body. After awhile a woman appeared. She was large and not very dark—of indeterminant age. In her hand she held a fan with a picture of "The Last Supper" on it, and the printed name of a funeral parlor. It was a warm day, but not hot.

"I'm looking for Mister Bodine Polite," he said.

The woman looked at him for a minute without speaking "Yes," she said at last. "You the insurance man?"

"Bodine works for me. I'm Mister McHenry."

"Yes," she said, looking at the crabbed left hand of Langston James and nodding. "I see you is. I thought you was the insurance man."

"Something the matter with him? He ain't showed up for two days now. I thought it might be he was sick or something."

"No," she said. "He ain't sick."

Langston James looked at her. "Well?" he said. "What's the matter with him?"

"He ain't sick." She paused. Twice she tightened the features of her face, pressing her lips together and swallowing hard. The movement was involuntary, but very definite, and Langston James suddenly realized that she was having trouble speaking. "He's passed on," she said. She measured her words slowly, slurring them as she spoke. Her voice held a charge of emotion, but Langston James couldn't put his finger on the exact nature of it. Sadness wasn't quite what it was, as far as he could tell. It might have been anger.

The tone of her voice diverted him, so that he didn't hear what she was saying. He looked at her for a minute before he replied. "Excuse me?"

"He's gone."

"Who *are* you?"

"I live here."

"Bodine's not married. He never told me he was married."

"I never said he was. Anyways," she said, pulling up the sleeve of her short-sleeved dress and wiping her eyes with it, "I don't *really* live here. Not no more."

Langston James looked around. "I asked all over. People been telling me this here is where Bodine Polite lives."

"He *used* to live here. I done told you. He's passed on. I used to live here too."

Langston James nodded his head. "I don't hardly see how he could be...passed on. He wasn't sick or nothing. Day before yesterday he was riding with me on the paper route. What did he pass on *of*?"

"Waspes."

"What?"

"He got bit all over by waspes."

"Listen," said Langston James. "Could I set down?"

The woman nodded. There was a rusty washing machine with a wringer attachment on the porch, and one straight-backed chair. Langston James sat down in the chair.

"We're talking about Bodine Polite?" he said.

"He gone up on the roof to fix a leak. They was a waspes' nest, and they bitten him and bitten him and he fell off." '

"Wasps?"

"Yassuh."

"Don't nobody die from no wasp bite."

"I'm just telling you what happened. Wasn't no *one* bite. They bitten him and bitten him. All over. He fell off and died." The woman leaned against the jamb of the door and covered her face with her left hand. For a minute her shoulders shook with her sobbing. When she collected herself, she pulled up the sleeve of her dress again and wiped her eyes.

So much crying made Langston James nervous and uncomfortable. He sawed his head from side to side, rubbing his good hand on his chest, while he tried to think of what he could say. "I don't know what to say, lady. I didn't mean to upset you. You ain't his wife?"

The woman shook her head. "I'm his daughter-in-law."

"What?" Langston James looked up sharply. "Who was it come to the door to begin with? The little one?"

"That's my daughter's child."

"Your *daughter's* child? How old *are* you?"

"We reckon I be thirty-nine—maybe forty. Depends on how you figure."

Langston James looked at her for a minute without speaking. "He told me he was forty-three years old. That's seven years ago. He'd be...," Langston James stopped to figure, "fifty by now."

"Yes," she said. "He like to do that. He be sixty-three, Mister McHenry. That's any way you figure it. I always thought he was two year older than that, but he says he was borned in 1900."

"His *great* grandaughter?"

"Well, *that's* for sure. I'm the one birthed her mama."

Langston James shook his head slowly from side to side. "What's the matter with her?" he said at last.

"Jenniwese?"

"The little one come to the door."

"You talking about her face, I reckon."

"That's right."

"She went to light the kerosene stove and it blowed up on her. The doctor fixed her that way. He say it might be they wouldn't be too big of a scar. I don't hardly see how, but you can't tell no doctor his business."

Langston James nodded. "I don't know if I can believe this. About Bodine, I mean."

"Suit yourself. Hard to take it in."

For a minute neither of them said anything.

"You want to see him?" the woman asked.

"He here at the house?"

"Not hardly. They got him laid out down to Dalton's. They done a good job on him. He look pretty natural. You ought to go see him. He thought a lot of you, Mister Eljay."

"Yes." Langston James took the pack of Old Golds out of his shirt pocket and shook out a cigarette. After he put the pack back into his pocket he stood up and took it out again. He offered the woman one. She accepted it, holding it between the first two fingers of her right hand, with her right elbow propped in the palm of her left while she waited for him to strike a match.

"Hit's hot for this time of year," she said, blowing a cloud of smoke into the air. "Reckon we going to have us a hot summer."

Langston James stood up and looked at the woman for a minute. "I never seen his house before," he said. "Would you mind if I took a look around?"

The woman looked at him, then shook her head and cleared

her throat. "You mean *inside?*"

"If it wouldn't be too much trouble. All that time I've known him, but I never been to his house before." When the woman hesitated, he added, "We was good friends, ma'm."

She nodded slowly. "It ain't fixed up. Daddy wadn't much of a housekeeper. You go ahead if you want to."

There was a front room and the kitchen behind it on one side, and a bedroom and another room on the other side, both opening off the front room. In the bedroom there was a small iron bed with an apple crate beside it. On the apple crate was a kerosene lantern and a Bible. A 1938 calendar with a picture of an Indian was nailed to the wall over the bed. The rest of the house had hardly any furniture in it. A sagging grey plush sofa with the batting coming out of it and a wooden straight-backed chair in the living room — a woodstove in the kitchen and an ice box. In a corner of the living room there was a white enamelled basin, and above it on the sheetrock of the ceiling was a large brown water stain shaped like a heart. Between the planks of the floor there were cracks — wide enough in places that Langston James could make out the texture of the dirt underneath the house. He looked for the yellow-eyed dog, but couldn't see him. As he walked through the rooms, Langston James thought what it would be like to spend time in a place as poor as this one was. The small child shadowed him from room to room, dodging out of sight whenever he looked her way.

There was food on the metal-topped table in the kitchen — the work of strangers and friends — fried chicken, a pot of greens, cornbread, and a cake with sugary white icing. Except for the faint smell of strawberries layered under the heavy smells of grease and kerosene, and a row of Tube Rose snuff cans on a shelf over the stove, there was almost nothing to mark the place as Bodine's the way Langston James had known him. He took one of the snuff cans off the shelf and walked back out to the porch.

"Can I have it?" he said to the woman, holding up the can so she could see it.

"You want a snuff can?"

"There wasn't much he left behind. He liked his dip. It's something I remember about him. I don't have me no picture."

The woman looked at him for a minute. "Course you can have it," she said. "They's a lot of them in the kitchen there. Take all you want."

"One's enough. Just, you know, there ought to be *something*. I reckon Bodine was the best friend I ever had."

For a minute neither of them spoke. The face of the woman tightened, and Langston James was afraid she was going to cry again. "Where you say that undertaker's was?"

She collected herself to answer the question. "Down to the end of the street and take a right. You can't miss it. He got a sign out front."

"Dalton's?" Langston James began limping down the steps.

"That's right. They done a good job on him. He was swole up something awful when they took him in."

Langston James nodded and got into the truck without speaking. As he pulled away he saw the yellow-eyed dog staring at him from behind the front steps. Jenniwese was peeking around her grandmother's skirt. He realized suddenly that he didn't know what the woman's name was.

* * *

Dalton's Funeral Home shared half of a ranch-style brick house with Maybelle's Beauty Parlor. The director was a large man with a serious manner and two gold teeth. In his lapel he wore a sprig of fern and a pink rose, both made of plastic. The way he moved and spoke was smooth and courtly, and somewhat fluttery for such a large man. With Langston James he was painfully deferential. Though he must have been surprised to see him in the establishment, he acted as if it was the most natural thing in the world for a white man to come visiting in a colored funeral home. He sweated heavily the whole time and did not offer to shake hands with Langston James, or to touch him in any way.

"Are you Mister Dalton?"

"Mister Dalton passed on several years ago. I'm his son-in-law, Demolay Keese." His voice was rich and deep, but it had a manufactured sound to it.

"Is *every*body dead around here?"

"Well, yes," said Demolay. "Mostly they is. We do be in the business. Was there something in particular I could do for you? We don't work on white folks."

Langston James nodded. "I've come to see Bodine Polite. Bodine worked for me."

"Ah, ah," said Demolay. He rubbed his hands together. "Yes, sir. Step thisaway."

He led Langston James into a small room which had once been a dining alcove, with panelled wainscotting painted over pink, and bookshelves painted white. There were no books on the shelves, only several dogeared copies of *Ebony* and a couple of *Reader's Digest*s. The casket was set up on trestles and the lid was open. Langston James walked up to it and looked down on his friend. Bodine's appearance jolted and shook him. His face had been kneaded into a grimace that was nothing like the way Langston James had known him to be in life.

"He's smiling," said Langston James.

Demolay nodded and rubbed his hands together. "We had us some trouble with that. You know, he was bit by wasps and he swole up something awful. Dealing with swole up features is a hard thing." He held up his hands and moved the fingers. "You got to have strong hands to do it."

Langston James looked up at the hands of Mr. Keese. "I never seen him smile in my life. That looks awful. Like he's got a mouth full of cotton."

A hurt look came over Demolay's features. "We got to consider the fambly," he said. "Generally they likes to see them looking restful and happy. It's a comfort."

"It ain't no comfort to me. I known him seven years and I never seen no expression like that on his face. Not in my life I didn't."

While they were talking, a small man came into the room. Demolay turned to him for help. "Tell me, Mister Washington. Don't he look natural?"

Mister Washington looked into the coffin. "Sure do," he said. He spoke in a high stuttery voice. "Just like he was goin' to get up and go. Just like. Just like."

Langston James rubbed his hand through his hair. "Who *are* you? Sounds like somebody off *Amos 'n' Andy*. For sure you didn't know him the way I did." He turned back to Demolay. "I ain't never heard of nobody died of wasp bites."

"Me neither," said Demolay. He thought for a minute. "You was talking to Wilma, wadn't you?"

"I don't know. Is that her name? His daughter?"

"She his daughter-*in-law*. The one to the house. Married his son Decatur. Kind of a light complexioned woman. Right nice lookin'? Wilma got it in her head hit was them stings caused the decease. Doctor said he had him a heart attack. Also broke his neck when he fell off the roof. You got you three choices. You can take your pick. Only takes one and...that's all she wrote."

Langston James reached for his pack of Old Golds.

"Excuse me," said Mr. Washington, stepping forward. "Could you spare me a cigarette?"

"Is it all right to smoke in here?" Langston James spoke to Demolay.

"Go right ahead. We try to make everthing natural as we can."

Langston James passed the pack around. Some of the edge went off Demolay's professional smoothness and he became mellow in a more genuine way. "You known the departed well, did you?"

"He worked for me." Langston James thought about his remark. "In a way he did. We was friends mostly. I got a paper route. He used to ride with me."

"And you'd say you was friends?"

Mr. Washington smiled and nodded and puffed on his Old Gold. "Old Golds is my favorite," he said. "Some people says Luckies is the best, but I never did think you could go more first class than Old Golds. That's what I thinks myself."

"There wasn't no real salary. I paid him now and then, but we never did settle on the money. How well did *you* know him?"

"Not very. Mister Washington there's the one you need to talk to."

"You known him, did you?"

"We done time together. You can't get to know a man no better'n that."

"You were on the chain gang with Bodine?"

"It was *hard* time in them days. I can tell you that." The way he sounded, Mr. Washington seemed proud of working on the chain gang.

"Sounds like you got fond memories of it. You proud of being put in jail?"

"It make a impression on you. Stick in you mind." Mr. Washington stubbed out his cigarette in an ashtray shaped like a map of Georgia.

Langston James offered him another. "You help him steal the hog?"

"What hog? I done time for stealin' peaches out Mister Colquit's packin' shed. They was culls at that."

"I mean the hog Bodine stole got him arrested."

Mr. Washington looked at Langston James, cocking his head to one side to keep the smoke from the Old Gold out of his eyes. "Bodine didn't go on the gang for stealin' no hog."

"He told me he did."

"I don't mean he was lyin'. Bodine stealed him a hog all right, but he didn't do time for it. Nobody ever caught him for stealin' no hog. Bodine's a smart fella. He pulled that one off slick as a whistle."

Langston James looked at him. "He told me he got five years for stealin' a hog."

"He got him five years all right, but that wadn't hit. Bodine went on the gang for bringin' charges against a white man."

"What white man?"

"Mister Sweat."

"Elrod Sweat? The John Deere dealer?"

"That the one."

"He brought charges against him? What for?"

"Mister Sweat headed up the bunch lynched Bodine's son."

Langston James looked at him for a minute without speaking. "Bodine never said nothing about no son getting lynched. Never said word one. When'd that happen?"

Mr. Washington pursed his mouth and looked thoughtful. "Long time ago. Before the waw."

"What'd they lynch him for?"

"Well. They *said* it's for rapin' one of the Sweat women, but that's a lie. Mostly it's for being uppity. He wouldn't stand and uncover when they talked to him. Looked 'em in the eye. That kind of thing. They taken him and nailed him to a stump and set him on fire." Mr. Washington looked thoughtful. "That's in '32. I *do* recollect about that. President Roosevelt done won the election, but he wadn't in the White House yet. Anyway, a lynchin' like that kind of stick in your mind."

"*Nailed* him to a stump?"

"They done some other things to him first, but I ruther not talk about that. Wadn't the best of times back then. Not for colored folks it wadn't."

"What'd they get Bodine for?"

"Paid somebody to name him for breakin' in the Gulf station out on the Waycross highway."

"And it wasn't no hog?"

"We et that hog."

For a minute or two there was silence. Finally Demolay spoke up. "Well. Anyway, we done got all that kind of thing behind us. It's a new day in the modern world."

Langston James shook his head from side to side. "He never told me none of that. Just said it was for stealin' that hog." He looked at Mr. Washington. "Never told me about his son. Nor the Gulf station. Nor none of it." He thought a minute. "He told me he's forty-three years old. That's another thing."

"Well, *did* he now?" Mr. Washington slapped his leg and let out a high-pitched, cackling laugh. "I bet he did. He like to do that."

"His daughter-in-law said he's sixty-three years old."

Mr. Washington nodded. "I'd say sixty-five, but it's close one way or another. I'se borned in '98 myself. We was almost of an age. Give or take a year or two."

Langston James walked over to the open casket and looked down at Bodine. "I never did know you couldn't trust me, Bodine," he said. "Why wouldn't you tell me about yourself the way it was?"

Demolay walked up behind him, almost touching. "I wouldn't take it too hard. Mister Polite had strange ways from what I hear. It don't mean he didn't trust you."

"That's right," said Mr. Washington. "He lied to *ever*-body. His own daughter thinks he was in the waw."

"But I was his *friend*."

"His daughter thinks he was in South America in the merchant marines. He didn't do that neither."

"When was that?"

"He come back in '55 . . . '55 maybe '56 . . . somewhere around there. I can't recall just when he left. Right after the waw sometime."

"Where'd he go?"

"It wadn't South America. I figure he was on the bum. Down to Florida maybe. He like it where it wawm. No tellin' really. Bodine was a close-mouthed kind of a man. Anyway, it wadn't none of my business."

"I met up with him in '56. First time. He didn't say nothing about Florida."

"I wouldn't swear it was Florida. Could of been just over to the next county. I ain't been out of Whippet myself. I wouldn't know."

"It's hard for me to take it in—all this. I thought I knew him pretty good."

Demolay stepped up and almost put his arm around Langston James. "Yes. Well. You want to look around and see our equipment? We very up-to-date."

Langston James put his good hand into the casket, laying it on the folded hands of Bodine. He stood there for a minute without saying anything. "Why you want to leave this thing open? He never did look like that. I'd ruther remember what he used to look like."

Demolay didn't answer. Langston James turned and started out of the room. As he passed, Mr. Washington put out his hand. "Could you spare another one of them Old Golds? For old time's sake. I was his friend as well."

* * *

Back at the house, Langston James moped and dragged. Finally he began to talk to Cowie about it.

"I don't know what you can count on in this world. We was good friends. I mean, we had our differences and all, but we was really *good* friends. I'd 'a done anything for that man—just about."

"Don't take it too hard, Eljay. Colored folks can't treat white people straight out. We haven't had time enough for that yet."

"Goddamn, Cowie. I known him for *seven* years. We ain't talking about some field hand walking on the side of the goddamn road."

"Well...you just didn't know him like you thought you did. That's all."

"I never would of expected he would lie to me."

"He didn't lie to you, Eljay. Just he didn't tell you all his business."

"What about the hog?"

"Maybe he lied to you a little bit. Friends do that all the time. It don't have to mean anything."

"He had no *cause* to lie to me."

"Well, yes he did."

"What? Why would he want to do that?"

"Because you're a white man."

"That ain't no reason, Cowie. What kind of a reason is that? I didn't never lie to him on account of him being a colored man."

"Come on, Eljay. You're forty-one years old."

"I told Bodine things I ain't never told nobody else. Why would he want to treat me that way?"

"There's some things that if you don't know them by the time you're forty-one years old, then you're not ever going to know them. *Twenty*-one, really. Maybe before that even. I can't explain it any better than that."

"You got awful wise all of a sudden. How come you think you

know so much more than me?"

"He wasn't so much of a friend of mine. I can see what it is better than you. At least right now I can."

He drank the last of his coffee and lit an Old Gold. "Okay. It ain't a good time for me to think things out just now. I had Mizres Fanshaw to put up with already. I feel like I don't know nothing about what's going on. A man ought not have to feel that way at my age. You need to coast on the downhill side."

"Never noticed much chance to coast myself." Her voice softened. "You're not going to figure anything out the way you are now. What you need is a good night's sleep."

"Maybe that thing in the coffin was really Bodine after all. He didn't look like the way I known him as. I only spent twelve hours a day with him. For seven years. How would I be sure?"

"Take you a hot bath and see can't you think of something pleasant."

"Give me a hint what maybe it could be."

"Well."

"Tell me something, Cowie."

She looked at him and waited.

"What's my name? I need you to tell me what my *real* name might be."

"You need to ease off, Eljay. Like I said. That's what you need."

"No, listen. Tell me what my name is. My real whole name. All there is of it. I need you to do that for me, Cowie. Right now that's something I really do need."

She looked at him and hesitated. "Langston James McHenry..."

"You sure?"

"My husband...Langston James McHenry. That's what your name is. Truly."

"You wouldn't lie to me, would you, Cowie? You wouldn't tell me no lie at a time like this?"

"Go get you some sleep, Eljay. I don't like the way this is going tonight."

Langston James went to bed, but he couldn't go to sleep. After awhile he got up and went into the room where Halstead and Gabriel were sleeping. For awhile he stood looking from one to the other of his sleeping sons. Finally he sat down on the edge of Halstead's bed and studied his face in the light from the hall.

"Who *are* you, Halstead?" He spoke softly so as not to wake him. Halstead was sleeping with his mouth open and a gentle gurgling sound rattled in his throat. "How can I know who it is you really are?" He put out his hand and stroked Halstead's narrow head. Halstead closed his mouth and turned over on his side.

Langston James adjusted the covers over Halstead, then went to Gabriel's bed. He picked up the child and took him into the bathroom where he studied the two of them in the mirror over the basin. "I never did know who *you* were, Gabriel." He touched Gabriel's fine yellow hair, stroking it into place. "That's something I *do* know." Afterwards he walked the house, holding Gabriel and humming cradle songs. Finally he went into the front room and sat on the couch, hugging the child while he rocked back and forth, humming and mumbling to himself. It was almost time for him to leave on his route before he put Gabriel back into his own bed and went in to Cowie.

"How you feel?"

"I been thinking it over. It's time I found out what all I don't know."

"You going to be all right? You want me to ride with you on the route?"

"I'll be okay."

"You sure?"

"I feel like I've been reamed out, but I'm not sleepy. It'll be okay. I like being out there in the dark by myself."

"Well," she said. She sounded sleepy.

"One thing," he said.

She yawned. "What's that?"

"Would you hold my hand?" He touched her under the covers. "Just for a minute or two?"

* * *

In the kitchen, he made his breakfast, then he cleared the table and got a piece of paper and a pencil. On the paper he printed his name, forming the letters with care and precision. For awhile he looked at his name on the paper, tracing over the letters with his pencil. Then he added the names of Cowie and Halstead and Gabriel, each on a separate line going down the page. At the end he printed Bodine's name, wetting the point of the pencil to make the letters firm and dark, and going over them twice. When he finished he studied the list, nodding his head and tapping the point of the pencil on the table. Finally he folded the paper over on itself once—then twice more, running a spoon over the creases to compact them. He held up the packet and turned it this way and that, looking at it closely to make sure it satisfied him. Finally, he took out his wallet and slipped the paper into the compartment with the photographs. After he got into the truck, he had a better idea, and he took the Tube Rose snuff can out of the glove compartment and put the piece of paper into that. Later he wrapped adhesive tape around the can, winding it over and over, sealing the lid on tight.

Fourteen

THE FUNERAL TURNED OUT TO BE an ordeal for him, as much as the visit to Dalton's had been, though he didn't have to look at the terrible dead smile again. He stood outside the crowd of mourners, leaning against a tree with his hat in his hand—chewing on his lip. The high, rolling pitch of emotion got on his nerves. And the preacher's chanting way of working up the funeral party struck him as an insult to Bodine's memory—whether or not he could be sure *exactly* who he was. Most of all he didn't like the group's responses to the incantations of the preacher. What he wanted was quiet grief. Instead he got something like the low end of a tent show, and snake oil for his true heart's misery. By the time it was over, he was wound so tight he felt like jumping over a steeple. There was only one word to bring him ease, and he ground his teeth on it as he walked away, saying it over and over under his breath—
"...niggers...niggers...niggers..."

Later, after the service had ended and everyone had left, he went back to mourn his quiet white man's grief.

Up close to the grave, he could see that the marker was a small block of granite, not much bigger than a common brick. The inscription read:

BODINE ALMA POLITE
1899 - 1963

On each side of the stone there was a blue Milk of Magnesia bottle with a plastic flower in it. The bottle to the right of the stone also contained a small American flag.

"It ain't even big enough to trip over." He spoke the words out loud, shaking his head from side to side as he calculated the dimensions of the stone, setting them over against the loss he felt for his dead friend. When he got back to the truck he looked at the lyre-backed drugstore chair in the bed—the one Bodine had sat on when they were driving around town. For a minute he stared at it with his hand on the handle of the door, while the resolution was forming inside his head. Finally he lifted it out and took it back to the grave, where he put it down at the head of the loose mound of dirt, pushing the legs in to anchor them.

"Temporary, Bodine," he said, speaking softly. "At least you can *see* the goddamn thing." He hesitated. "I can do better for you than that. Maybe I don't know who in the hell you was. But I know you was my friend...my friend...my friend..."

* * *

For the second time in his life, Langston James went down to the Whippet Monument and Funerary Adornment Company to do business with Wicklow Grant.

When Wicklow found out where the headstone was going, he began to show signs of deep reluctance to do business.

"That's a nigger graveyard, Eljay. Something like that is going to have repercussions—deep repercussions. I got to think what all it might could mean—you know—in a business way."

"Goddamn, Wicklow. It's just a dead man out there. What the hell difference does it make?"

"There's a colored monument place over in Slabtown. Why don't you go over there and see what they can do for you?"

"I don't want no nigger gravestone, Wicklow. I'm looking for first-class work."

"Well," said Wicklow.

Langston James looked him in the eye. "Listen," he said. "I'm ready to go for *two* doves."

Wicklow doodled on a pad without answering him.

"Two doves, Wicklow." Langston James hesitated. "Two doves and a angel."

Wicklow stopped doodling and looked up at him. "Two doves *and* an angel?"

Langston James nodded. "That's right."

Wicklow took out his handkerchief and wiped his brow. "How about some Old English text?" he said. "Tell you what. Throw in four lines of Old English text and it's a deal."

Langston James nodded and took out his wallet. He didn't shake Wicklow's hand. He counted the money into it instead.

Wicklow tore the top sheet off the tablet. "What you want for the inscription?"

Langston James didn't look at him. "I'll have to think it over."

"Could you let me know tomorrow? Takes a little time to do four lines."

"Yes," said Langston James. "I'll let you know tomorrow." He hesitated. "Listen, Wicklow," he said. "What's it mean when they've got the birth date on a stone and they don't put down the date when he died?"

Wicklow looked at him. "Means they got it made up before hand."

"What?"

"Pre-need. Went ahead and bought the stone ahead of time. I do that right often."

"I see," said Langston James. He thought a minute. "Don't tell nobody about this, Wicklow. I want to keep it a secret."

The expression on Wicklow's face was a mixture of surprise and relief. "You do? Why didn't you say so in the first place?"

"Don't nobody need to know about this. It's *my* business."

"You can count on me." Wicklow doodled on his pad. "Would it be all right if I carried it out there after dark?"

"Don't they lock the gates at sundown?"

"What for? Nothing but niggers, ain't it?"

* * *

Halstead gave him a quotation out of a poem he was studying in his English class at school.

> *This be the verse you grave for me,*
> *Here he lies where he longed to be;*
> *Home is the sailor, home from the sea,*
> *And the hunter home from the hill.*

"It's Robert Louis Stevenson."

"It is?"

"Yes, sir."

"That's okay."

After supper, Langston James told Cowie about the funeral. "His middle name was 'Alma.'"

"That so? Never heard of any man named 'Alma.' Where you reckon they got that from?"

"I never heard of *nobody* named that."

"My daddy had a cousin named Alma. Only she was a woman. Lived over near Hahira. Alma's not a man's name really."

"Bodine was a man."

"You know what I mean."

For a minute or two he didn't speak. "What would you think if I got rid of the truck?"

Cowie turned and looked at him. "I'd think it was high time. You been nursing that thing for seventeen years. "You'd do better to *bury* it."

"It's *your* truck. I wouldn't do nothing didn't you want me to."

"More yours than mine. I wouldn't drive it out the yard if I didn't have to."

"I thought I might drop by Shoefelt's and see what kind of a trade he'd give me."

"You going to get you a Cadillac? That'll be a step up."

"I need something I can depend on."

"Why don't you get you a Lincoln?"

Langston James answered quickly. "I don't want no goddamn Lincoln."

"Uh huh. Well. You need transportation you can depend on all right. Can we afford it?"

"Money ain't no problem."

"Well, well. How about that?"

"I been thinking about it for some time. Halstead's been talking about it for a couple years now."

"Listen," she said. "Is a Cadillac automobile going to make you happy, Eljay?"

"This is a business proposition, Cowie. It ain't something I'd be doing for the fun of it."

Cowie turned back to the sink. "I don't care about the truck, Eljay. Just do something to put a smile on your face. I'm worried about you, honey."

He got up from the table and put his arms around her from behind. "I'm worried about me too," he said. "I just can't ride around in that truck no more. Not by myself."

She turned and put her arms around his neck. "You just get you a Cadillac automobile if you want to." She kissed him on the mouth. "Get you a Cadillac convertible, if it's going to make you happy."

"I hope it will," he said.

"Make it blue," she said. "Baby blue."

"Blue as Gabriel's eyes?"

"Honey," she said. "They don't make them *that* blue."

* * *

The next day he stopped by Shoefelt's Oldsmobile-Cadillac dealership and talked to Fulton Shoefelt about trading in his truck on a 1959 Fleetwood. A black one.

Fulton was a large, shy man, who wore Madras jackets with tattersall shirts and argyle socks. Nothing found its way onto Fulton's person that was not parti-colored and strident. And though his commitment to plaid was especially deep and abiding, every now and then he would risk a stripe or two. The patterns and colors changed from time to time, but the impulse stayed the same. Fulton was one of those people who like to ride their groove once they've found it. His only deviation was the suit he wore to funerals and weddings. It was dark blue—pinstriped, of course. With it he wore a three-inch tie with orange-and-white vertical stripes.

He also wore a straw hat like Sam Snead, the golfer, and the hat was if anything more permanent than the plaid. He took it off to shower. And Sunday mornings when he sang in the choir of the First Methodist Church. But he wore it working in the yard, and around the house, and to the dentist's. At night it

rested on the stand beside his bed. In the morning it was the
first item of clothing he put on. His argyle socks were the second.

In his lapel he wore a World War II veteran's button. Those
had been the golden years for Fulton. His service had been in
the 3rd Army, and his remembrance of the breakout from St. Lo
and Patton's dash for the Rhine was something that he could get
seriously emotional about. They were grand days, the likes of
which he knew he would never see again—certainly not in
Whippet. Someone once put the case that Fulton was with Patton the way Mary was with child. Nobody knew what it meant,
but everyone agreed it applied.

He wasn't all that good at selling automobiles, but then a
Cadillac dealer didn't have to be. With customers, his manner
was affectionate, and his voice was low and confidential. He put
his arm around Langston James's shoulder while he walked him
over the lot. When they got down to the details of the trade, his
voice went lower yet.

"I'll tell you, Eljay. That's a classic truck you've got there. Classic. But I'm not going to be able to give you what it's worth. If
you want to know the truth, I'd recommend you put an ad in
the newspaper and sell it yourself. Mostly our type customers
wouldn't be interested in it. I don't want to insult you with the
price I'd be able to allow."

"Well," said Langston James, "what would it be?"

Fulton hesitated, then cleared his throat. "Twenty-five dollars."
He was embarrassed, and his voice dropped so far Langston
James could hardly hear him, even with his good ear. Fulton was
clearheaded in his business dealings, but he didn't relish the
moment when he had to go into the details. Most of the time
he didn't think of himself as being in business at all. Selling
Cadillacs was more like a calling to him. Closings brought everything into focus and made him uncomfortable.

"Twenty-five dollars?"

Fulton looked pained. "I told you. I know it's an insult. I hate it's the best I could do. I love to put people in an automobile, but I just about can't stand the *selling* part."

"Well," said Langston James. "Twenty-five dollars, eh?"

"Why don't you run that ad?"

"I'll pay cash," said Langston James.

Fulton looked relieved.

He parked the truck in the back yard and drove the Cadillac for two days while he thought over what he wanted to do about it.

The first thing he did was take the Tube Rose can out of the dash pocket and wrap it up in a neater package. Then he painted it with gold spray paint he bought off of the model airplane counter in the ten-cent store. He tied it up with a red ribbon and hung it from the rear view mirror in the Cadillac.

The second thing he did was go around to see Brother Moates about buying a gun from him.

Mrs. Moates answered the door, and when she called Brother Moates he came into the room walking on crutches. There was a very large bandage on his right foot.

"What happened?"

Mrs. Moates spoke up before Brother Moates could answer. "He thought he heard a burglar."

"What?" Langston James couldn't take his eyes off the bandage.

"He thought he heard a burglar, so he got up in the middle of the night and shot himself in the foot."

Brother Moates had a small, half smile on his face. He seemed to be in pain. "I filed down the sear. That Magnum's got a hair trigger on it."

"Did you shoot the burglar?"

"Wasn't no burglar. I think he dreamed it all in his head." Mrs. Moates didn't sound very sympathetic.

"It ain't all that bad, really." Brother Moates sat down in a Barclay Lounger with his foot extended stiffly. He moved slowly and with care. "Kind of on the side and to the front."

"He blew his little toe away." Mrs. Moates pointed to a spot in the lime green shag rug. "I don't know how we're going to get that hole fixed. I spent a month looking for that *exact* color. They won't never be able to match it."

There was a large hole in the rug with black powder stains around it.

"Put a chair over it. Won't nobody be able to tell." Brother Moates shifted himself carefully in the Barclay Lounger.

"In the *middle* of the floor?"

"I'll get you a coffee table." Brother Moates groaned in a controlled way. "I don't really want to talk about it just now, honey. Give me a rest."

Mrs. Moates nodded. "I pretty much got the bloodstains out with salt water and Ivory soap. It's the hole I'm worried about."

Langston James stepped over and examined the spot more closely. "That's a pretty big hole."

"Three fifty-seven magnum. You could hunt Kodiac bear with a three fifty-seven. I seen a picture of a feller shot one. In a magazine." Brother Moates shifted himself again, carefully. He seemed to be having a hard time finding a position that suited him. "Cain't seem to get comfortable," he said.

"He had on his new wing-tip cordovan shoes too." Mrs. Moates shook her head. "That's another forty-five dollars down the drain."

"What if it *had* of been a burglar?" Brother Moates shifted his position again, and the strain came up in his voice.

Mrs. Moates looked at her husband. "He'd of had to have him a Mayflower moving van to haul off enough stuff to put him ahead of what it's going to cost us now." She ticked the items off on her fingers. "There's your cordovan shoes and the rug and what the doctor's bill is going to come to." She stopped and looked at Langston James. "He said he's going to have to do some rebuilding on that foot." She looked at the bandage and shook her head. "I couldn't get a price out of him, but you don't have to be any Einstein to figure it's not going to be cheap."

"Listen," Brother Moates had a strained sound in his voice. He started to get up. "I think I better go lie down. I cain't seem to get comfortable somehow."

"Preachers generally get a good price from doctors. I don't know what he's going to say about a gunshot wound."

"Listen," said Langston James. "What I come to see you about is—you got a gun you could sell me? You know—cheap?"

Before Brother Moates could speak up, Mrs. Moates answered. "Mister McHenry, you're going to get you the deal of a lifetime. Take your pick. Take the whole lot. You wouldn't believe the price I'm going to give you. I'll sell 'em to you by the pound."

"Don't pay no attention to her, Eljay. She's upset just now. Step this way."

Mrs. Moates put her hand on her hip. "He don't have to step that way. He hadn't blowed no hole in his foot."

Langston James settled on the H&R twenty-two.

"That'd cost you thirty-five dollars now, and it's in tip-top condition. I take care of my armaments." Brother Moates thought for a minute. "What you say to ten dollars?"

"That's the same one you showed me before, ain't it? I recall you said you paid twenty-five."

"Thirty-five is what it goes for now. The price gone up. I'll throw in a box of long rifles. Ain't as good as holler points, but they'll do the job."

Langston James didn't want to argue. He paid him the ten dollars.

"Is it loaded?" he asked.

"Course it is. What good's a gun got no bullets in it? Don't wave it around. It can't do you like a three fifty-seven, but wouldn't be no joyful experience neither if you winged yourself."

"Much obliged," said Langston James. He walked out of the house holding the pistol at arm's length. After he got into the Cadillac, he put it into the glove compartment with the barrel pointing away from him.

The next day he drove the truck down to the Oakmulgie River, onto the bluff next to the bridge on State Road 41. He pulled it right up to the edge of the bluff then got out and started stripping things off it and throwing them into the water. Everything he could pull off with his hands or pry loose with a tire iron he flung into the river—the hub caps, radio antenna, the radio itself, the seat cushion, the knob off the gearshift, the loose wires under the hood. When he couldn't find anything else that would come loose, he got the pistol and shot out the glass and blew the tires. Then he opened up the hood and took aim at the engine. The bullet whined and zipped around for what seemed like a minute or more before it came buzzing out, just by his ear. It scared him, so he put the pistol down and went to work with the tire iron again, banging and whacking in a general way. He started at the tailgate, working toward the front, then around and back to the tailgate again on the opposite side. He didn't really do much damage, but by the time he was through he felt a whole lot better—though he was red in the face and drenched in sweat.

He sat on the tailgate and smoked two Old Golds while he cooled down, then he let off the hand brake and pushed the truck over the bluff into the river. It drifted off a ways before it sank out of sight in the black water. Langston James watched until the eddies had all died out and the placid movement of the river erased all traces of the mark.

He flipped his cigarette into the river and watched it float off on the current.

"Well," he said at last. "It's a new day."

* * *

On the Saturday after the funeral Langston James took Gabriel
to ride in the Cadillac. He wanted the child to be pleased, but
he could tell it wasn't the same for him as riding in the Lincoln.
In the Lincoln there was Calloway to do the driving while Mrs.
Fanshaw petted and talked to him in the back seat with the two
of them wrapped in the laprobe.

He put Gabriel on his lap and let him steer the car, but even
that wasn't as good as the Lincoln was. Nothing he could think
of to do with the child could be undiluted. There was no way
he could be as single-minded in his affection as Mrs. Fanshaw
could be. He could let Gabriel play at driving, but he had to
keep his eye on the road and shift the gears. Though Gabriel
might be an obsession for both of them, Langston James had to
balance the residue of responsibility all by himself.

Anyway, letting Gabriel steer the car didn't last long. A highway patrolman stopped them and gave Langston James a lecture
about highway safety. It ended with a written warning.

"You're old enough to know better, mister." The patrolman
had a deep voice and was as big as a bear. "Fooling around like
that and being a menace. Get that child off your lap and pay
attention to what you're doing."

"I ain't breaking the law, officer. I see people doing this all the
time."

"Want to give me a little lesson in the law, I see." The patrolman leaned down until his face was level with Langston James's
and gave him an intent look. "Tell you what. I don't much like
your face, mister. You want to work this up into something *really*
worthwhile?"

"No, sir."

"Then get your ass out of here."

"Much obliged."

The siren and the flashing lights scared Gabriel. The reflecting sunglasses the officer wore made him cry. After that he didn't want to ride in the Cadillac. He even had to be coaxed to get into the Lincoln.

Mr. Washington began to presume on the connection he had made in the meeting at Dalton's to elevate his lifestyle. Soon after the funeral he started coming around to the drugstore to beg Old Gold cigarettes and Coca-Colas. Langston gave them to him in the hope that what he had to say about Bodine might give him some ease and comfort, and a clue to who his friend had been. He even had Mr. Washington ride with him on the route for a couple of days, thinking that the feeling they would have riding together in the dark, and in a Cadillac automobile at that, would loosen him up and produce more valuable bits of information about his dead friend. But the fact of the matter was that Mr. Lincoln Thomas Washington didn't need any loosening up. He was a talker—by nature and constitution. The trouble was that the information he furnished was only of two kinds—neither of which was useful or consoling. He either talked about himself in such boring detail that it made Langston James's head ache, or he revealed things about Bodine that were not so much valuable as depressing, since they just confirmed Langston James in his sadness over the way Bodine had treated him. Whichever direction the conversation took, Mr. Washington only reminded Langston James of how much he missed his dead friend—and of how deeply he had been hurt by him.

"Whyn't you see you a hand reader?"

"What?"

"I knows a woman reads hands pretty good. She help straighten out you mind."

"You know what, Lincoln Thomas? You're full of shit. What's

she going to see in my hand that's going to help me with my present troubles?"

"She tell you what all going to happen. Then you got time to think it over."

"Like I'm going to take a long trip and meet somebody beautiful?"

"Maybe that too."

"She ever done you any good?"

"Saved my life."

Langston James looked at him and frowned. "Saved your life? How'd she do that?"

"Tole me she seed something got a truck in it, and a rope tied up in a noose, and fellas in white robes cover they faces. All that gone happen on a certain day, which she name. I tarried over to my sister's place in Fly for a spell. Give it three days each side of what she say. You know, just to be safe. Sit out a week."

"Well?"

"I *here* ain't I?"

Langston James thought about it for awhile. "You listenin', Lincoln Thomas?"

"You say somethin'?"

"You going to have to pay attention to this now. You need to be tuned in. Watch my mouth." He waited to make sure he had Mr. Washington's attention. "What she did was predict you a thing that *didn't* happen. That's what she did."

"Well. She were *right*, weren't she?"

"What?"

"Here I is." Mr. Washington slapped the seat. "Sittin' right beside of you in this here Cadillac automobile."

Langston James thought about that for awhile. "There's something wrong with this, Lincoln Thomas, but I can't put my finger on what it is."

"I figure she save me life." Mr. Washington lit an Old Gold

from the pack Langston James had given him. "And I mighty grateful for it myself. *That* the thing I put my finger on." He looked up at the Tube Rose package hanging from the rear view mirror. "What *is* that thang?"

"Just a keepsake."

Mr. Washington thought it over for a minute. "Whyn't you get you some pink dices? Some baby shoes from that sweet lookin' chile you got? Give it a touch of *style* and such."

"Uh huh," said Langston James.

None of the conversations he had with Mr. Washington were any more profitable or satisfying. The way things went reminded Langston James a little of the way they had gone the time he had Will Ed Freemont riding with him. Mr. Washington was more cheerful and agreeable, but, in his present state of mind, about equally unsettling to deal with. Langston James began picking up the papers half an hour early, and avoiding the drugstore in the daytime on the premise that he didn't need Mr. Washington in his life after all. Not just then he didn't.

* * *

He talked to Cowie about it.

"I thought it was maybe him being a colored man would make it like it was. But that ain't working."

"He doesn't sound like very good company."

"No company at all, really. I never known a man open his mouth so much and so little come out of it." Langston James thought a minute. "Fair's fair," he said at last. "His heart's in the right place. Only he bores the shit out of me."

"Well."

"Makes me feel bad too. I don't need it just now."

"What *would* make you cheerful, Eljay? The Cadillac automobile didn't do it."

"It ain't some *category* makes you a friend. It ain't like—'sixty-year-ole nigger, got a name start with *B*.' You can't go out and get one like you're buying groceries at the store." Langston James shook his head. "I need something special. Just for me. Something to put myself into."

"You've got *me*."

He didn't look at her. "Don't take this hard, Cowie. I love you for my wife. I truly do. But you don't *need* me. That's the thing. I'm the one needs you."

She nodded her head. "You reckon I aught to take that as a compliment?"

"Don't get on me now. You know what I'm talking about."

"Got to be Gabriel? What about Halstead?"

"Halstead's of a piece. You know—*collected*. I love Halstead too, but he don't need me any more than you do."

For awhile neither of them said anything. Finally Langston James spoke. "It don't pay to be truthful. Does it?"

"I'd hate to be the one to say that."

"Sometimes there's more *meanness* in the truth than anything else. Hurting other folks, *that's* what some people like about telling the truth." He looked at Cowie. "I hope you wouldn't think that's what *I* had in mind."

"No," she said. "That's not what I'd think."

* * *

Langston James drew in his thoughts to a central point, like focussing a magnifying glass to start a fire. He felt that he had to do something—perform some act against Mrs. Fanshaw, make some move that would be concrete and definite—to put him on an equal footing in his battle with her over Gabriel. On his way to pick up his papers on Sunday, he drove by the Fanshaw house. At two o'clock in the morning there wasn't much to be seen; still he had the feeling that some kind of a revelation might come to him out of the proximity itself—a stratagem to arm and bolster him in the uneven campaign he was waging. Nothing occurred to him that first time. On Monday night he parked and watched the house with his lights off. On Tuesday, he got out of the car and walked across the lawn to the structure itself. He went twice around it, looking in at the darkened windows and talking to himself. Some kind of curve in his thought brought him back on Wednesday with a box of rock salt, which he sprinkled on her rose bed. Afterwards, he stood in the moonlight contemplating the house with his chin in his hand, then he crept up onto the porch and pried the house numbers off the jamb of the front door and threw them into the shrubbery. Those acts of pure vandalism, premeditated, but senseless, as even he would admit, brought a momentary peace to him, but it was a peace that hardly lasted beyond the city limits as he drove out of town to deliver his papers. Something more seemed called for, but he couldn't think what it was.

When he noticed the first dead possum in the road, a small alarm rang in his head. He lit an Old Gold and tried to think what it meant. The second one rang a little clearer, but it wasn't until the third one that he stopped and shaped the thought. He got out of the car and lined the trunk with newspapers. Then he peeled the dead animal off the asphalt, opened the trunk and dropped it in. By the time he finished the route, he had thirty-seven of them packed in there—nearly five cubic feet of squashed and ripening possum. When he got back to town, he drove directly to the Fanshaws' house. First light was breaking, but he was caught in the momentum of the thing and couldn't weigh the risk. Six at a time he emptied the trunk of the Fleetwood, carrying mashed and mangled possums by their tails, like stringers of fish, making a pink and furry mound in the middle of the Fanshaw's well-kept lawn. For a minute, he stood and contemplated his work. "There," he said at last. "That ought to hold her."

He went to the faucet in the rosebed with the intention of washing his hands, then thought better of it and wiped them on his pants. Back in the car, he took the pistol out of the dash pocket and held it in his hand while he stared across the lawn and thought about the one further step he might take. While he watched, the first vulture appeared. Circling down in a slow and cautious spiral, until it came to rest on the roof of the house, then sidestepping slowly along the ridge, all the while looking with hump-backed concentration at the heap of possums below him. A second vulture appeared. And then a third. He held the pistol up, taking aim — balancing one of the sad, angular birds on the blade of the front sight. Then slowly he moved the sight down the slope of the roof, lowering it until it came to rest on an upstairs window. Perhaps it was the bedroom in which Mrs. Fanshaw was sleeping at that very minute. The thought came over him in a rush, and his finger began to tighten on the trigger. Suddenly a light came on in the window, breaking yellow into the greyness of the morning. No one was moving behind the drawn shade as far as he could tell, but he found himself drenched in sweat and his hand with the gun began to shake. He put the pistol into the dash pocket, and slammed it shut. Then he turned on the engine and pulled slowly away from the curb with his lights off.

Back at the house, he wrapped the pistol in a towel and put it into a section of drainpipe that was lying across the rafters of the garage.

"Sweet Jesus!" he said. "I must be losing my mind."

Cowie heard about it from Mrs. Fanshaw, who thought it was a little out of the ordinary, but didn't seem to be disturbed by it. She didn't know who had done it.

"I don't know what you had in your mind, Eljay. I don't even *want* to know. Just don't let it happen again. That's all I've got to say."

Langston James shook his head. "I don't know either. I really don't know either."

For awhile neither of them said anything. "I even thought about shooting Mizres Fanshaw. Shooting in her house anyway."

"What?"

"I got me a pistol from Brother Moates."

"Eljay!" She sounded stricken.

"I said I *thought* about it. You don't think I'd really *do* a thing like that, do you?" He posed it as a question. As if he wasn't sure himself what the answer might be, and was waiting for her to tell him.

"Dead animals... that's crazy. A pistol is something serious. I mean you can't get any more serious than what you're talking about."

"I know. I put the gun up out the way. Ain't got no bullets for it anymore. I threw those in the river. I *know* when I'm thinking crazy. I ain't gone out of my mind yet. Just heading that way. It seemed like the best way out at the time."

"You say you put the gun away? Maybe you better tell me where you put it."

"It's out in the garage. In a piece of drainpipe up on the rafter. I'll get it for you and you can put it up yourself if you don't trust me. I couldn't never use it on nobody. Not really I couldn't."

Fifteen

IT WAS APRIL 12TH, the afternoon of Good Friday. Langston James was sitting on the top step of the back porch, watching Gabriel play with his Donald Duck pail and shovel in the loose dirt of the back yard. It was a serious undertaking, which required all of Gabriel's powers of concentration. He would fill the pail deliberately and with care. When it was exactly full and even on the top, he would dump it in a pile at the end of the row of piles he was working on. Cowie came to the screen door and stood with her arms folded, watching Langston James. Finally she pushed open the door with her shoulder and stepped out onto the porch.

"The eggs're ready," she said.

"You going to let him help you color them?" He spoke without turning his head to look at her.

"I guess so," she said. "It's going to be a mess."

"Well," he said. "Easter don't come but once a year."

She came to the top step and sat down beside him. For awhile the two of them sat side by side, their arms hugging their knees, watching Gabriel.

"What you reckon you'd do without him?" she said at last. She didn't look at him when she spoke. Only the softness in her voice went over to touch him. Gabriel looked up at the two of them and smiled. He held the shovel in a military manner, pointing it towards them, the way a small general might indicate the movement of troops with his baton.

"Don't put your fingers in your mouth, Gabriel." Langston James spoke in admonition, but gently. "No telling what all germs in that dirt."

Cowie leaned her shoulder against him in a gesture of affection. "He ain't nothing but your eyeball," she said. "That's all he is."

For a minute Langston James didn't speak. "I don't hardly think what he looks like no more." He spoke slowly and thoughtfully. "I don't really *see* him, you know. After awhile it gets to be that way." He sucked his lip. "Just all I can think about is the sweetness." He turned his head and looked at Cowie for a minute, then he looked back at Gabriel. "That there's the sweetest child God ever put on this earth. It wouldn't matter *what* he looked like."

"That's right," she said. She smiled and put her arm through his, hugging it to her. "Sweet as he is, it don't matter none what he looks like, but it doesn't hurt anything that he's beautiful. Does it? Does it...anymore?" She put her head on Langston James's misshapen shoulder.

"Women *got* to be right, don't they? No matter *what*? Just don't you say 'I told you so.'"

She looked at him for a minute without speaking. "I told you so," she said.

Langston James didn't move.

"Beautiful," she said. She relished the sound of it. "He's our angel child." She whispered it softly, as if she were telling him a secret. "That's what he is...our angel child."

"Yes," said Langston James. "Ours...and Mizres Fanshaw's."

That night he walked with Gabriel long and hard. And the cradle songs he sang to the child were more mournful than ever.

When Langston James came in off his route on Saturday, he found Gabriel playing with a white baby rabbit on the back porch.

"Where'd *that* come from?" He looked at Cowie while he waited, though he already knew what the answer would be.

"Mizres Fanshaw gave it to him for Easter. Gabriel calls him 'BeeBee.'"

"I ain't up to it, Cowie. It's gotten to be just too much."

"He loves it, Eljay. Try to think of it that way. He was afraid of it at first. I told him it was the Easter Bunny."

"Too many things been happening too fast. I feel like you're taking sides against me."

"We can't take it away from him now, honey. He loves it."

Gabriel held up the rabbit in both hands. "BeeBee," he said.

Langston James went up the steps and into the kitchen. Delmer was sunning himself on the windowsill above the sink. Langston James picked him up and threw him onto the back porch. "Go piss on a live wire, Delmer. You been *de*-posed."

For a minute he stood at the screen door, watching Gabriel and the rabbit. "Goddamn," he said at last. "I ain't only got to fight *pretty* things and *sweet* things...I got to fight *cute* things as well."

Langston James went into the bedroom where he dropped down on the bed and looked up at the ceiling of the room for a long time. He felt like he was coming apart and the pieces were floating off in different directions and he had to do something to get them back together again. But he couldn't think of what there was he could do. Finally, all the pieces were swirling around loose and the only thing left was the misery down in the center of everything. The killing machine took shape on the ceiling of his room. And right there beside it Mrs. Fanshaw was standing, smiling her sweet, grandmotherly smile. He could almost see inside it now. And Gabriel wasn't the one who was there. He was. Gabriel was standing off somewhere—behind Mrs. Fanshaw—where he couldn't be seen. When he couldn't stand it any longer, Langston James got up and went out to the alley behind the house—walking past Cowie and Gabriel without looking at them. Gabriel was taken up with his rabbit and didn't notice his father.

Langston James paced the alley, kicking rocks and looking for live things to step on. Passing the hedge behind his garage, something lodged in the branches caught his eye. When he stepped up for a closer look, he discovered the hand-tooled leather wallet Mrs. Fanshaw had given him on her first visit to the house. He retrieved it from the shrubbery and turned it over in his hands. He tugged and twisted at it, trying again to tear it apart, but it had weathered hard and brittle, tougher than ever, and he could make no more headway with it than he had the first time. He took the lid off the garbage can and dropped the wallet in, but after he had taken a turn down the alley, second thoughts came to him. He went and got a pair of metal cutting shears, dug the wallet out of the garbage and cut it into tiny pieces.

He considered going for the shovel and digging a hole to bury the pieces in, but he finally thought better of it and walked down the alley dropping them into the garbage cans of his neighbors, one piece at a time. The last small square he nailed to the fence post at the corner of his property.

"There, you sonofabitch," he said as he pounded home the nail, "*Now* come back together." Afterwards he dropped the

hammer into his own garbage can, then sat on the lid. He tried
to think, but that only brought hard breathing on him. Nothing
that made any sense would come. Instead, a resolution began to
take shape inside his head. There wasn't anything reasonable
about it. He could recognize that clearly. And it didn't appeal
to him in any way. But he couldn't get it to leave him. Nothing
better would come to take its place. He sat in the alley until dark,
hoping that some other choice would turn up. When Cowie
came for him to call him in to supper, it was still the only
resource he had.

* * *

The resolution strengthened on Easter Sunday because of the
horehound candy.

For a long time there had been one, single thing that Langston James felt he could keep away from Mrs. Fanshaw—one
thing that he could give to Gabriel that she could not. He could
bring the child sticks of horehound candy out of the jar of it he
kept for him at the drugstore—it was his ace in the hole. Gabriel
loved it—and Langston James was the one who knew this and
Mrs. Fanshaw did not. Until Easter Sunday.

Maybe she had smelled the sweet, sharp odor of it on
Gabriel's breath. Or got him to ask for it—though Gabriel could
hardly speak his own name in a way that a sharp-eared person
could understand, much less get his mouth around four syllables
at once. Whatever it was, somehow she had found out. When
he came in off the route Gabriel was sticky with it—smeared all
over his face. The box weighed five pounds—a huge orange and
yellow one, with a red ribbon tied around it. Inside, nested in
the candy, there was a second box—a small wooden one with a
sliding cover that contained a painted tin soldier wrapped in
tissue paper. The name of the company and the address were

printed on the side of the box. It came from Asbury Park, New Jersey.

While he drove the route on Monday, his resolution fed on the darkness out beyond the beams of his headlights, growing bigger and stronger and mixing at last with the dream of the killing machine. By the time he got back to the store, there were three simple thoughts riddled out in the sieve of his desperation. His friend Bodine was dead — smiling his terrible unknown smile forever under the sandy plot in the Slabtown cemetery. Mrs. Fanshaw had become his nemesis — if ever so sweetly. The dream of the killing machine played in his head, not always when he was asleep.

And then there was Gabriel. The angel child. Gabriel was at the center of it all. Moving in all three.

"I got to do something..." he said, speaking to himself out loud, "even if it's wrong."

During supper and afterwards he tried to act in a way that was natural. Cowie noticed, but the particular odd behavior of the evening faded into the generally peculiar way he had been acting for the past two weeks, and she didn't make anything of it. Any upswing at all — even a jittery one — was something she welcomed. She had expected that he would have to go off in the other direction eventually, and she was happy to think he might be coming out of his depression.

"It's a new day," he said — several times.

"I hope so."

"Truly it is. A new day tomorrow. That's what it's going to be." He gave her a kiss on the mouth, then picked up the rabbit and walked up and down the kitchen stroking it and talking baby talk. He even let Delmer rub himself against his leg.

In the bedroom he laid hands on her in a way he hadn't done in years. Afterwards he talked love talk to her in whispers until she went to sleep.

He lay quietly in the bed without moving, so as not to disturb her and attract her attention—looking at the ceiling, and watching himself as he climbed into the killing machine time after time.

At one-thirty he slipped out of the bed and went into the kitchen. He tried to remember the things he did in his morning routine, so as not to break it and wake her. After he put on the coffee, he tiptoed into the room shared by Halstead and Gabriel. Halstead was sleeping on his back and snoring. Langston James was grateful for the racket, which covered the sound of his movements. He picked Gabriel up and walked the house with him, singing cradle songs and humming as he had been doing for the past two weeks. At one point he went into the bathroom, where he turned on the light and looked at the two of them in the mirror. When he leaned up close to look at himself, he was surprised at how unfamiliar his own face had become.

"Lordy," he said. "I'd forgotten how ugly I was."

He took a towel from the rack, then went into the parlor where he put the child down on the couch with the towel spread under him. Gabriel opened one eye and yawned. The puff of breath smelled like horehound candy. Langston James hummed "Baby Bunting" to him and stroked his hair until he went back to sleep.

In the kitchen, he took the butcher knife from the drawer. That afternoon while Cowie was delivering her papers, he had sharpened it. He tested the edge with his thumb. His touch was light, but the blade was sharp and it drew blood. There was a bottle of turpentine under the sink. He took it out and poured it along the blade to sterilize it. When he looked up at the window above the sink, his reflection on the dark panes of the glass caught his eye. He turned his head from side to side, looking at his features. "Was there somebody else I might of been?" he said. "What if I had of been somebody handsome?" He held up the knife and slanted it to catch the light. For several minutes he stared at himself and at the knife in his hand. It was a large and cruel knife, the one that was used for all the serious cutting jobs they had to do—butchering and boning meat—a foot of use-dulled steel, with the bright honed sweep of the cutting edge. He thought of the whiteness of Gabriel's skin, and of his soft, red mouth. For a long time Langston James stared at his own grotesque features in the panes of the window. Then he opened the cabinet door, carefully, making the hinges move without a sound, and took out the turpentine bottle again to pour more of it along the blade—drenching it and letting the drops fall off the point into the sink.

Finally he set his jaw and spoke to the reflection in the window.

"Hurting is the only way you know you're alive. If I'd had it easy, I wouldn't of known who I was." He put his thumb to the blade of the knife and drew blood again, pressing harder this time. "It's too sharp to feel the cut," he said. He put his thumb over the mouth of the turpentine bottle and upended it, washing the wound, feeling something like atonement and vindication in the sting. "Being hurtful don't pleasure me none," he told himself in the glass panes of the window. He laid the blade of the knife against his cheek, pressing it down until he felt the light prick of the tip. "I thought into it far as I could." His face was drawn and strained as he turned to go back into the parlor. He took a piece of the horehound candy out of the box Mrs. Fanshaw had sent and put it in his pocket.

Gabriel was asleep on the couch, the light from the hallway falling across the side of his face. For a minute Langston James stood looking down at the serene face of the child, in sleep more like an angel than ever.

"He ain't never hurt at all," he said. "Not never in his whole life." He nodded. "Nor Mizres Fanshaw neither."

The rehearsal of his scheme played over and over in his mind as he stood looking down at the sleeping face of the child, framed by the night sounds of the house as it creaked and groaned. For several minutes he stood there, motionless beside the couch, trying to arrange a picture of what Gabriel's face might look like after he had done the thing.

"Mizres Fanshaw's not going to like you no more, Gabriel. Not when you ain't pretty. You're going to be *mine*. You're going to be one of *us*." And then he noticed something on the towel. At first he didn't know what it was. When he looked down, he saw that he was gripping the blade of the knife. The blood was dripping out between the fingers of his hand, running along the blade and falling onto the towel. He opened his hand and looked at the long gash which had opened up across his fingers. He could feel nothing, not even the blood flowing. Knitting his brow, he concentrated on feeling the pain, but it was not there to be felt.

"You're not going to do it, are you, Eljay?"

He looked up and saw Cowie standing in the doorway leading to the hall. Her statement fell flat and toneless. Not a question. For a minute he stood looking into her eyes, then he shifted his gaze to a point just above her head, under the lintel of the doorway. He seemed thoughtful and very calm. Finally he frowned and looked back at the gash in his hand, bringing it up close to his face.

"I smelt the turpentine," she said. She didn't move. "You're not really going to do it, are you?"

He didn't answer right away. "I can't feel it," he said at last. "It don't hurt at all. Look," he said, "I can't feel nothing at all." He drew the knife across the open palm of his hand, slowly and deliberately. Halstead had stopped snoring and the room was deathly quiet. She could hear the sound of the blade, soft and whispering, like an indrawn breath.

"Give me the knife," she said, not moving from the doorway, holding out her hand. "You don't know what you're doing. You're going to hurt yourself bad."

"It don't hurt, Cowie. What you reckon? It really don't hurt." He sounded surprised. "I can't feel a thing. I could cut my hand off and I wouldn't feel nothing at all." He looked up at her. "You reckon it's something I could get used to?"

"Give it to me," she said, coming forward into the room. "You've got to get a bandage on that. You're bleeding over everything."

Their talking awakened Gabriel, who stirred sleepily, rubbing his eyes and smearing himself with the blood. "BeeBee," he said.

Langston James stood looking down at his son. "Bunny's all right, Gabriel." He put his hand into his pocket and drew out the stick of horehound candy, holding it up for him to see. On his face there was a strange half smile. "We're going to have him for supper," he said.

Cowie studied the expression on her husband's face. She came a step closer, then stopped. She didn't know whether to laugh or cry.

"Honey," said Langston James, reaching out to her. "Could I hold your hand? Just for a little while?"